PRAISE FOR SNOWBOUND STAGECOACH

"History plus fiction is a potent combination, and
author Lenora Whiteman's enthusiasm for this genre
is enthusiastically evident in her new title *Snowbound
Stagecoach*. The incorporation of her extensive research
along with gritty homespun dialogue characteristic of the
West in the mid-1800's combine to keep the reader front
and center as the hapless adventure dramatically unfolds.
For Western history buffs, for those who enjoy a well-told
yarn, pick up a copy of *Snowbound Stagecoach!*"

— ELLEN WATERSTON
Author of *Walking the High Desert, Encounters
with Rural America along the Oregon Desert Trail*,
University of Washington Press, 2020

SNOWBOUND
STAGECOACH

Lenora Whiteman

Moonglade Press
Publishing New Works by Uncommon Voices
www.moongladepress.com

Distributed by IngramSpark

ISBN: 978-0-9987639-6-5
Library of Congress Control Number: 2020903029

Printed in the U.S.A.

Many thanks to Charlene McLain, Charlotte Powell, Jeannine Cook, Judy DeSpain, Lorri Allphin, Charlotte Christian, Gail Morse, and Susan N.S. Johnson. They gave me encouragement, ideas and specialized information to supply answers when I had questions. As always I am deeply grateful to my husband Tom for everything.

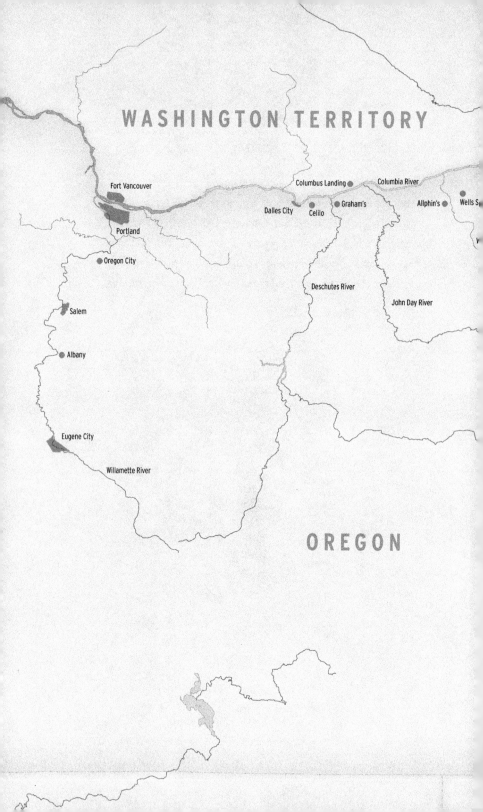

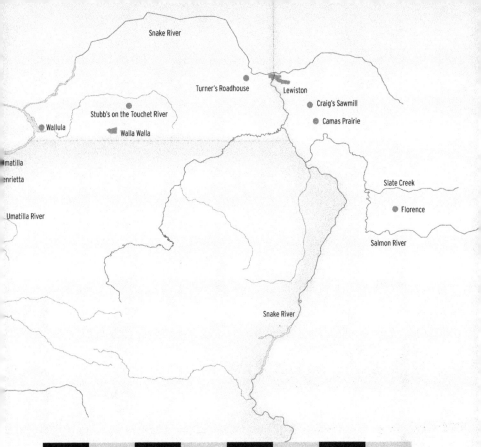

Snake River

Turner's Roadhouse

Lewiston

Stubb's on the Touchet River

Craig's Sawmill

Camas Prairie

Wallula

Walla Walla

matilla

nrietta

Slate Creek

Florence

Umatilla River

Salmon River

Snake River

The Tragic Journey
of the
SNOWBOUND
STAGECOACH
in Oregon, 1862

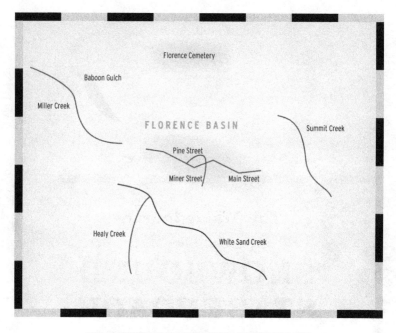

FLORENCE MINING DISTRICT
1862

INTRODUCTION

Being an old geezer can have its good points. Nobody expects me to do much work anymore. And every now and then I get asked some good questions. Just the other day, one of my nephews, Tommy Hale, asked me, "Uncle Jack, what was the hardest time in your life?"

What came to mind right away was the winter of 1862 and the worst blizzard I ever seen. I was pretty young then, about thirty-five-years old. I had a wife and two little daughters, and we were living in Dalles City, Oregon. I hauled freight for a living, using a team of big horses and my wagon.

My younger brother Frank had got himself a job working for the local stagecoach company, tending a waystation out east of town. He had his wife and family with him. At the time, we all thought that was a good job with a real future. If we had known how it was going to turn out, we would have thought differently.

Remembering it now, I can't blame anything but the circumstances for what happened. The summer of 1861 had seen the terrific excitement of the Salmon River gold strikes. In December, there were still hundreds of men trying to get home out of those mountains. That glut of men and the timing of the blizzard combined for a terrible tragedy.

Now, Lewiston was the first town of any size the miners would come to from the gold fields ...

CHAPTER ONE

December 27, 1861

At Lewiston, Washington Territory, the holiday party was still going strong hours after midnight. The crowd of miners celebrated stoutheartedly even though Christmas was already past and the coming year of 1862 was still several days distant. After all, it was a Friday night. Most of the revelers paid no attention when the sharp crack of gunfire rose above the raucous merrymaking.

In the canvas-walled dining room of the Palace Hotel, five traveling companions were enjoying a late dinner consisting mostly of large, rare cuts of beef, accompanied by baking powder biscuits, fried potatoes, black coffee, and straight whiskey.

"Eight shots?" asked Tom Jeffries around a mouthful of steak.

"Eight or ten," agreed Doc Gay.

"Sounds a lot like we never left Florence," said Jeffries, recalling the frenzied atmosphere of that miner-infested wilderness. The saloons and gambling houses there operated all day and all night, seven days a week. The hurdy-gurdy music hardly ever stopped, and a brief dance with one of the hurdy girls would cost a man fifty cents. Whiskey was expensive, too, and some of the saloons were not above watering their product.

"Pass the biscuits there, Swede," requested Richard Bolton, the calm Englishman.

"Sounded like down to the river, like Ragtown proper. You don't suppose old Skillet Jack is still down there hoorawing the community?" Charles "Swede" Wilson said, passing the platter of biscuits to his mining partner.

A diner at the next table, with his back turned to Wilson said, "It weren't Skillet Jack."

"You sure?" asked Wilson. "He was sure doing a rare job of it about an hour ago."

"Naw, it couldn't of been him just now. Couldn't of been because I am Skillet Jack, and at your service," he said, turning in his chair and grinning at Swede Wilson, hand extended. Wilson and Skillet Jack shook hands, and everyone in the dining room laughed in appreciation of Skillet Jack's humor.

"Well, if it be altercation and not celebration, we should hear about it pretty soon," said the city dude, John Jagger.

Sure enough, within a couple of minutes, a man came running from the riverfront, shouting up the muddy, half-frozen street. "Murder," he cried. "Murder down in Ragtown. We got us a dead Dutchman. Dead tailor Dutchman. The robbing murderers is getting away right now," he finished, already moving down the street to spread the news in front of the Grand Hotel, the Miner's Rest, Clearwater House, and the other ramshackle establishments of Lewiston.

"Any of you know any Dutch tailors?" asked Jagger, chewing steadily, looking around the table. No one spoke up.

———◆◆◆◆◆———

Most of the men at Lewiston had recently departed the Florence mining camp just like Jeffries and his traveling companions. Florence sat in a shallow, thousand-foot-long natural basin, steeply descending the mountainside and running roughly from west to east downhill. Although long, the basin is less than one hundred yards wide in the middle, tapering down somewhat at each end. Located at over 6,000 feet, Florence is flanked by a rocky ridge rising high to the west, and another steep hillside to the east. The basin forms a natural meadow, with few tamarack and pine trees. After the arrival of the miners, the forests on the surrounding slopes retreated further and further from the camp.

The mining camp consisted of three streets, Main, Miner, and Pine. Main Street zigzagged down most of the length of the basin intersected by Miner Street about halfway down. Pine Street ran parallel to Main for a few short blocks. Most of the ten butcher shops, seven bakeries, eight lawyers, six gambling saloons, and the dance house were located on Main Street. Sylvester Smith's store sat in the center of town at the corner of Main and Miner. If there were a church, it would have been located on Main as well, but not surprisingly, there were no churches.

Surrounding the camp were the mining claims, several creeks, and the Florence Cemetery. Baboon Gulch starts at the top of Main Street and drops steeply off to the north. One of the earliest arrivals, Peter Bablaine, staked a claim over much of Baboon Gulch. Other early arrivals staked smaller claims at Miller Creek, which runs down the drainage of Baboon Gulch.

White Sand Creek runs south of the Florence Basin with tributary Healy Creek, named after John Healy, coming in from the southwest. Summit Creek runs roughly north to south to the east of Florence. The Florence Cemetery is located just north of town and east of Baboon Gulch.

The early arrivals at Florence staked the best claims, with John Healy and George Grigsby staking the prime Healy Creek claims.

Doc Gay had several mining claims, at least one of which was on Miller Creek. Leading citizen Sylvester S. "Three-fingered" Smith had claims on Miller Creek and several other areas.

———•◦•◦•———

The five traveling companions – Tom Jeffries, Doc Gay, Richard Bolton, Swede Wilson, and John Jagger – finished their meal with thick, pungent cigars. Each man was feeling satisfied about the work he had done this past season. Each was also looking forward to going back to civilization.

Thomas S. Jeffries was a settled, responsible family man in his mid-forties. He had a farm on his donation land claim in the Bethel District of Polk County, Oregon. He had gone to the mines so he could buy more land, some farm equipment, and more stock. He was pleased with his success at the mines but was sorry he had missed Christmas with his dear wife Susan and his small son Theodore. Little Teddy was only four years old, but real sturdy, and just as cute as he could be. Jeffries had plans to buy both of his dear ones' presents once he got to a real town. He decided he would hold off on shopping for them until he got back as far as Portland. He wanted to bring back some memorable gifts, and he thought only Portland might have enough selection to suit his tastes.

Jeffries grinned at his friends around the table. He had first met each of them at "Three-fingered" Smith's store in that untamed mining camp, Florence, Washington Territory. Jeffries had been working a sluice box for the storekeeper on one of Smith's many claims near his store. Arriving too late to file on a rich claim himself, Jeffries had wisely hired out his services to Smith. Neither Bolton nor Wilson had arrived in time to stake any valuable claims, either. They had gone to work for wages instead, working other men's placers as a team. Each of these men had, in this way, earned the unbelievable sum of about three hundred dollars a day for the entire season. They had been paid in gold.

Richard Bolton, from England by way of the California gold fields, knew right away that the Florence diggings were rich. He had spent ten of his thirty years mining gold. Florence was better than the mines he had worked near Placerville, California. It was richer even than the Sailor Diggings, up near the Oregon border. The profits to be made from claims at the new Florence mining camp were staggering.

However, having no claim of his own Bolton was more than happy to work a claim for John Healy and George Grigsby. They had discovered gold near Florence on Healy Creek back in August, and they paid well. Until the discovery of gold, the area was only an up-and-down wilderness, full of gullies, ravines, and steep-sided canyons. Since then, it was estimated that more than three thousand miners had each and every one taken out over four thousand dollars worth of gold for themselves. Bolton certainly had done much worse on claims of his own back in California.

Charles "Swede" Wilson was another experienced miner, also about thirty years old. He had mined in Josephine County, Oregon, in the Williamsburg district. He had been living in Salem, Oregon, in the heart of the Willamette Valley when he got the news of the strike at Florence. While he wasted no time getting there, he was too late to stake a good claim. He had worked first briefly for Peter Bablaine, owner of most of Baboon Gulch. When Bablaine and his sixty pounds of gold left for Walla Walla, Wilson then went to work for Healey and Grigsby, meeting Bolton. They worked well together and got along. They had been partners ever since.

Doc Gay had arrived at the camp early on. He and Smith had been among the very first men to file claims. They had been present for the organization of the mining district in September. Smith had filed his claims on Smith Flat, later buying more claims all over the area. Doc had filed claims on Miller's Creek, on Smith Flat, and in the area known in the records as The Ranch. They were both respected as "old-timers" in the camp. Smith's store was the unofficial social center of Florence.

Thirty-four-year-old Gay was certainly going to be able to buy whatever he wanted when he got back to his comfortable family home in Eugene City, Oregon. He had left his wife Frances to care for their three children. She had another baby on the way. While he was sure his parents and brothers would look after his wife and young family, Gay was relieved that his absence of four months had been well worth the trouble. He wanted to get home as soon as possible. He found himself wondering five times a day if the new baby was going to be another girl. Having three daughters already, he certainly would welcome a son.

Jeffries met John Jagger at Three-fingered Smith's store a few days before leaving for home. Smith's general store was bringing in big profits, and his placer set-ups were each yielding him more than a thousand dollars a day. He had another paying sideline in acting as banker and unofficial post office for the mining camp. Smith was in the middle of trying to convince Jagger to act as his expressman when Jeffries came into the store.

"I got to have me a man, a trusted man, to take out the express and the mail," said Smith. "Ain't no Tracy expressman gonna come way out here. And Wells Fargo done pulled out of this whole country, gone south, and no help for it. They don't care if there's money to be made in Florence. They got enough business without bothering theirselves to come way out here. Now, Mr. Jagger, you are probably the most important, respectable man left on this here hill. I can't turn the mail and all that gold in the express over to just anybody.

Why, it's your duty as old R.R.'s son-in-law to do this for me, for all of Florence. Besides, you only got to take it to Walla Walla."

Jeffries got the impression that this fellow Jagger was not very interested in carrying the express for Smith. But Smith kept at him. "Now, come on, it won't be no trick at all for you to take the express. It'll all load onto just one mule. No trouble at all. You done told me you're going back to Portland, anyway."

Jagger did not say a word.

Smith tried a different tack. "I'll pay you good. Why; I'd even give you a big gold nugget to take back to that fine wife of yours, or maybe to show to her good old daddy," coaxed Smith.

"How big a nugget?" asked Jagger, finally showing some interest.

"Oh, let me just show you," said Smith. He brought out a tobacco sack full of gold nuggets and dumped the contents out on the table. "Tell you what," said Smith sizing up the gold, "How 'bout this 'un?" he asked, nudging a thumb-sized nugget away from the rest.

"How 'bout these, too?" asked Jagger, separating out a half dozen more big nuggets. "I know you got lots more, you old miser."

"You drive a hard bargain, sonny," said Smith. "That's maybe a hundred dollars worth of nuggets you got there. That's pretty good wages for leading a pack mule someplace you're already going," complained Smith.

"Well, that's what it's going to take, you old sharper," said Jagger. "Providing," he continued, "Providing you know someone to ride out with me, then you got a deal. I ain't doing this all by my lonesome. I'd end up robbed and dead along the trail."

Smith's beady little eyes immediately swung over to Jeffries. "Tom, you're about fixin' to head back home, ain't you?" he asked.

"You know I am, you decrepit reprobate," said Jeffries. He had a good idea what was coming next and really didn't mind. He was well-acquainted with Smith and could guess that the old man was going to try to rope him into this enterprise, too. That was alright. He was about ready to leave Florence, having made excellent wages working for Smith. There was already a foot of snow on the ground, and he did not want to get caught in the mining camp for the winter. Jeffries agreed to accompany Jagger, and Smith made the introductions. "Tom, this is John Jagger. Son-in-law of an old friend and a right respectable man," Smith said. "John, this here is Tom Jeffries. He's been workin' with me all season, and you won't find a more reliable man out here than Tom."

Jeffries took note of Jagger's town frock coat with the fancy black fur collar, his stylish gray and black checkered trousers and his fairly clean, white shirt. His mode of dress marked him as a city dude, and one with a fat wallet. He was not a miner, and Jeffries wondered what he had been doing at Florence. He wasn't a merchant, and Jeffries had not seen him running any of the games of chance. Nor had he seen the man involved in any of the brothels. Smith had seemed to set some store in Jagger being somebody's son-in-law. He had called the city dude important and respectable. That, Jeffries thought, remained to be seen. He knew that it was more than two hundred miles to Walla Walla, and the trip would take a full week. Correctly, he figured to find out all about this city dude Mr. Jagger on the upcoming trip down to Walla Walla.

"You hear about that Oregon City man who bought up part of Baboon Gulch after Bablaine left?" asked Smith.

"His name was Bridges, wasn't it?" asked Jeffries.

"That's the man. You know he only worked that claim for four days before he pulled out, too," said Smith.

"What happened?" asked Jeffries. "Did he get hurt?"

"Naw," said Smith. "First day he worked that claim he got fifty-seven ounces of gold. The second day he got one hundred fifty-seven ounces. On the third day, he did even better. He extracted two hundred fourteen ounces for his day's work. On the fourth day, he only worked for two hours and took out two hundred ounces more. That adds up to more than twenty-two pounds of gold, Tom. The reason he only worked two hours on the fourth day is that he was on his way down the trail by that very afternoon. I think he figgered he was rich enough. He ought to be about back home in Oregon City by now."

Of the nearly five thousand people who had swarmed into the area since August, only about four hundred were left by the first week of December. Of those only about three hundred intended to stay over the winter at the six thousand foot elevation of Florence. They did not know exactly what to expect since no one had ever stayed there during the winter before. They had hopes of doing some useful mining during the cold months. So they built the best shelters they could, digging into the hillsides for warmth and using canvas, mud, and the sparse pine and tamarack trees to roof over their shelters. As men deserted the camp, any materials they left were immediately taken for use by others.

———•◦•◦•———

It was the week before Christmas when the news reached Florence about the devastating flooding in the Willamette Valley. It had been a very wet October and November; the rainfall amounts broke all records. All the rivers and creeks were running high. It was during the night of December 2nd that the Willamette River totally destroyed the town of Champoeg. The high-water mark was later shown to be fifty-five feet above the normal level of the river. The miners who called the Willamette Valley home were understandably anxious to return to their homes and families.

CHAPTER TWO

Tom Jeffries and John Jagger left the mining camp of Florence early in the morning on Monday, December 23rd. Mounted on saddle mules, each man also had one pack animal along. While Smith had given Jagger a regular pack mule for the express load, the mail and his own personal baggage, Jeffries had trouble finding a pack animal of any kind. At the last minute, he had made a deal with the professional packers, John Creighton and Ralph Bledsoe, for a burro, short in the legs and long in the ears. Jeffries was glad to get the little fellow and was secretly thankful not to have to deal with a big horse or even a full-sized pack mule in addition to his saddle mule on the narrow trail down the mountain.

Calling the route up the side of the mountain a trail was being generous. The edge of the cliff was never far away, and the path was covered in places by slippery, rolling gravel. Now, there was ice and snow on the route that had not been there back in the summer and fall. A missed step could send man and beast thousands of feet down into the rocky gorge of Slate Creek.

No wheeled traffic of any kind had ever yet been able to manage this trail. Because of this, every bit of material brought into Florence had come in on the back of a man or an animal. Since Creighton and

Bledsoe were making such huge profits from the labors of each of their animals, it had been difficult to get them to part even with a small burro.

On this frosty morning, Jagger had augmented his attire with a stylish wool topcoat, matching scarf, and a hard, round derby hat. Jeffries had a wool topcoat of his own, much thicker and bulkier than Jagger's. He wore the thick topcoat over wool long johns, heavy canvas trousers, and a padded, quilted cotton shirt. His wide-brimmed hat was made of oiled felt. Thick wool socks and heavy boots covered his feet. He would be comfortable on the way down the mountain.

It was a long, steep twenty-five miles down Slate Creek to the Salmon River supply camp. At least twice a mile Jeffries was sorely tempted to dismount and lead his animal down the treacherous, narrow trail. He never did though, knowing perfectly well that the animal enjoyed much better footing than he could ever hope for. The men rode single file, with Jagger trailing behind Jeffries' pack mule, making conversation difficult. With heads tucked into their collars to avoid the cold, the men occupied the time with thoughts of home and their families.

The sun had come up as the two men left the Florence camp. The thermometer in front of Smith's store had indicated ten degrees above zero. The two men rode all day long, and it did not seem to get any warmer. Though the sun would occasionally break through the clouds, sometimes for half an hour at a time, they never felt the benefit of it.

Jeffries figured they must be making decent time down the mountain since no other parties caught up with them before they reached the camp at the mouth of Slate Creek several hours after dark.

There was no place to stop, no shelter to be found before reaching the ramshackle camp where Slate Creek emptied into the Salmon River. The camp didn't consist of much, just a few lean-tos, some wall tents, some A-tents, and a couple of dug-out cabins with canvas roofs. The men stabled their stock and hauled their valuables along to the lighted wall tent serving as the hotel.

Upon entering the tent, Jeffries immediately spied his friend Doc Gay taking his ease near the plain box stove, talking with several other men who had recently come down from the mining district.

"Howdy, Doc," he sang out. "I see you didn't die coming down off the mountain."

"Well, Tom Jeffries," said Gay, rising to shake hands, "I guess you survived that miserable excuse for a trail, too." Gay and Jagger were unacquainted, so Jeffries made the introductions. Gay noticed the mail among Jagger's possessions and chuckled.

"I guess you're the poor fellow Smith roped into bringing down the mail."

Jagger gave a curt nod but said nothing.

"Well, there's a big pot of beans back there on the other stove," said Gay, indicating the cookstove in a back corner of the tent. "The fare ain't fancy, but it's warm, and there's plenty. Claim yourselves a stretch of ground for your bags and bed, maybe right over there. I'm set up there out of the breeze from the door. The landlord only wants a dollar a night to sleep in this here palace. Provide your own bedroll, of course."

A party of a dozen miners came in from the trail off the mountain shortly after Jeffries and Jagger had gotten themselves settled. These men also had something to eat and then wedged themselves into the remaining straw-covered floor space to try to get some sleep. They would be among the very last men to leave the Florence camp that season. Ice and snow would soon close the Slate Creek trail completely. Then no one but a madman would even attempt to come in or go out until the thaw came in March or April.

Jeffries, Jagger, and Gay rested, fed their animals and rearranged their burdens at the Slate Creek camp. On the morning of Tuesday, December 24th, the three started out together with their pack animals. Two inches of frozen snow covered the ground. The thermometer stood just below freezing. It was forty miles to the big wall tent at the forks of the trail on Camas Prairie. The frozen snow was packed down and traveling was smooth. By pushing hard, the group made it there by midnight. Unlike the trail down from Florence, the route now was fairly level, and the men could ride beside each other, rather than following in single file. This gave them a chance to talk, and Jeffries learned more about both of his traveling companions.

Doc Gay, Jeffries found, was not really a doctor at all. "That there is just a nickname," admitted Gay. "My real, given front name is James. Ain't nobody calls me that, though, not even my wife. You see, from the first, I was a kind-hearted child. Any animal ailing on the home place, I'd try to nurse it back to health. One time I cured a pony of the colic, staying up with him, walkin' him, and pettin' him, and seein' him through it, and after that, that's when Daddy started calling me Doc. Back then, I was just a sprout. I always have had me a soft spot for animals, even way back then. But no, I got to admit I ain't no sawbones, not by a long shot, more of a farmer and a carpenter for a living," he said.

Jeffries asked, in jest, "How do you find the life of an expressman, Mr. Jagger?"

Jagger apparently took him seriously. "Sir," he declared, "I am no expressman. I am no more expressman than our friend Mr. Gay here is a physician. Smith hornswoggled me into hauling his express, or I wouldn't be doing it."

Jagger sat up straighter in his saddle. "I'll tell you what I really am, gentlemen. Why I'm even here, what I really am, is a captain of industry, in training. You might say I am an apprentice business magnate," he said proudly.

Neither Jeffries nor Gay knew what to say to that.

Jagger enlightened them further. "You see, one of the major, no, the absolute most major capitalist on the western seaboard has taken me under his wing. He tells me he saw my potential from the very first time he laid eyes on me. He's instructing me in commerce and economics. He trusts my judgment. He has put me in charge of some of his most promising enterprises. And he sent me out here to be his eyes and ears, to spy out the land, to make the right contacts, and report back to him about the best ways we can increase his fortune out here."

"Is that so?" asked Gay noncommittally.

"Yes, it is exactly so," said Jagger.

"Just who is this world-beater you are apprenticing under, anyway?" asked Jeffries.

"Oh," said Jagger, "He's my father-in-law."

"Yes?" encouraged Jeffries.

"Yes," said Jagger, "My dear Eliza's daddy, old R.R. as our friend Sylvester Smith called him, the head of the Oregon Steam Navigation Company, Mr. Robert R. Thompson."

———◆◆◆◆———

By 1860 Robert R. Thompson was, indeed, one of the richest and most powerful men in Oregon. Upright, strong and active, as late as 1850 Thompson had still characterized himself as a working man, a cabinetmaker. Since that time Thompson had used a fortune brought back from the California goldfields and the famous "Thompson luck" to make himself a power in Oregon transportation.

Thompson first used his newfound wealth to compete with other businessmen and win freighting contracts from the federal government to supply Fort Dalles, Oregon. He next bought up every boat he could find, forming a fleet of river bateaux. He hired skilled boatmen and fulfilled the government contracts, becoming rich. He then acquired enough stock to become the principal stockholder in the Oregon Steam Navigation Company. That enabled him to make decisions on policy, set the transport rates, and make settlement deals with the company's competitors. He had new steamships built and inaugurated new routes, raking in the profits. Under his guidance, the company became extremely successful. Thompson's good business judgment shortly made him a millionaire.

His sound judgment also made him very wary when his eldest daughter Eliza started receiving attentions from a young man named John Jagger. Jagger attended the same church as the Thompson family, First Presbyterian Church, organized in 1854 and located on the corner of Tenth and Alder Streets in downtown Portland. Thompson was suspicious that Jagger had singled out Eliza not because she was a charming young lady, but because she was the daughter of R.R. Thompson. But Jagger was slow and careful in his courting of Eliza Thompson. One Sunday after services, Jagger approached Robert R. Thompson. Formally, he asked the older man if he would please be allowed the privilege of accompanying his daughter Eliza the several blocks to their home, walking with the family group. This made a very good impression on Thompson. Jagger was allowed to walk with Eliza on Sundays from then on. Soon Sunday dinners with the Thompson family were a weekly event.

A few months passed, and seeing that Eliza seemed fond of the young man, Thompson had him thoroughly investigated. The report he received was most positive. Mr. I.E. "John" Jagger had been born in Albany, New York. His actual name was Ira Eugene Jagger. He was the eldest son of Ira Jagger, who owned the local blast furnace and was president of the Corning Iron Company, a major Albany enterprise. Ira Jagger was also active in local politics. Everyone in Albany knew who he was.

Ira Jagger had begun his professional life as a humble millwright, machinist, and minor inventor. He was now one of the richest men in Albany. He was exactly the kind of successful, self-made man whom Thompson could understand and respect.

Ira had sent his son to a fine private school, and the boy had completed his formal education before the allure of the untamed west had brought him to Oregon. Actually, glowing letters from his newly married sister Carrie had a lot to do with young Jagger's desire to go to Oregon.

Caroline Jagger had married Henry W. Corbett in 1853. The young couple then went to Portland, Oregon, where Corbett became a very successful merchant. Caroline subsequently had outlined the many opportunities to her father and her brother.

Young Jagger did not come west seeking any favors. Arriving in Portland around 1858, he would not accept employment from his brother-in-law Corbett. Instead, he had secured employment from John R. Foster at his downtown hardware store. Foster found Jagger's work to be very satisfactory. He seemed to have a good head for figures and the customers, both men and women, liked him. He was always neat and made a good impression. His suits showed fine tailoring. He kept up on current events and generally found it easy to talk to people. Thompson decided that Jagger was exactly the sort of young man he would want for Eliza.

Thompson was especially pleased that young Jagger had never mentioned his wealthy father or his close connection with Henry Corbett. He was obviously determined to succeed on his own merits.

Jagger lived in a room he had taken in the large, respectable Funkstein family home, within walking distance of the hardware store. He attended church regularly. He spent an increasing amount of time calling on Eliza Thompson. Even the Thompson family dog was growing fond of Jagger.

While the young man was somewhat egotistical and a bit over-confident, Thompson did not hold that against him. Thompson had always believed in himself and his own abilities. If Eliza's beau had the same kind of attitudes, that was all to the good.

In the spring of 1860, Jagger asked Robert R. Thompson for his daughter's hand in marriage. Thompson then subjected Jagger to an intense, private moral and financial catechism. All the young man's answers were acceptable. Jagger seemed to dote upon Eliza. He was confident in his ability to provide for her and make her happy. He was willing to work hard for her welfare. Thompson gave permission for the couple to wed in the summer of 1860. R.R.'s wife, Harriet, wept through the entire ceremony. She had always been a very sentimental woman.

The Jaggers set up housekeeping in a recently constructed house only two blocks from the Thompson residence.

In September of 1861, Thompson sponsored Jagger in opening his own business. I.E. Jagger and Company was a wholesale dealer in dry goods and hardware. Jagger found himself in the novel and delightful position of supplying goods and making a profit from his old boss, John R. Foster.

Jagger had been in business less than a month when Thompson sent word for him to drop by his office.

"How are you, son? And our girls?" asked Thompson, referring both to Eliza and the newly arrived baby, Hattie, named for her grandmother.

"We are all fine, sir. Thank you for asking. Yourself, sir? And Mrs. Thompson and the family?" asked Jagger politely.

"Oh, fine, just fine," said Thompson. "What I want to talk to you about is this. You know I can't be everywhere at once. But I need information. And I can't just go traipsing up and down the river whenever I feel like it. I'm needed here, whether I like it or not. You know that."

"Yes, sir," said Jagger.

"What I need," said Thompson, "I need some eyes and ears to go on up to Dalles City and further, up to the new gold strikes. There's a mort of gold coming out of there, and a mort of freight wanting to go up. There's freight just sitting on the docks because it is impossible to keep up with the demand for transportation. There's dollars just sitting there. We know that already, but we don't know about the availability of pack animals way upriver, the quality of the available timber or when and where the ice might block navigation. And we need to contact the important men in the area. Who has a lot of money? Who might cause us some grief as competition? And more, who can be bought out?"

"Yes, sir," said Jagger. "I see what you're saying."

"Good," said Thompson. "I know you just got set up at your store, and you got the new baby and all, but I sure would like it, I sure would be grateful if you would go for me, real quiet, and get a handle on the whole mining district. People are starting to call it "the inland empire." It has exceptional business potential. Pay special attention to the best routes in and out. It shouldn't take too long. Observe our employees, too. Have a word with the supervisors. Stop and talk with Lawrence Coe with Oregon Steam Navigation at Dalles City and Lewis Day at the Walla Walla office. They should have some good local information for you. Introduce yourself to anyone you judge might be valuable to the company in the future. Go out to the actual gold workings and get an eyeful of those camps."

"I'd think you could do that and be back here before Christmas. I'll send over one of my clerks, a good man, to help at your store until you get back. And if you would like we can have Eliza and little Hattie move back in with us until you return. How about it?" asked Thompson.

"I'd consider it an honor, sir. You will find that your confidence in me is not misplaced," said Jagger pridefully. "I'll get your information and talk to the important people. I'll make sure your employees are doing their best for you and the company. You can rely on me, sir."

Jagger rightly saw this errand for his father-in-law as a great opportunity. If he did well this time, Thompson would send him on other economic missions. If he did well, Thompson would take him into his confidence in the future, teach him more, perhaps start to place trust in his judgment.

Jagger was in the best of spirits as he said goodbye to Eliza and the baby. Leaving in the last week of October, he was confident of his return before Christmas. He would come back to them successful and triumphant from this trip. After all, he was going as the representative of a rich and powerful man. This mission would be the beginning of an exciting, profitable future. He would meet valuable business contacts, and this trip would establish him in the business world. He had been preparing for this his whole life. His father would be proud.

———◆◆◆◆◆———

Jeffries, Jagger, and Gay struggled into the camp at Camas Prairie at midnight, December 24th in a snowstorm. Travel throughout the daytime hours had been uneventful, but as darkness fell, the snow started to fall, too. After several hours of riding in the cold dark snow, the three men were grateful to sight the lighted tent. They tended to their animals and got themselves under cover as quickly as they could.

The next day was, of course, Christmas, but there was no way for them to observe the holiday properly. Most of the two dozen men at the Camas Prairie camp had verbal Christmas greetings for one another, and the camp cook conjured up a lopsided cake as a treat for all. It snowed off and on all day, adding another two inches to the foot of snow already on the ground. The temperature never rose above freezing.

One of the older men at the camp was reminiscing about the lost days of his youth. "Every Christmas when I was a young'un, my mother would make us all some molasses candy. It was the only time a year she would make it. It was right prime, right prime," he said. "Then, on Christmas Day, my granddaddy would read to us out of the Good Book. He'd read us the story about the birth of Jesus, every year. I sure do miss them days," he said with a sigh.

Jeffries, Jagger, and Gay took their ease, ate, and slept. Each man took time to think about their loved ones back home. Gay couldn't help but wonder if the new baby had arrived and if this time Francis would introduce him to a son or another daughter. Jeffries and Jagger thought about their wives and little ones at home, too. Jeffries pictured four-year-old Theodore, opening his present, playing joyfully with his new toy, and eating Susan's pumpkin pie. Jagger thought of beautiful Eliza laughing and smiling around her parents' table, with little Hattie asleep in her arms.

They did not travel again until Thursday, December 26th.

CHAPTER THREE

---- ✵ ----

Early on the morning of December 26th, a moderate earthquake struck the area between Portland, Oregon and Olympia, Washington Territory. There was no serious structural damage, but people were shocked by the tremor. No one had felt an earthquake in that area before. Later that same day serious, region-wide snowfall began.

----◆◆◆◆◆----

At Eugene City, Frances Gay had enjoyed the Christmas holiday with her in-laws, Martin and Ann Gay. Her children, Susan, Martha, Mary, and even the new baby had been shamefully spoiled by their grandparents. It had been a very good Christmas and would have been perfect if only Doc had gotten home. She could hardly wait for him to arrive. She was anticipating telling him the news and introducing him to his new daughter. She knew Doc had wanted a son badly, but she also knew he would appreciate the name she had chosen for this fourth daughter. She had thought about it a great deal. She planned when he came in the door to say, "I know you left Florence to come back to us, but I'd sure be proud for you to meet your very own daughter, Florence." Frances was tickled with herself to have chosen such a witty name for this child.

———◆◆◆◆◆———

Susan Jeffries was thankful that Tom had left her with a full larder before he went to the mines. She estimated that she probably had enough staple groceries to last until spring, if need be.

She had made every effort to make this lonely Christmas cheerful for her son Teddy. Being four years old, Teddy was thrilled with the new stick horse his mother had made for him from a broken broom handle and scraps of tanned deer hide. She had wrapped the horse in a new quilt she had made for Teddy's bed. So he enjoyed the unusual luxury of two gifts for Christmas. And he dug right into the special foods she made for the occasion. Mincemeat and pumpkin pies were his favorites. Carefully observing the last piece of pumpkin pie, he asked his mother if maybe they should save that last piece for Daddy. "No, honey, you go ahead and eat that one. I'll make another when Daddy gets home," she said.

———◆◆◆◆◆———

Christmas at the Thompson household in Portland was full of good food, expensive presents, and laughter. While Eliza's husband had not made it home for Christmas, everyone was confident that he would return shortly. His brightly wrapped presents were waiting, untouched, for his arrival.

In Albany, New York, Ira Jagger enjoyed an opulent Christmas, full of extravagant gifts and rich food. Holiday greetings had been received from his daughter Carrie and from his new daughter-in-law Eliza. He was very pleased to learn that John had been sent on a business mission by R.R. Thompson. He had great confidence in his son. The boy would be a big success.

———◆·◆·◆———

Leaving the tent at Camas Prairie early on Thursday, December 26th, Jeffries, Jagger, and Gay had another forty miles to go to reach Craig's sawmill. The level, treeless meadow at Camas Prairie extended north nearly to Craig's settlement. Snow fell on the group of travelers all day, getting heavier again after nightfall. They reached Craig's buildings around ten o'clock that night. Cold and weary, they made fast work of getting settled, and the three men were asleep in no time.

Upon rising the next morning, the men were glad to see that the snow had stopped. After a dismal excuse for a breakfast, which was also fiendishly expensive, the three men hit the trail for Lewiston, now twenty miles away. The weather was cold but clear, and the three men covered the distance quickly.

Arriving at Lewiston around noon, they found six inches of snow on the ground, and the town polluted with scores of miners on their various ways back to civilization. They also found their old acquaintances, Richard Bolton and Swede Wilson, enjoying a leisurely lunch at the crowded Palace Hotel dining room. Jagger was introduced to Bolton and Wilson, greetings were exchanged, and hands were shaken all around. Jeffries, Jagger, and Gay joined Bolton and Wilson, and the five men enjoyed a decent meal together. Bolton and Wilson had been lucky enough to secure a room with a real bed at the canvas-walled Palace Hotel. Since there were no other rooms now to be had, they generously offered to share their space with the other three. Jeffries, Jagger, and Gay were grateful, even if they would have to sleep on the floor. At least they would have an actual floor to sleep on. The shooting down at Ragtown during dinner disturbed no one's subsequent rest.

Jeffries, Jagger, Gay, Bolton, and Wilson agreed to ride together west to Walla Walla. Starting from Lewiston early on Saturday, December 28th, the group of riders first needed to cross the Snake River in order to start heading west.

The ferry was not at the landing as the men rode down to the Snake River crossing. An angry man, the ferry operator, paced back and forth at the water's edge. Briefly, and with plenty of invective, he told the five men that drunken Indians had stolen his ferry boat in the night. Being ignorant of how to control the craft, they had drifted downstream and gotten stuck on a sand bar near the far shore, a couple of hundred yards away, yet still in sight. The unfortunate ferry operator had sent his son to get ropes, pulleys and a team of horses to try to get the ferry back in business. It would take some time.

The five travelers decided to swim their mounts and pack animals across the river. They found the water at the ford to be only three feet deep. By lifting their feet clear of their stirrups, the riders kept their boots dry. They crossed without incident, and continued on their way, heading west and uphill. The snow held off that morning, but the temperature hovered near freezing.

It was about thirty miles to Turner's roadhouse, where they could again find shelter for the night. But the going was slow. There was a foot of snow on the ground as they crossed over the divide. Jeffries wondered how the short burro could keep up, but the snow didn't seem to slow him down at all. As they came down the western slope, the wind was blowing hard, spitting tiny ice pellets at the riders. They struggled against the weather and finally made it into Turner's after ten o'clock at night.

The following morning the men hit the trail again; they traveled for about thirty miles in a big, ugly snowstorm. The men rode on quietly, each grateful to have a mount to ride and looking forward to getting out of the weather. It took them until eight o'clock at night to reach Stubbs' establishment on the Touchet River. It had snowed all day and was still snowing hard as they stabled their animals.

Stubbs himself was at the door to greet them. His inn consisted of a single twelve by twenty foot room, dominated by a large wood stove in the center. The warmth from the stove felt good to the tired men. A large number of travelers were already making themselves comfortable around the room.

"Come on in," said Stubbs. "We're kinda short on floor space, so if you have any baggage you could leave out in the barn, I'd sure appreciate it." Catching sight of Jagger, laden with four large canvas bags, Stubbs exclaimed, "You there! We ain't got room in here for all of that. You'll have to take most of it back out to the barn."

"Sir!" cried Jagger, "These bags contain the United States mail and the certified express shipment from Florence. I will not leave them in the barn. They come with me."

"Oh, well that's alright then. You fellows can settle into this corner, here. If I might ask, how do you like working for the express company? I heard they pay real good," said Stubbs.

"I am not now, nor have I ever been an expressman," declared Jagger. "I let myself be talked into carrying this shipment out of a sense of civic responsibility. My good nature was imposed on."

"Sorry to hear that. That'll be a dollar for the night for each of you. There's a pot of beans on the stove, if you're hungry," said Stubbs.

The next morning, the men awoke before dawn to find there was a foot of new snow on the ground, making a total of almost two feet. Tom Jeffries consulted with John Jagger.

"It's getting pretty deep. Should we stay or should we git while the gittin's good?" asked Jeffries.

"I wouldn't want to intrude upon Mr. Stubbs for any longer than is necessary," said Jagger, already gathering together his baggage. Everyone else was also anxious to get to Walla Walla, so they decided to ride on in the frigid dawn. By five in the afternoon on Monday, December 30th, the men succeeded in reaching the thriving burg of Walla Walla, Washington Territory.

"Now we're a-cracking," said Swede Wilson. "Finally, a real town. One with hotels that aren't made out of canvas. Hotels that are real buildings, that have upstairs rooms, and real beds. And look there, an eating house, I bet with real tables. Maybe they even got stores where they stock something better than dry beans or mining equipment."

Looking around, Bolton said, "The sign on that mercantile claims they also repair clocks and watches. You might ask them about that gold pocket watch you want to buy so much."

"Ain't I been telling you?" Swede laughed as he asked Bolton, "Ain't I been telling you I'm gonna have me a fine, big gold pocket watch when we get where I could buy one? And I'm gonna find me a goldsmith who can mount that prize nugget I found on that watch's case. I intend to have me a pretty-for-nice. I intend to have me a right prime braggin' piece; you know I do."

"Just let us get shed of our animals and our baggage," said Bolton, "And I'll come along with you. I've got a notion to buy me something, myself. Don't know what, yet, besides maybe a shirt that won't itch my neck so bad or maybe some shoes that don't weigh twenty pounds apiece. I don't need another watch, already got me my good old turnip. She may be a little bulky," he said, patting his bulging pocket, "But she keeps fine time."

The hotels in Walla Walla were of better quality and construction than those in Lewiston, but no less crowded. Jeffries, Jagger, Gay, Bolton, and Wilson were fortunate again to locate a room to share among themselves.

Wilson had been correct in his initial assessment of Walla Walla. Here there were stores and services that had been unavailable to the men at the mining camps. Miners who had needed the attention of an actual physician could finally find him. Some had carried boils, festering splinters and bandaged limbs for a hundred miles and more. There was a brisk business for the medical community of Walla Walla. The bath houses and barber shops stayed open long hours and brought in excellent profits. Most of the returning miners were looking forward to reunions with family and friends and wanted to appear not only clean and respectable but well-dressed and prosperous. Thus, the clothing and shoe merchants did a booming business, also.

Wilson and Bolton both located what they desired in Walla Walla. The elegant gold pocket watch, complete with his prize gold nugget affixed to the case, would be ready for Swede to pick up the next day. For himself, Richard Bolton bought a boiled shirt with five collars and a sober black frock coat with a silk lining. Unable to find a pair of shoes in his size, he continued to wear his heavy boots.

The festive, holiday spirit pervaded the town. On every side, there were people celebrating. There was plenty to eat, and no Indians were currently on the warpath. The many miners in town had almost all had a very profitable season at the diggings. Merrymaking was in order.

Walla Walla was the first place the men had noted women to be in residence, not just passing through or camping out for the convenience of the miners. It was good to see women, decent women living in the town, going about their business. Walla Walla was perhaps not much, but Walla Walla was the beginning of civilization.

The first order of business for Jagger was the delivery of the express and mail baggage to the Tracy and Company Express office. It was with relief that he unloaded his burdens and received a written receipt from Mr. Jonathon D. James, express agent.

His responsibility fulfilled, Jagger then hurried over to the nearest livery stable, where he caught up with his companions. Each was in the process of selling their saddle and pack animals, with their assorted traveling gear. They would be continuing on from here by stagecoach and river steamer and would have no further use for their stock.

Jeffries briefly considered keeping the burro and shipping him to Portland, to then take home as a pet for his son. He gave up the idea, though, finding it might cost more than the little fellow was worth.

The men located a hotel room and hauled in their remaining belongings. They enjoyed a decent dinner and retired early. They were exhausted from the cold, arduous trip and most of them slept in until almost noon the next day. Leisurely meals, prolonged soaks in bathtubs, and shopping took up the next day.

New Year's Day, 1862 fell on a Wednesday. Citizens and guests in Walla Walla spent the day sleigh-riding, target-shooting, loafing, eating, and drinking. In the evening, Bolton and Wilson found themselves a congenial card game. Jeffries, Jagger, and Gay decided to go to the theater. They went to see Miss Susie Robinson and the entire Robinson Family perform a play called "Perfection." The house was packed, and the performance was greeted with waves of applause and cheering from the appreciative crowd.

Early the morning of January 2nd, the five traveling companions enjoyed a breakfast complete with real eggs. The floorboards in the dining room were wet with tobacco juice, notwithstanding several strategically placed spittoons in the room. The smell of cigar smoke was strong, though the fog was lighter in the morning than it would be later in the day.

The bartender was in fine form, even in the early morning. "Belly up to the bar, boys," he called. "Pick your poison. We got it all, red eye, skunk juice, strike-me-blind, or rotgut. You name it. We got the best." He had quite a few customers, even at this early hour.

Breakfast conversation centered around leaving Walla Walla. Tickets would be needed for the next portion of the journey. A stagecoach ride of thirty miles would take them west to the Wallula steamboat dock on the Columbia River. Jagger and Gay volunteered to find out about the travel schedules, and purchase the tickets.

Upon reaching the office of the Oregon Steam Navigation Company, the two emissaries found a note tacked on the door. Steamers departing from Wallula delayed until further notice due to weather was written on the note. That did not look promising. Through the window, they could see no one in the office, and they found the door locked when they tried the knob.

Jagger said, "It's business hours. Somebody, probably the station manager Lewis Day, is supposed to be here, weather delays or no. If he's shirking, he is going to be sorry."

Gay suggested, "Let's go talk to the stagecoach office. They probably know what the story is with the steamboats."

Jagger and Gay approached the ticket office for the stagecoach company. Their stable, stage barn, harness shop, blacksmith forge, and corrals were located next to their tiny storefront office. The sign above the office door read "Miller and Blackmore Stage Coach Line, Walla Walla to Dalles City, Est. 1861."

"My good man, what is going on with the steamers, and what is your schedule?" asked Jagger, striding up to the ticket window.

Instead of giving Jagger a direct answer, the clerk launched into his practiced spiel regarding the merits of riding with Miller and Blackmore.

"Now, sir, we offer the finest nine-passenger Concord coaches, which have superior leg room and a velvety smooth ride. In this winter season, we provide buffalo robes for the comfort of our patrons, and the coaches are equipped with heavy leather side curtains to seal out the inclement weather. Our drivers are highly trained, experienced men who always come in ahead of schedule. There is no finer mode of travel, gents," he concluded.

"I'm sure that is true, but, if you will, what about the steamboats and what is your schedule?" Jagger asked again.

"Why, yes sir, one of our fine coaches is due to depart from bustling downtown Walla Walla tomorrow, the third of January, at eight in the morning. Straight shot through to Dalles City with guaranteed arrival in three days, meals included," said the ticket agent. "Another will be leaving here next week, on Friday, if you care to wait, sir. I don't got no idea about the steamers. That ticket office been closed up since yesterday and what I hear is the big one, The Colonel Wright, she's supposed to be at Wallula now, but she ain't."

"Thank you. In that case, we will take five tickets on the stage leaving tomorrow morning," said Jagger, bringing a well-filled bag of gold flake from his topcoat pocket.

The ticket agent reached under the counter and produced a set of scales. As he expertly weighed out the amount needed to purchase the tickets, he said, "Miller and Blackmore are offering a generous two for one discount for gold over cash. That means each of you gets your ticket for twelve dollars and fifty cents in gold instead of twenty-five dollars in United States currency. You sure can't beat that. And you got here just at the right time, gents. Five seats is all we got left on tomorrow's stage. That comes to sixty-two dollars and fifty cents, just over three and one-eighth ounces out of your poke, sir."

CHAPTER FOUR

In Portland, Captain John C. Ainsworth, president of the Oregon Steam Navigation Company and skilled river man, pondered the latest information he had received. According to the report, it had rained or snowed every day and every night for the entire month of December in Portland. He correctly assumed this to be true for all of western Oregon State and Washington Territory. This was creating flood conditions for the entire region. He knew that high water was even more dangerous for navigation than low water. And it had been snowing in earnest from south of Portland to north of Olympia, which was unusual. So far, traffic on the lower and middle portions of the Columbia River, Astoria to Dalles City, was almost unaffected. The conditions at Dalles City and further east would, of course, be much more severe.

Each captain had total responsibility for his ship. The steamship The Colonel Wright, captained by the capable Leonard White would stay above the falls, eight miles upriver from Dalles City at Celilo and not make the run to Wallula if the water was too high. The snow wouldn't bother her at all. Ice, however, would be a different matter. Ainsworth trusted Len White to keep his vessel out of danger while still delivering passengers and cargo if it was at all possible.

———•◦••◦•———

Swede Wilson bought a newspaper early on Friday, January 3rd. While waiting for the stagecoach and breakfasting with his friends, he read to them. "Listen to this here advertisement," he said. "Wallula, January 3, 1862. Notice – Until Further Notice, the Steamers of the Oregon Steam Navigation Company will leave Celilo for Wallula As Follows, *Steamer Col. Wright* Tuesday and Friday, Celilo for Wallula. Returning will leave Wallula for Celilo Thursday and Sunday, at Five A.M. signed Lewis Day, Agent. Kind of goes against what they got posted on the door at their office, don't it?" he asked.

"There seems to be some incompetence in our Walla Walla office," said Jagger. He was irritated. He had spoken with agent Lewis Day on his way up the river and had gotten the impression that the man was doing a fine, capable job for Oregon Steam Navigation. Now upon Jagger's return downriver, the man was not to be found. The Walla Walla office of the Oregon Steam Navigation Company remained unmanned and locked. This would certainly be included in Jagger's report to R.R. Thompson.

Wilson said, "I do wish one of your nice big steamboats would have been just waiting to take us all down to Dalles City."

"As do I, Mr. Wilson, as do I," Jagger agreed. "You know, The Colonel Wright, she is absolutely beautiful. Brussels carpets, mahogany woodwork, brass everywhere. She's a hundred and ten feet long, twenty-one feet in the beam, and can go anywhere there is five feet of water to float her in. It really is too bad she ain't docked at Wallula, or we'd be in Portland just thirty hours after she got underway. Think of it gentlemen, only thirty mere hours to Portland."

"Thirty hours would sure be an improvement over three days on a stagecoach to Dalles City, and then who knows how long to make connections back to the Willamette Valley," said Wilson.

"Don't speak so soon," said Richard Bolton, coming back to the table after a short walk to the stagecoach ticket office, located across the muddy, frozen street. "This is going to take longer than we first thought. Our stagecoach has been delayed. The incoming stage is late, making our departure out of here late, too."

"How late, any idea?" asked Doc Gay.

Bolton said, "Man at the ticket office, he said forget about getting out today. He said we should all be ready to go tomorrow, at eight in the morning."

Groaning about the delay wouldn't do any good but, groan they did.

One more day and night was then spent in Walla Walla. Jeffries, Gay, Bolton, and Wilson ensconced themselves in the dining room of the Bonanza House Hotel, intending to eat, drink and play cards all day. They stayed to themselves and did not participate in the organized games of chance offered by the establishment, such as three-card monte, chuck-a-luck, rouge et noir, and roulette.

The saloon orchestra, consisting of fiddle, banjo, cornet, piano, and piccolo, was loud, if not very good. The musicians commenced to mangle "The Arkansas Traveler," "Turkey in the Straw," "Devil's Dream," and other assorted favorite pieces of music. As darkness fell, the revelry and noise increased. "Old Dan Tucker" brought dancers out on the floor. What they lacked in talent they made up for in enthusiasm.

"What kind of step do you call that there?" asked Wilson, indicating the heavy-footed dancers.

"That," said Bolton, "That is what you might call some kind of gallopade, I think. It sure ain't no Virginia Reel."

"Ain't no polka, either," said Gay.

Jagger took the opportunity provided by the delay to visit the offices of the Oregon Steam Navigation Company again, trying to locate the elusive Mr. Lewis Day. And Mr. Day was again not to be found. If he had had more time, Jagger would have made the thirty-mile jaunt down to Wallula, to see what he could learn at the landing. As it was, he went back to the hotel and took a nap before dinner.

At six in the evening, Jagger joined his friends at their table in the dining room, disenjoying another dinner of steak, biscuits, and potatoes. One of the major benefits of reaching Portland, he thought, would be the chance to eat decent food again. Jagger remembered the feasts created by his father's housekeeper back home in New York and the wonderful dishes served on the Thompson family table, created by their devoted cook. He thought of his beloved Eliza and dear little Hattie. He was becoming more irritable about enduring the discomforts of travel. He wanted very much just to get home quickly.

——◆•◆◆•◆——

When Miller and Blackmore had gone into business, the plan had been to have offices in the main cities at each end of the line. They set up one in Walla Walla to the east and the other in Dalles City to the west. Two stagecoaches and two four-horse teams would be kept at each home office. There would be five waystations in between, starting from Dalles City heading east they were, the Deschutes River Station, the John Day River Station, Willow Creek Station, Fort Henrietta, and Umatilla Landing Station. They would keep four replacement horses at each station, and eight replacements would be kept at the halfway point at Wells Springs. As the stagecoach drivers left tired horses on the way, the fresh horses would be taken.

Several months ago, there was one major change to the plan. The stagecoach company decided to abandon Fort Henrietta and move the station keeper to Willow Creek. Now Fort Henrietta might be used for a rest break, but there were no horses or stage company personnel there.

Every Friday, a coach would leave from Dalles City and one from Walla Walla on a three-day turnaround trip. The Dalles City coach would head east, stopping to feed the passengers and change horses at Graham's Hotel at the Deschutes River Station before continuing on. They would eat their evening meal and spend the night another twenty-eight miles east, at Scott's home station on the John Day River. At the same time, the Walla Walla stagecoach heading west would reach its day's destination in Umatilla in about ten hours, with no change of horses. The westbound passengers would eat and stop for the night at the Umatilla Landing Station, allowing the horses to rest. On the second day, the east-bound Dalles City coach would start from Scott's, change horses and feed the passengers at the way-station on Willow Creek. They would continue east, reaching Wells Springs in the early afternoon. There they were supposed to meet the Walla Walla stagecoach, which had made its way west from Umatilla. When they got to Wells Springs, the coaches would exchange passengers, change horses and go back the way they came.

The passengers on the returning Dalles City coach would eat and spend the night at Scott's on the John Day, after changing horses at Willow Creek. The Walla Walla coach would change horses and feed the passengers at Wells Springs before heading back east to Umatilla.

The Walla Walla stagecoach would spend that night in Umatilla. The third day would see the Dalles City coach change horses and eat at Graham's hotel on the Deschutes River, and pull in to Dalles City in the early evening. After leaving Umatilla, the Walla Walla coach would now have no relief horses on the route and would take at least ten hours to reach Walla Walla.

Every couple of weeks a freight wagon was sent out to supply the waystations with firewood, horse feed, and some basic groceries.

As the weather deteriorated, the schedule did not hold up. The freight wagon failed to arrive with supplies. The stages were typically late and sometimes had to spend the night short of their usual goals. The drivers were taking extra horses from the stations, and leaving none behind. Horses began to accumulate in Walla Walla and Dalles City. Then the hosteler at Wells Springs deserted, taking a big bag of groceries and the last two horses in the barn.

It had gotten so bad the drivers were never sure if they were going to make connections. They had to be ready to go further than they had expected. Blackmore and Miller had said as much to their drivers, but said nothing to the potential passengers.

———◆◆◆◆———

In Dalles City, December 30th, R. Emmitt Miller was worried as he watched and waited hour after hour for his stagecoach from Walla Walla. Veteran driver Rafe Garrity was a day late on his expected run of three days. It had been snowing at Dalles City, off and on, during that entire time. The wind kept picking up, and the temperature kept going down. Just before sundown Miller finally heard the coach pull up in the street outside his office.

Coming outside, he watched with alarm while the passengers climbed down from the stagecoach. Only three men had ridden in with Garrity. They were dressed for the storm, heavily coated and booted. Two of their hats had chinstraps, and one was held on with a thin scarf tied under the owner's chin. Miller contained his curiosity while the passengers collected their baggage, thanked Garrity and hiked off toward the Umatilla House Hotel.

"Mr. Garrity," said Miller, "I'm awful glad to finally see you. Just where have you been and where in tarnation are the rest of your passengers?"

"Emmitt," said Garrity, "Believe me or not, I'm right glad to see your ugly face, too." Garrity turned to speak with the hosteler, A.J. Kane. "Give them big boys extra everything. They deserve it."

Garrity turned back to Miller. "There was no coach to meet me at Wells Springs. I guess you got a good reason for not sending one out?"

"Damn good reason," said Miller. "Our Mr. Kane, he had a bit too much to drink and managed to run the stagecoach into the gate and up over the watering trough in the stableyard. Broke a front wheel and ruined some of the running gear. He'll get it fixed, or I'll have his hide."

"If it ain't one thing it'll be another," said Garrity. "You will notice I come in with an extra pair, giving me a hitch of six, and still we just barely made it in here. There was no replacement stock at all at Wells Springs, at Allphin's on Willow Creek, or Scott's on the John Day River. I left my poor, worn out starters at Graham's Deschutes River station, and took all six horses they had from their barn. If John Stephens ever makes it to Wells Springs, he's gonna be right unhappy with me. There ain't a relief team left to be had between the Deschutes and there."

Miller said, "That's as may be. Horses is horses. Passengers is passengers. What I asked you is just where your other six passengers are, Rafe."

"Now don't go getting all hot and bothered," he said. "They are fine, every one of them. But we hit some real deep drifts, Emmitt. When the horses couldn't pull no more, I had to have the passengers get out, walk, and push of course."

Miller gave him a questioning look.

"None of them had no broken legs," Garrity said, defending his actions. "They could all walk alright. But four of them, they claimed they couldn't walk no more when we got to Wells Springs. So I told them that if they couldn't walk no more, they should stay there at the swing station because whoever goes further with my stagecoach is going to have to be willing and able to walk when I tell them to walk. And push, too, if we need it. We come within a gnat's whisker of getting totally snow-blocked right there at Wells Springs, Emmitt. I didn't find no horses there in the barn, no regular relief team. Nobody was there to help. The place was deserted. So we just had to keep coming with my poor frazzled starters. Even then, I had to have a couple of passengers break trail for us to get rolling again."

"What did the ones you left behind have to say about you leaving them there?" asked Miller.

"Oh, they grumbled some, but they stayed there when I headed back out," said Garrity. "They had shelter, and they had food. They could start a fire to stay warm. I left them their bedrolls and baggage. They will be fine until this storm breaks, and maybe Stephens or another one of our drivers can pick them up. There was no way I could take them any further."

"Alright, what about the other two?" asked Miller.

"Those two were with me clear to Tom Scott's house at the crossing of the John Day River. They decided to stay there at Scott's after I warned them that once we crossed over, they would have to walk all the way up to the top of the rise on the west side."

"Well, I guess there's no help for it," said Miller. "But I sure wish you could have got here with all the dadburned ticket holders."

"I tell you, Emmitt, I was lucky to get here with this many of them," said Garrity. "Besides, I done brung the mail and the express treasure box. I done my best. The horses done their best, too. Horses can't pull for beans in this much snow."

Miller complained, "Yeah, but there will be talk, you know. This could hurt the company's reputation. I ought to get you a fresh team and send you right back for them other passengers."

"Emmitt Miller, you are just a consarned old slave driver, an old tyrant," said Garrity

"Who's old?" demanded the twenty-seven-year-old Miller. "I know for a fact that I'm all of two years younger than you are, Rafe Garrity."

"Is that so?" asked Garrity.

Miller said, "I'm here to tell you."

Garrity grinned. "Is that what you're here for? I been wondering about that," he said.

"Aw, hush your tater taster, Rafe. Let's get the mail sack and that express box down and secured in the office, and I'll stand treat down to the Umatilla House. We'll get them to rustle us up some grub, and we'll have a couple of drinks. Once you get some good hot food in your gut, you'll be more in the mood to go back after them passengers. I just know you will," said Miller with a laugh.

———————

Umatilla House Hotel, three stories high with many tall windows, stood on the waterfront next to the Columbia River. During the busy season, the steamboats tied up right in front of the building. A fancy covered porch ran across three sides of the gray-painted establishment. The elegant hotel showcased one hundred and twenty three guest rooms, each with its own stove. There were two bath rooms in the hotel and a new-fangled toilet in the basement. The interior featured dark, heavy carved woodwork, flocked brocade wallpaper, and gilded chandeliers. Glass kerosene lamps brightened every room. To the rear of the opulent barroom there was a card room and another room with pool tables. There was a cigar store conveniently located between the barroom and the dining room. A tailor shop was accessed through the hotel lobby. There was a reading room with the latest magazines and newspapers. In the main barroom, the piano sat up on a platform and behind a metal pipe fence designed to protect both the instrument and the pianist from any boisterous dancing or fighting by the drunken patrons. The dining room had seating for over two hundred fifty diners. The rectangular tables seated eight and boasted immaculate white linen tablecloths. At the busiest times, sixteen waiters served the dining room. A meal or a room cost twenty-five cents. The owner of the Umatilla House Hotel was making a fortune in mining the traveling miners.

———◆·◆·◆———

At Walla Walla Jeffries, Jagger, Gay, Wilson, and Bolton were ready to go early Saturday morning, January 4th. The other four passengers were also on hand. Three of these passengers were miners returning home. Jagger recognized the fourth as the local Tracy and Company Express agent, Jonathon D. James.

Mr. James had over three hundred pounds of gold in the express, and the mail delivery from Walla Walla entrusted to him on this trip. He also carried, as part of his employment, two forty-four caliber Colt Special handguns and a sawed-off ten gauge shotgun loaded with double ought buckshot. James was an experienced professional messenger. He was alert, and he was no fool. He had never yet failed to deliver an express consigned to his care.

James himself loaded the mailbag into the chain-supported, rear platform compartment on the Concord stagecoach. He rolled down the heavy leather shroud and padlocked it in place. Then he and stagecoach driver John Stephens between them hoisted the heavy strongbox up and deposited it under the driver's seat. Thanking

Stephens, James stood to one side, waiting for the hosteler to finish with the team. James would be the first passenger to board the stagecoach. He would take the seat in the left rear corner, facing forward. This was, he thought, the best interior position to defend the stagecoach from, should trouble arise.

Standing outside the stable, near James but not too close, waiting to board the stagecoach was W.A. Moody. Moody was a returning miner, twenty-eight years old and married with four young children. He had lived all over the Willamette Valley, spending time at Albany, Portland, and the Salem area in particular. Moody now made his home in Eugene City and usually followed the trade of carpenter. He had enjoyed a very good season at the mines. He was carrying a lot of gold and was anxious to get home.

Tall, full-bearded H.S. Niles also waited to board the stage. He was going back to his Eugene City home with a sizeable sack of gold himself.

The ninth passenger on the stagecoach would be H. Wellington, an experienced miner from the California gold fields. Wellington was forty-one years old and not married. He had been living with the Eyre family in Salem, Oregon when he heard about the Florence gold strike. The season in Florence had been very good for Wellington, and he carried about thirty pounds of gold in a specially made belt. He also sported an outfit to compete with the attire of John Jagger.

Wellington had packed away his rough miner's garb and completely decked himself out from the shelves of the Walla Walla stores. He wore the latest in fashionable city gentlemen's dress. His shiny half-boots had short heels. His trousers, a dark purple color, featured a thin line of gold braid down the sides. His white shirt had a pleated front and a standing collar. Over his shirt, he wore a fancy black shawl-collared waistcoat with wide lapels and sixteen metal buttons. His flaming red necktie was tied in a wide bow. His broadcloth frock coat was a dark purple, matching the trousers. Over all this, Wellington wore a black overcoat with a fur collar and cuffs. A shiny black stove pipe hat sat on his head. His white kid gloves he did not wear but carried in one hand.

Stagecoach driver John Stephens loved the Walla Walla end of his route. The people at the Walla Walla home station made it run like clockwork, and there was always a crowd of ready stable help on hand. While stable boys sometimes weren't of much use, they could usually be coerced into running to the mercantile and getting a fellow a brick of plug tobacco if a body didn't have the time himself. Having several hostelers around was nice too, with always at least a couple on hand to hold horses, secure baggage, hand reins, and generally be useful to a driver.

Things would be different along the route, out in the puckerbrush. At the swing stations, the company usually employed only one man to a station, especially in the winter. The driver had to take care of himself at these stops designed mainly to change horses. The hosteler would have his hands full changing teams and may not even have anything for the passengers to eat. There sure wouldn't be any supplies like tobacco to be had.

One of the stable boys held the harness of the near leader, talking to the big horse, ensuring that the stagecoach did not move. The passengers handed their baggage up to the roof of the stagecoach. It would be tied in place to the baggage rails by another stable boy. The passengers were then invited to board the stage, as the driver walked around the coach doing a final check. He looked to make sure nothing was wrong with the stagecoach or with the team. He made sure nothing was missing, twisted, or torn and nothing was under undue stress.

Mounting the box, Stephens settled his wide leather belt and checked the big handgun he wore on one hip. His Bowie knife he carried in a sheath on the other. He doubted whether he would have any use for either weapon on this run. Neither hostile Indians nor road-agents much liked the cold. As a matter of fact, thought Stephens, the frigid weather was probably doing more for the security of this stagecoach than a man riding shotgun would.

It was fairly common to find horsemen, alone or in groups traveling in company with the stagecoach. There appeared to be no outriders today. Maybe they didn't much like the cold, either.

Stephens buckled the strap of the heavy leather lap apron, making sure he could still access the foot brake, located on the right. He settled himself on the seat to drive from just to the right of center. The hosteler Irish Mike unwrapped the lines from the foot brake and handed them up to Stephens, backing away from the stagecoach once he did so. The driver then disengaged the brake and nodded to the stable boy at the horses' heads. As the stable boy let go of the team and backed away, Stephens called out, "Sit tight. Hang on. We're off." He snapped the cracker on his custom-made hickory and leather whip. The polished stock of the whip was seven feet long, with a ten-foot braided leather whiplash. The braided silk cracker, designed to make noise, never had touched an animal.

Exiting Walla Walla at a brisk clip, Stephens talked to his team, settling them into the work for the day. "Bear, Bear now you take up that slack. Hey, there, hey hup, boys. That's it, steady now, that's it," he encouraged.

Blackmore's stage, with John Stephens handling the ribbons, departed Walla Walla shortly after eight in the morning. It was a fifty-mile drive section south to Umatilla Landing, and it would take all day. The temperature was just below freezing, and the west wind was starting to blow. Six inches of frozen snow covered the ground.

The passengers gave a loud cheer as the stagecoach started moving.

"I can't wait to get back to the Willamette Valley, land of them big, juicy red apples," said Niles.

"I got to get back to get my webs wet again. Us Oregon birds can't take too much of that dry weather," said Jeffries, with a smile.

———•◦•◦•———

Driver John Stephens, twenty-four years old, had been handling this route for several months. Proficient and experienced, he liked his job very much. He was good with the hoofed stock, and he had control of one of his favorite teams for this trip. All four in this hitch were bay, and they were just a mite over the size of most horses owned by R. Emmitt Miller or by Mr. Blackmore and in use on this stagecoach line. Stephens thought of them as his "Team of Wild Beasts." This reflected not their behavior, but their names. The near leader was named Bear. The off leader was Lion, Tiger held the near wheel position, and the off wheeler was Hippo. Spirited and strong, they had never let him down.

The coach itself was a standard Concord, made of ash wood, leather straps and forged iron by J.S. Abbott and Company of Concord, New Hampshire. It boasted inside seating for nine and room for more on the top. However, in this winter weather, no one would ride out in the open with Stephens. Blackmore and Miller did not want any passengers to perhaps freeze. Something like that might be bad for business.

Driving stagecoach in winter was dirty, numbing work. Stephens had special equipment to help him keep out of the worst of the weather. He wore a pair of long elk hide gauntlets with supple fingers made of light deerskin. There was an extra pair stored under the driver's seat, in case these should get wet. He had heavy ox hide boots on his feet, over wool socks. He wore an oiled, broad-brimmed leather hat with a chin strap and a knitted wool liner. His canvas coat was lined with sheepskin. The heavy leather lap protector he had strapped in place was attached to the footboard and the sides of the driver's box. This would do a lot to keep him dry and comfortable.

John Stephens and the Walla Walla head hosteler, Irish Mike had talked early that morning as Mike supervised the harnessing and hitching of the team, getting the stagecoach ready to go.

"You sure you don't want another pair added to your hitch?" asked Irish Mike. "It would be no trouble at all, none at all."

"Oh, thanks anyway Mike, but I think we'll be fine the way we are. Them four wild beasts are all big and strong. Besides, the snow ain't gonna be that deep," said Stephens.

———◆◆◆◆———

"Say, gentlemen," said Swede Wilson as the passengers seated themselves in the stagecoach and settled in, "Perk up your ears now everyone, because I see we got us a list here on this side by my head, and it's the rules for our conduct on this here stagecoach." Swede waited until he had their attention. He cleared his throat. All conversations stopped, to be resumed again after the reading of the rules.

Swede cleared his throat again. In a loud, clear voice he read, "Notice For Information Of Passengers Of The Blackmore and Miller Stagecoach Line Regarding Their Comfort and Safety;

"First Rule, Know That Your Driver's Word Is Law. Disobedience Or Disrespect For The Driver Will Not Be Tolerated.

"Second Rule, There Will Be No Consumption Of Alcoholic Beverages Unless You Have Enough To Share With Everyone.

"Third Rule, Please Refrain From The Use Of Firearms While The Coach Is In Motion, Except, Of Course, In Case Of Indian Attack Or Robbery. Firing From The Moving Coach Is Inadvisable, Since It May Disturb Your Fellow Passengers, Your Driver, Or The Horses.

"Fourth Rule, Please Place All Trust In Your Driver. He Is An Experienced Professional And, In The Unlikely Event Of A Runaway Team He Will Gain Control And Bring The Coach To A Safe Stop. To Jump From The Coach Is Unnecessary And Could Result In Personal Injury.

"Fifth Rule, If Sleeping, Please Do Not Snore, Drool, Or Use Your Fellow Passengers As A Pillow. It Is Rude And Will Not Be Condoned.

"Sixth Rule, During The Winter Months Please Share The Buffalo Robes Fairly. Passengers Who Are Selfish And Unable To Share Will Be Made To Ride Outside The Coach Exposed To The Weather.

"Seventh Rule, There Will Be No Discussions Of Hostile Indian Actions, Stagecoach Robberies Or Unfortunate Accidents. Conversations Involving Religion Or Politics Are Also To Be Avoided As Conducive To Contention And Discord.

"Eighth Rule, If Ladies Are Present On This Stagecoach, Every Courtesy Will Be Accorded Them And Their Children.

"Ninth Rule, If Ladies Are Present On This Stagecoach, There Will Be No Smoking Of Tobacco. Chewing Is Allowed, But Passengers Who Are Chewing Tobacco Must Seat Themselves At A Window And Spit With The Wind.

"Tenth Rule, If Ladies Or Children Are Present On This Stagecoach, No Cursing Or Foul Language Will Be Tolerated. It Is Offensive To Ladies and Corrupting For Children.

"Any Passenger Found To Be Offensive Or In Willful Disobedience To Any Of These Rules Is Liable To Be Set Afoot. The Fate Of Passengers Who Are Set Afoot Is Neither The Concern Nor The Responsibility Of The Blackmore And Miller Stagecoach Line. Signed R. Emmitt Miller, Co-Owner," finished Swede.

"Pretty standard," said Niles.

"Yep, sure is," agreed Doc Gay.

Bolton said, "I've ridden stagecoaches in California with twice that number of rules. This here ain't unreasonable at all."

Conversations resumed. The stagecoach passengers had a chance to get to know each other during the day-long ride to Umatilla Landing. Discussions ranged in subjects from expectations of the future to reminiscences of the past. Mining was a big topic, and stories of mine disasters and of sudden wealth were told. Plans for the future were outlined.

James did not enter into the conversations. Besides Jagger, James was the only passenger who was not a miner returning home. He was working. He never said much, watching carefully, paying attention, earning his salary.

Jagger and Wellington fell into an animated conversation, perhaps due to their shared sartorial splendor. "I would definitely choose an ebony walking stick if I were you. It would complement your hat. A gentleman can't be too choosy when it comes to accessories," said Jagger.

"My father always carried a carved rosewood walking stick. I never considered ebony before," said Wellington.

Moody and Gay found that they knew each other from years past. They had lived in the same section of Eugene City and had met before. Each man had worked on new buildings near the ferry landing.

"Say, ain't you the fella who was having such a time a year ago last spring getting the walls level in that fancy new brick-fronted store on Olive Street?" asked Moody.

"Sure was," answered Gay. "First, I couldn't use a plumb bob because of the gusty wind. Then I was lent a water level, but the darn thing leaked. It took me a long time squaring and measuring to get that job right. Didn't I see you on that crew remodeling the hotel down near City Hall?"

"That was me, alright. Have you noticed how everyone wants sawn lumber now? They are all too modern for log construction," said Moody.

"Eugene City is sure growing and changing. I know a lot of frame houses are going up. And most businesses now are made out of brick. Prices on town lots have doubled since I bought my place seven years ago," said Gay.

"I'm glad I situated there in the Willamette Valley," said Moody. "I like the weather better than on this side of the Cascades. It gets a lot colder out here than it ever gets at Salem, or Albany, or Eugene City."

"I like it in the Valley there, too, except sometimes when it rains day after day," Gay admitted. "I can hardly wait to get home."

Tom Jeffries dozed, slumped in the middle row, far left-hand seat. He stretched his booted feet out into the space alongside the front seat and the side wall of the stagecoach. He leaned his head against the side wall, lulled by the motion and the murmur of voices. Fading off to sleep, he heard disconnected portions of several conversations.

"They were serving meat so tough," said a voice, "so tough I couldn't even chew the gravy."

"Funny thing about them Dutchmen, my dear old mother used to say every single one of them was touched in the head and just plumb crazy. She knew what she was talking about, too. Her parents was both from Prussia," said another.

"Had me a dog once," said a voice, "That dog, right nice dog, his name was Flash, and you never seen a slower animal."

"And I said not to come no further, or I would shoot," claimed yet another.

"Oh no, that there you see, that there is just a nickname. I always was a kindly child," began a voice which had to be Doc Gay.

Jeffries slipped off into sleep.

CHAPTER FIVE

By the end of December, more than a foot of wet snow had fallen over most of the region. This fallen snow then froze hard as a rock.

The cold, wet weather had slowed or halted transportation. Regular supply runs were postponed, and steamers and ferries were docked. The widespread flooding was more than just an added headache. Every low spot was full of water, usually with a crust of ice on top. Bridges washed out, isolating large areas, and people were running out of supplies all over the region.

Stock, mostly cattle and horses, were dying. Some simply froze to death. Others starved when the grass they usually ate disappeared under the petrified snow. And others died of thirst while surrounded by frozen water. Ranchers were unable to get out and help their animals, even if they had feed or water to offer. It was public opinion that this was quickly becoming the worst winter anyone could remember. In later years it would be referred to as "The Hard Winter."

After ten hours of riding in the gusting wind and frozen snow Stephens was glad to see the Umatilla station up ahead. The stagecoach arrived at Umatilla Landing at six in the evening Saturday, January 4th. The hosteler greeted Stephens and the men as they piled out of the coach. There were fifteen frozen inches of snow on the ground, and the wind was gusting from the northwest. The only food to be had at Umatilla Landing was cold beans and cold biscuits with cold coffee. The accommodations consisted of a large drafty warehouse building which had only one small box stove for heat. The passengers all unrolled their blankets somewhere near this inadequate heat source.

Early the next morning, Sunday, January 5th, the stagecoach full of passengers was on its way again, now with a fresh team.

Stephens had again been offered a hitch of six horses.

"Depends," he said. "Which team do I have?"

"We got you that team of blacks you like so much," said the Umatilla Landing hosteler, a good-natured jokester named Joe.

"They'll do. We won't need no more. Them blacks may be a mite on the small side, but they're stronger than some of Blackmore's bigger horses. Got more heart, too," said Stephens.

The team which Stephens thought of as the "Bitty Blacks" was indeed reliable and strong. Stephens also privately thought they were a lot more intelligent than some of the teams owned by the company. Coal, Midnight, Jet, and Sable didn't startle easily. They pulled well together, and they were smart enough to trust their driver.

"What kind of temperature are we looking at this morning?" asked Stephens, pulling on his gauntlets.

"Oh, you know she's a frosty one," said Joe. "Along about four this morning I checked and the thermometer, she was down about a foot and a half below zero," he said, laughing at his own wit.

It was indeed a very cold morning. Stephens checked the thermometer himself. It actually was a remarkable fifteen degrees below zero.

Stephens guided the stagecoach out of Umatilla Landing at a walking pace. The team had been stabled for about a week, and he wanted them to get a feel for the slippery footing. Making the turn to the south, he let the team start picking up speed even though the way was slightly uphill. "Ya-hup there, boys, stretch 'er out, limber 'em up there, that's it, that's good there," he called.

The team responded, seeming glad to be out in the cold, feeling the brisk wind, smelling the snow underfoot and on the breeze. The fifteen inches of snow which covered the ground at Umatilla Landing thinned down to about a six-inch depth south of the settlement due to the wind action on the exposed face of the slope. Most of the snow which would have been covering the road rested in the gully to the east.

Stephens was glad for the snow cover as the coach approached the area known to stagecoach drivers as "sticker alley" or "thorn hollow." In the late summer and early fall, this stretch of road was especially hazardous. Terrible long, sharp, unbelievably hard thorns grew all along this part of the route. These thorns could disable a horse. Stephens had faith that the snow cover would protect his team from harm on this trip.

The stagecoach made fairly good time even though there were no tracks in the snow ahead of the team. In about five hours they reached the lower crossing of the Umatilla River. Fording the two-foot deep river, they came up on the abandoned site of old Fort Henrietta in the big meadow on the west side of the river. Stephens allowed a five-minute rest stop for the passengers and himself. The horses seemed in favor of a break, too.

In the past, this had been a bustling place. The United States Government used to headquarter its Indian Agency there, in a very nice little frame house. When the house burned down in 1855, the Indian Agency had moved down to Umatilla Landing. The United

States Army had later built the fort, but they no longer used any part of it. At various times there had been a trading post and a post office at Fort Henrietta. Neither existed now.

Since the Blackmore and Miller Stagecoach Company had moved its home station very little remained at Fort Henrietta. Only a crumbling barracks building and parts of the stockade still stood.

After less than five minutes, the passengers were grateful to pile back into the stagecoach. A vicious, icy little wind was blowing. Stephens started the team off again with a cry of "Hey, hup!"

Crossing the meadow and climbing up the bluff to the west, the stagecoach now followed the route of the Oregon Trail. Reaching the top of the rise, they would proceed along on the fairly flat terrain of the Columbia Plateau. The roadway there was sandy and covered with less than a foot of snow. Stephens could see the trail crossing the gently rolling prairie ahead as an unswerving white ribbon, extending straight as an arrow and disappearing into the snowy distance.

The wind had picked up, even more, blowing directly from the west, right in Stephens' face. It was very cold and carried tiny bits of icy snow. Fortunately, the team didn't seem to feel it. Stephens eyed the horses with appreciation. They made a pretty picture jogging slowly along through the falling snow. They were willing to work, full of spunk, and not at all lazy. He would be glad to bring them in to shelter at Wells Springs. He would give them something extra in the feed trough, too. They deserved a good, warm barn and lots of fodder after this day's work. He hoped to arrive at the swing station before dark.

Stephens squinted into the frigid wind. Ice was starting to form on his eyebrows and his mustache. He estimated the distance left to Wells Springs to be less than ten miles. The stagecoach followed the trail where thousands of wagons had passed before. At least there was no possibility of losing their way.

Stephens recalled the first time he had come down this road. It had been very different than today. It was early fall, 1844. The sun was shining, and the day was hot. He remembered the choking clouds of dust. He had been six years old, traveling with his family in a large party of wagons, coming from Illinois to the promised land of Oregon. Passing through Wasco County, they had gone on to settle in Washington County, southwest of Portland. The Stephens family had done well. Ma and Pa lived on the old home place to this very day. Stephens thought he sure could use some of the heat from that day long ago. But they could keep the dust. He didn't miss that.

Nearing the Wells Springs station the trail wound down and through a couple of shallow ravines. The snow had drifted over the roadway at the bottom of each gully. The stagecoach slowed considerably while the team struggled through the drifted snow to come out of the first low spot. Tackling the second gulch, Stephens gave the team a few good words and began to wonder if maybe he should have taken that hitch of six horses, after all. The snow was over three feet deep at the bottom of the second gully. The stagecoach body dragged in the snow and almost stopped for a brief moment. Then, with just a couple of encouraging words from Stephens, the horses gathered their strength and hauled their burden up and out of the gulch. The buildings of the Wells Springs swing station could be seen ahead in the near distance.

It was five in the afternoon when the stagecoach reached the small oasis of Wells Springs, and it was quickly getting dark. No lights showed from the station building, or from the large barn. The wind howled, and nearby the noise of a banging door could be heard, whacking against the side of a building. The place looked dismal and deserted.

Guiding the stagecoach under the barn's covered portico, Stephens shouted out, "Haloo, stage coming in here, haloo." He halted the team and set the foot brake. No one appeared from the station or the barn. The irritating door continued to bang. Stephens could now see that it was the door to the station house, swinging open and slamming closed, making all the noise.

Already cold and tired, John Stephens was now starting to get angry. Where was the hosteler? He would sure like to know. He knew very well that someone had been paid good money to be here and meet this stagecoach and, by golly, that someone was not here. He also knew that there was supposed to be another stagecoach here from Dalles City, to take his passengers on west. He could then take the passengers from the Dalles City stagecoach and bring them to Walla Walla tomorrow. There was no Dalles City coach here, either. This was happening more and more often. He would have to keep going to the next waystation to the west and hope he met the Dalles City stagecoach there.

Stephens freed himself from the leather apron and wrapped the reins around the foot brake, talking to the horses the whole time. They were tired from their long day's work. They stood quietly, seeming to enjoy the feeling of the portico over their heads. Stephens jumped down from the box. The passengers were starting to emerge from the stagecoach, eager to stretch their legs again after the long ride.

"Poor welcome we're getting here, I'm sorry to say. You all can go on into the station. There should be something we can fix to eat, and some wood to make a fire. I'm just gonna check out the barn. It looks too quiet. I got a sneaking suspicion I ain't gonna find no relief team in there," said Stephens.

By investigating the barn, Stephens confirmed what he had feared. There were no relief animals to act as replacements for his tired team.

The nine passengers entered the Wells Springs station house, a building about twenty feet by thirty feet in size. They firmly latched the banging front door. Lighting a lantern kept just inside the door, they surveyed the room. The floor was dirt. There were two or three benches to sit on. An apology for a table lurked in one corner. There were two wood-burning stoves, one at each end of the room, but curiously neither had any stove pipe attached. An armful of firewood rested near one stove, but a search of the room revealed no lengths of stove pipe. A coffee grinder with its drawer full of ground coffee was the only grocery item found.

"I suppose we're goin' to bed on empty stomachs," grumbled Wellington.

"Say," Niles said, "I got about a pound of crackers in my carpet-bag. It may not be much, but let me go get it, and I'll share them around."

"I'll go with you," said Jeffries. "I'll ask our driver where to get some water to go with this here coffee. Or should I just get some snow to melt?" he asked the group in general as he picked up a bucket from the bench nearest the door.

"I don't know how you aim to melt snow or heat water if we ain't got no stove pipe," said Wilson.

"I'll tell you something, I want coffee so much I'll haul one of them stoves outside to fire it if I have to," said Jeffries.

"I'll help you, too," said Bolton. "But first, let's mount a bit of a search outside. We know there's no pipe hiding in here."

"If we find some stove pipe or not," said Jagger. "You shouldn't use snow unless you have to. Snow won't yield you near as much water as you might think. You would be much better off starting out with water instead."

"Alright, I'll go fetch some," said Jeffries, following Niles out the door.

Bolton came out of the building a second later. "I'll walk a circle around the building a few times, and see if I can find anything," he said.

"Where's the springs?" Jeffries called to Stephens and James, who were busy unhitching the team and bringing them into the barn. The Tracy Express agent had come back out of the station building after a quick look inside and was assisting Stephens while staying close to the mail and the express.

Niles climbed up on top of the stagecoach and quickly located his stash of crackers. "I'll go in and divvy these up. And I'll save yours for you fellows and keep them nice and warm," he said, laughing as he walked back to the station building.

"A very amusing gentleman," he continued. "The springs are over past the barn here and south of the trail a bit," said Stephens. "Wait for me to feed these horses, and I'll bring this here lantern and help you. Them springs, they're kind of miry near their headwaters. If you don't watch out, you could lose a boot in the mud."

"That would be nasty with the weather like it is," said Jeffries. "Here, let me give you two a hand with feeding the team," Jeffries offered setting the bucket down near the barn doors.

The three men soon had the horses fed. The stable barn provided fair shelter for the team once the double doors were secured.

"I'll come back and curry them down once we get them some water," Stephens said. He carried the lantern and two big buckets from the barn to bring back water for the horses. James carried two more. Jeffries came along with the bucket from the station house.

Stephens led the way to the springs; lantern held high. Over a foot of snow covered the ground, making walking difficult. The wind had let up a little, but it was starting to snow again.

"Give me strength," he said, upon seeing the state of the springs.

"What in Tunket?" asked Jeffries.

"It looks to me like some fool stuck a bunch of pieces of stove pipe upright into the main pool. What in blue blazes did he think that was gonna do?" asked Stephens.

"Say, we just found there ain't no stove pipe for either of the stoves back in that station house," said Jeffries. "Bolton's out in the snow walking circles around the building, trying to find them."

Stephens put down his buckets. "Then I'd bet these belong back there. Let me just fetch a couple of them back with us. Here, give me your hand," Stephens said to James, leaning far out and plucking two lengths of pipe out of the water.

"It ever snow enough up here so you lose where the water is?" asked Jeffries. "They might of been trying to use the pipes as markers to locate the springs in case the snow got too deep."

"I never seen the snow even this deep here before," admitted Stephens. "We may have ourselves a time getting further west to Willow Creek. Here, we'll each take two buckets back to the horses if you can take the one you got and handle the lantern and them pieces of stove pipe."

"Sure thing," said Jeffries.

Leaving Stephens' lantern with the men in the barn, Jeffries trudged back to the station building with the pieces of stove pipe and his bucket full of water.

Once back inside, he was hailed as a hero for finding the stove pipe. Bolton had already come back inside after finding nothing around the outside of the building. Moody helped Jeffries with the stove pipes, and in short order one stove was back in business, and a fire was kindled. Bolton took off his boots to dry them and warm his freezing feet in front of the fire.

Water was heating when Wilson found a notice on the wall. "Listen to this, gentlemen," he said. "This is the schedule of prices we need to pay for the wonderful selection of goods we have found here today. As a matter of fact, that firewood we're burning is going to cost us two dollars."

"Two dollars!" several voices complained in unison.

"That's robbery," said Bolton.

"Sure is," agreed Swede Wilson.

"But I guess we'll pay it," said Bolton.

"Of course we will," said Wilson. "We learned that back at the mines. Just because the price is robbery, that's no reason not to pay."

Jagger set about finding cups for the coffee. He could only locate four tin mugs among the meager kitchen supplies.

"Gentlemen, it looks like we will have to share cups," Jagger said, holding up the four mugs.

"As long as I get some hot coffee, I'll be happy," Wellington replied.

"Me, too," said Bolton.

All the rest of the passengers agreed, and the four mugs were filled and passed around.

Stephens and James came back in from the barn, glad to finally have a chance to thaw out next to the stove and share in the hot coffee. The first pot of coffee was emptied quickly between the ten men.

Everyone ate their crackers, thanking Niles.

"Would anyone care for a little dinner music?" asked Niles, drawing a harmonica from his inside coat pocket.

No one made a comment. Jeffries inwardly cringed. He had heard more than his fill of raucous, blaring harmonica music back at Florence. So, he was absolutely amazed when Niles commenced producing an airy, light, beautiful little tune on his instrument.

"You're pretty good on that thing," said Jeffries.

"Good enough to play for my sister's wedding and my granddaddy's funeral," said Niles. He softly played a slow, plaintive version of "Taps."

As the second pot of coffee brewed, Stephens called a meeting. "I want you all to know," he said, "I want you to know that we might just be in a pickle here."

Everyone listened.

"There was supposed to be a stagecoach here to meet us and take you all on to Dalles City. There was supposed to be a hosteler here, too. And there was supposed to be a fresh, rested team here to relieve my buddies out there in the barn." Stephens paused and took the time to look at each of the men in the room. "We're gonna have to go on west at least to Willow Creek. We just maybe could have us a lightning of a time getting through. There's about a foot to a foot and a half of snow up here on the level. I know for a fact it's got to be drifted worse in places. Right before we pulled in here, we were almost in trouble. I don't know if you boys could feel it, but you all were on the bare edge of having to hike back there. If the team hadn't pulled up over the lip of that gully with me just talking to them, well, we wouldn't have made it. I wasn't about to strain them. Not when they are tired like they are. You would have all been walking over the top and pushing, too, you bet."

"So you foresee then, sir, that we may soon have some walking to do?" asked Jagger.

"That I do," said Stephens. "I won't be surprised a bit if you all have to walk a certain amount of the distance between here and the Willow Creek home station. It's a good fifteen miles. There are a few hills between here and there. That's where we will have trouble if we're going to. Is everyone able to walk?" he asked, looking at each man for his response.

Each man nodded his agreement that he could, indeed, walk.

Stephens continued, "Mr. Blackmore done told me back at Walla Walla that if anything went wrong, we should just keep on coming until we meet that other stagecoach. That is what I intend to do.

"Only other thing I think we got to worry about is the temperature. If we get a Chinook wind and the snow starts to melt, we'll never get out of here. It'll be so slick we can't move. I been studying on it, and I think our best bet would be to skin out of here in the dark when it will be the coldest. I'm thinking to get some rest and maybe be out of here and back on the trail by midnight. Anybody got anything better to suggest?" Stephens asked.

No one was quick to speak.

Express agent James finally spoke up. "Mr. Stephens, you are the expert here. You know that stagecoach and that team a whole lot better than any of us do. I, for one, will completely trust whatever decisions you make."

"I thank you, sir," said Stephens. "Call me John."

Stephens and James rested until about eleven at night. Working together, they then got the team hitched and ready to go. The men had burned the last of the firewood, and the room was cooling down rapidly. The passengers were all ready to go by midnight.

Stephens lit the square-sided oil-burning lamps mounted to the stagecoach body just behind and below the level of the driver's seat. Walking out of the yard and west down the trail, he spent some time stomping down the snow where the horses would have to pass. He hoped it would be enough to get them moving. He hoped they wouldn't get stuck. Another two inches of snow had fallen in the short time the stagecoach had stopped at Wells Springs.

CHAPTER SIX

———— ❋ ————

One week previously, Rafe Garrity was making some hard decisions. The miles from Fort Henrietta to Wells Springs had been a nightmare of almost getting stuck in snowdrifts and having all the passengers get out and walk several times. Each time they had to get out and walk, two of the men would protest loudly about poor service and frozen feet. Garrity's patience was wearing thin, and the two passengers' constant complaining was adding to his burden. The fact that it was all too likely no Dalles City coach would meet them at Wells Springs also weighed heavy on his mind. He decided, even before getting there, if that was the case, then he would be leaving some complaining passengers there, and going on to Willow Creek with the quieter, more able ones. If he still did not meet the Dalles City coach, he would just have to keep coming west as best he could.

Pulling into Wells Springs station, Garrity's suspicions were confirmed there was no coach there to greet them. He would have to keep pushing on westward. Finding the Wells Springs station cold and dark, with no replacement stock in the barn, took Garrity by surprise. After a quick assessment, he decided they needed to keep moving. He took the shortest of breaks, wanting to get to Willow Creek before the snow got any deeper. Garrity lost no time in unloading four of his passengers. They were unable or unwilling to walk further, so they would have to stay in the shelter of the station.

Garrity first addressed the two passengers who were complaining the most, and, he noticed, having the worst time getting through the snow on foot. "Say, you two, for your own good, I'm unloading your baggage so you can stay here, with food and heat. There's going to be more walking to do between here and Willow Creek. Neither one of you is up to it," he flatly stated.

They started to protest, but Garrity was not going to listen. "Anyone else who might have trouble walking further, you should stay here, too," he said.

One of the other passengers came forward. He was a young man with very worn boots. "I guess I'll have to stay, too," he said.

"I've walked as far as I can in the snow, at least for today," said another. Both men's baggage was soon unloaded.

When the coach was gone, the passengers Rafe Garrity had just left behind held a meeting of their own.

"I paid full value in gold for my ticket. I got a right to a seat on that coach. Can you believe the nerve of that driver?" demanded Johnson Mulkey, a big, powerful man of fifty-four years, accustomed to being in charge. He was angry about being left by the stagecoach, even though he could not walk any further through the snow. He was even more disturbed when he considered that he had come close to freezing his feet while walking part of the way here.

"No, really, I can't. I never heard of such a thing. Not in all my born days," said William Riddle, fifty-six years of age. Riddle was another big, beefy man. He was in good physical condition from his season at the mines. But his boots were worn, and he was afraid he had frozen some toes while walking behind the stagecoach. He would be relieved to remove his boots and inspect his feet once they got a fire going inside the station building.

Texas native, red-headed Pat Davis, didn't say anything. He had spent most of his thirty years on a cattle ranch, only becoming a miner in the last few months. He had no desire to chill his feet further and was glad to stay at the Wells Springs station with a roof over his head. He thought the driver had been right in leaving behind those passengers who were unable to walk any further. He'd had more than enough of trudging through the snow during the day and was glad for the chance to thaw out.

The fourth man, J.E. Glover, also remained silent. While he was only nineteen years old, Glover was the largest of the men. He was well over six feet tall, and he was wide, not fat, but thick with solid bones and muscle. He was very fit and strong from his own season of hard work spent mining.

Following the directives of his upright and morally strict mother, Glover had never used tobacco, and he had never had a drink of alcohol. He did not gamble. He did not swear. He did not cavort with loose women. A quiet man by nature, Glover also never complained. He usually spoke only when asked a direct question. Coming from a large family, he knew how to stay out of people's way. He knew how to get along.

Glover would never have allowed himself to be left behind if it hadn't been for the awful condition of his boots. With good boots, he could have gone on with the stagecoach and even walked most of the way. As it was, he was going to have to find something to repair his footwear with or he would soon be walking barefoot.

Davis lit the lantern he found hung on a nail just inside the door and then busied himself with starting a fire. There was plenty of firewood stacked at one end of the room.

Mulkey and Riddle continued to grouse and grumble while they arranged their bedrolls and baggage against one wall.

"Anybody know where the water is?" asked Glover, picking up the bucket.

"I think the driver said the springs are over across the trail and in back of the barn," answered Davis.

"It ain't quite full dark out yet. I'll bring us back some water. Send out the hounds if I don't come back soon." said Glover, going out the door.

"I got a wife and a house full of youngsters to get back to," complained Mulkey.

"Me, too," said Riddle. "Where did you leave that wife of yours and your young'uns?"

"Oh," Mulkey said, "I got me a nice land claim about three miles west of the Willamette River down in Benton County. Staked it back in 'forty-five and been raising cattle and horses on it since I brung a bunch back from the States in 'forty-seven. Heaven on earth, my friend, that's my heaven on earth."

"That's right fine to hear. I got me a little of that for myself. I got me a nice claim down in Douglas County near Canyonville. It's not too hilly, but not too flat. And my Maxamilia, she's been making my life a joy for nigh on to thirty years now. Can't speak highly enough of my woman," said Riddle.

"I know exactly what you mean. My Susan has been by my side about that long, too. When I first went to mining back in 'forty-nine down to California, I didn't know what she'd think. Well, apparently it didn't bother her much at all. She took care of the youngsters, minded the ranch, and shot a bear while I was gone," said Mulkey. "I can't wait to get home and see how she's got along this time."

Glover came back with the bucket full of water. He had managed to sink one run-down boot deep in the icy mud at the edge of the water, nearly losing it. The falling snow had practically covered his coat and hat. "If it keeps snowing like this I won't be able to find the springs again," he said.

"We can't have that," said Mulkey.

"You know what they used to do back in Texas out on those sandy plains," said Davis. "They used to stick a length of stove pipe in the waterhole to keep the grit from blowing in and covering up the water. You could see it from a ways off, too."

"That might work. It might just be the ticket," said Riddle.

"Well, we don't need to fire both these stoves. Let's take the pipes off one to use as markers," said Davis.

Davis volunteered to take the pipes out to the spring and set them upright in the pool.

"Watch the bank it's pretty boggy near the edge, nearly lost my boot," warned Glover.

"Appreciate the warning," replied Davis, looking down at Glover's soaked and muddy boot.

"There," he said upon his return. "At least now we won't lose our water source. We could melt snow to use, but it would only give us a couple of inches of water for a whole bucket of snow. It's tedious. I know. I've done it."

The fire soon took the worst of the chill off the room. Finding coffee to brew, the men took further stock. They found about a pound of flour, some bacon grease and some shriveled apples in the food box. Glover was glad to find some odds and ends of harness to use in repairing his dilapidated boots.

"I thought there was supposed to be something here for us to eat. You can bet your bottom dollar we can't stay here with no food," said Mulkey, eyeing the grease, water and flour pancakes just concocted by Davis. He privately vowed not to touch them. "We'll have to see what the weather looks like come morning. If it ain't storming too bad, we should probably walk on to Willow Creek. I heard the driver say it was only fifteen miles further."

"Good cakes," said Glover, quickly finishing his share. "You gonna eat yours?" he asked Mulkey.

After a short discussion, everyone agreed to wait until morning and see what the new day would bring.

Glover had no trouble finishing off Mulkey's share of the pancakes.

———•••••———

The men woke early the next morning and they used the last of the water in the bucket to make breakfast. Davis made coffee and then another batch of pancakes with the last of the flour. The snow had stopped, and the men agreed they should start the long walk to the next station. Mulkey, Riddle, Davis, and Glover started walking toward the Willow Creek home station at daylight on December 30th.

Before they left Davis insisted on taking down the remaining pieces of stove pipe and standing them in the pool at the springs, too.

"These are longer than the other pieces of pipe. They can be seen better," he said.

The last man out of the building was Glover. He thought he had secured the door, but the latch had stuck and had not dropped. The wind buffeted the door for a few minutes before successfully prying it loose. The door then banged in the gusty wind for the next week.

The four men followed the tracks left by the passage of Garrity's stagecoach. It had broken the icy crust on top of the snow and cleared the way a little, making walking easier. While the depth of the snow was only about a foot on the level, the blowing wind had created big snow drifts. It was shallower on some of the rises, but wherever there were dips in the terrain, it was quite a bit deeper. Even with the already-broken trail, it was cold, hard work every step of the way.

It took eight full hours for the group to walk the fifteen miles to Willow Creek. Each man carried two of the shriveled apples as his share of the remaining food to eat on the way. They had nothing to carry water in except the coffee pot or the bucket from the station building. No one wanted to carry either of those in addition to their bedrolls and bags, so they had no water. They saw nothing wrong with eating snow if they got thirsty.

By the time they sighted the station building and barn on the far side of Willow Creek, both Mulkey and Riddle were limping and starting to struggle. Each hoped again that he had not frozen any of his toes. Mulkey's deerskin money belt was digging into his sides and making his life a misery. He was going to have to adjust how it rode on his waist once they got to Willow Creek. Riddle was afraid of how his feet would look when he finally took off his boots. He had lost feeling below his knees at least three miles back, and he knew that was a bad sign.

Pat Davis was grateful to get to the Willow Creek station himself. If he hadn't gotten out of the weather soon, he knew he would have been in real trouble. Although his boots were fairly new and had thick soles, his feet were still starting to freeze. His coat was too thin for the low temperature, and Davis had only kept his body warm through exertion. He knew he did not dare to stop until he reached shelter. He weighed the irony of the dilemma. You had to keep walking in order not to freeze your body. But by walking, you increased your chances of freezing your feet. Reaching shelter and warmth would be the only answer.

Nineteen-year-old Glover was making every effort to get back to his family home with as much gold as possible. He was, however, beginning to regret that he hadn't bought some clothing in Walla Walla when he came down from the mines. His boots, pants, shirt, and coat were the same ones he had worn when he left his family home near Salem, four months earlier. They were now patched and threadbare. Glover kept curling and uncurling his frozen fingers wishing he had some gloves, or better yet, some mittens. His hands were numb even though he had them buried in his coat pockets. His feet were starting to freeze, too. He could feel the cold creeping over his toes, and pounding through the soles of his feet. He wished he had some decent boots. Thankfully his wide hat was good thick oiled felt. It shielded his face and kept his head warm.

As he trudged through the snow he thought of his family. His parents needed money. They were elderly and had a lot of children to feed. Glover was one of the middle children and had never had much of a chance to stand out in his family circle, aside from his size. If he could come home with a lot of gold, he would be an economic knight in shining armor.

While Glover may have been young, he was being cautious regarding his gold. He had it hidden in several small pokes in several different pockets. He tried to balance the weight so it wouldn't drag on his coat or pull down his trousers. He was carrying over twenty pounds of gold flake, nuggets, and coarse dust.

———•◦•◦•———

As I mentioned in the beginning, my younger brother Frank Allphin had this promising new job working for the Miller and Blackmore Stagecoach Company. He was the station keeper for the Willow Creek home station. He was outside chopping firewood with his nephew Allen when they spotted the four exhausted men toiling their way down the opposite slope to the creek. He had been halfway expecting this. Garrity had told him about the passengers left at Wells Springs. "Allie Ann, we got men on foot coming in," he shouted to his wife inside the station house. Loading Allen's arms with firewood and grabbing up an armload himself, they hurried back into the house.

"Allen," Frank said to his nephew, age eleven, "Bring in the rest of that firewood we just got cut. I'll go and meet them men and show them where best to cross the creek. I'll be right back. Allie Ann, put on some more coffee and fix up some extra vittles," he instructed his wife.

CHAPTER SEVEN

Since the morning her husband had boarded the eastbound steamboat, Eliza Thompson Jagger had prayed daily for his safe return. She began to worry when the snow started to fall in Portland. She hoped John was safe and warm. She became even more worried when during the first week of January, 1862 she never saw the thermometer rise above freezing.

Now that John was considered overdue, Eliza prayed morning and night. However, she voiced very little of her concerns to her parents. She especially did not want her father to think she blamed him for John's absence. Only baby Hattie was taken into her mother's full confidence. And she was too young to understand.

Eliza kept her hands busy and tried to appear cheerful even though her spirits were actually as low as the mercury in the thermometer.

Allie Ann Allphin wished she had a thermometer. She would like to know just how cold it had been now for more than a month at the Willow Creek home station. She had to tend the fire constantly to keep the one-room house at all warm. Her son William, almost three years of age, was made to wear his coat in the house. He didn't like wearing his coat, but he did just what his mother said. He knew from experience that she could swat if he gave her any backtalk. Allie Ann's eleven-year-old nephew Allen escaped having to wear his coat in the house only because he wore a thick, long sheepskin vest.

Allen was the only son of Cary McClain, Allie Ann's elder brother who lived near Albany in Linn County, Oregon. The boy had been staying with the Allphins since late summer. He was proving to be a lot of help. Though he was a little shy around strangers, he was good with the animals. He already had a deep sense of responsibility and definite ideas about right and wrong. He was very willing to learn and trailed Frank around like a shadow. Allie Ann privately thought Allen was well on his way to becoming a fine man.

Young William had sized up the new arrivals and correctly identified Glover as the best possibility for a friend. Glover had been a little boy himself not so long ago, and he had small brothers of his own back home. Young William reminded Glover a lot of his little brother Sam at that age.

"Say there, young man," said Glover. "Did I hear your father call you young Billy?"

"Yup, Mister, that's me, young Billy," said the boy.

"Now, how come you're young Billy?" asked Glover.

"I'm young Billy 'cause I ain't Uncle Billy and I ain't Grampaw Billy and I ain't Cousin Billy and I ain't Billy goat," he soberly answered.

Glover broke into surprised laughter. "I like you, young Billy. You're quite a fella," he said.

"Sometimes I go by young William, too," the boy confided.

———•◦•◦•———

Mulkey, Riddle, Davis, and Glover had several days to thaw out, rest up, and enjoy the good meals cooked by Allie Ann. Glover may have had the poorest footgear in the group, but it was Mulkey and Riddle who had ended up with frozen toes. Mulkey was the most vocal in his condemnation of the situation.

"Miller is gonna hear from me, you can bet your bottom dollar," said Mulkey. "I didn't pay out good gold to end up getting dumped by the side of the trail and freeze my feet."

"Me, neither," agreed Riddle.

"If I lose any toes, I'm gonna make Miller pay," Mulkey declared.

"Me, too," said Riddle.

They continued to repeat the same basic thoughts for the next week. Everyone, including little William, grew tired of hearing the same old thing. But they were polite and didn't say anything, knowing Mulkey and Riddle were both injured, and knowing they had a point in what they said. It still got tiresome to listen to them complain.

Both Davis and Glover tried to be helpful during their stay at Willow Creek. They felled some juniper trees a hundred yards down the creek and dragged them in to be cut up for firewood. They felt useful doing this, and they did not have to listen to Mulkey and Riddle's endless complaints if they busied themselves outside.

Young William was loyal to his new friend Glover. He did not even try to converse with Mulkey or Riddle. He was polite to Davis, but the man did not interest him. Although he was not allowed to go outside because of the cold, William followed Glover around whenever he was inside the house.

On the second afternoon of their stay, Glover brought in some short, finger-length pieces of half-inch thick willow twigs.

"Looky here, young Billy, did you ever see a willow whistle?" asked Glover.

"No, sir, I never," said the youngster.

"I seen my Daddy make them before," said Allen.

"I bet you did," said Glover. "Maybe you can tell me then, am I gonna have any luck making a whistle out of these this time of year? I know they'll work fine come May or June, but I don't know about now. What do you think, Allen?" Glover asked.

"I surely don't know, sir," said Allen.

"We might ruin them, but I guess we'll just have to risk it," said Glover, getting out his knife. "Now, they need to be just about this big around and this long. You cut the ends nice and straight and clean, see, like this. Then you make your first cut that goes just through the bark, like this, about an inch down. See that? All the way around, just like that. Now, gentlemen, we got ourselves what you call your moment of truth," he said. "What do you think, Allen? Is that bark gonna slide nice and easy off the last inch of this whistle I'm making? Or is it gonna stick and be a bugbear?" asked Glover.

"I don't know. I guess we'll just have to risk it, huh?" asked Allen.

"Just have to risk it," agreed young William.

"Well, friends, that's just what we'll do," said Glover.

Grasping and twisting the piece of willow, Glover managed to dislodge the bark, though it did not come off cleanly.

"I thought that might happen. This here may not be the best whistle by the time I get done with it," he admitted. "But I bet Allen here can make a real good one come spring. That is; if you can help him, young Billy. You'll have to help him remember just how to make one, what size twig to use, where to cut it and all. I seen how you paid good attention so you can recall all the steps, huh?" asked Glover.

"You bet your bottom dollar," agreed young William, finding a use for the phrase he had picked up from listening to Mulkey and Riddle.

Later that evening, Glover continued to work on repairing his boots. Allie Ann watched him for a while and finally spoke up.

"My dear old Daddy was a shoemaker," she said. "I wish I knew what happened to his cobbler tools after he died. They'd come in right handy sometimes."

"I got my knife and quite a bit of old harness here. And these pieces of canvas are just right. I'm doing fine," Glover said.

"Sure, you're doing alright. It would just be easier if you was to have some nice tough oiled twine and the use of a good, sharp hollow punch needle. I wish we had one to lend you," she said.

"That's alright," he said. "I appreciate the thought, ma'am."

Glover put another wrap around the instep of his left boot, securing it with one of the strips of oiled canvas given him by Frank. Glover consoled himself with the thought that at least his boots would be in better shape if he had to walk out of Willow Creek than they had been when he staggered in.

———◆◆◆———

Stephens' stagecoach pulled out of Wells Springs swing station heading to Willow Creek at midnight. The coming day would be Monday, January 6th. If there had been a moon that night, it wouldn't have mattered. The cloud cover was thick and low as it continued to snow, sometimes less, sometimes more.

The sizeable lamps on the stagecoach weren't throwing off enough light to see ahead. After almost driving off the trail twice, Stephens stopped to ask for a volunteer to go ahead of the team with a lantern. Dutiful Tracy Express agent Jonathan James said he would take the first turn.

The snow was drifted over three feet deep in places forcing James to take slow steps lifting his feet high and pushing through with his thighs. The trail surface was soft and sandy under the snow creating a feeling of unsure footing. It made for heavy going for the horses, too. Stephens could feel how his team fared through the reins. They were moving only at a deliberate walk. There was a roughness, a raggedness to the pull now that had not been evident the day before when the team was fresh. It was also becoming evident to Stephens they might need someone else to help break trail for the team as well as carry the lantern.

After less than twenty minutes, James had to call it quits in front of the team and gave up his place to Moody. After just a few minutes with Moody out in front, Stephens then called for a second man to help with breaking trail for the team. Gay jumped down from the stagecoach and took a turn with Moody. When they started to tire, Niles and Jeffries took over. When Wellington and Jagger took over, Stephens thought they were quite a sight. The two men duded up in their city clothes pushing through all that snow.

The hours of darkness passed slowly, like a nightmare. The men continued to take turns in front of the stagecoach. At times everyone had to get out and help push. The shifts in front of the team became shorter and shorter as the men grew more chilled and more fatigued. After each turn, the tired men were grateful to climb back into the relatively warm coach and tuck under the buffalo robes to rest before their next shift at the front. Finally, the horses could haul the full stagecoach no further. Everyone had to get out and walk, with two men in front to break trail and the rest following behind in the tracks of the team and stagecoach, pushing when needed. As the hours wore on conversations dwindled and eventually stopped altogether. Numb and exhausted, the men needed all their focus and energy to put one foot in front of the other. Fifteen miles may not have sounded far, but each man began to wonder if they would ever make it to Willow Creek.

Just at daylight, with Bolton and Wilson leading the way, the stagecoach topped the last rise before the downhill run to Willow Creek. Looking out over the rise, they could see smoke rising from a small house beyond the base of the hill and on the far side of the creek. It could only be the Willow Creek station. The men were relieved to see their destination was within reach.

"Hop back in, gentlemen," said Stephens, halting the stagecoach. "You can all ride the last half mile."

The horses were fatigued and ready for a rest. The passengers and the driver were cold and exhausted. They made it down the final half mile into the Willow Creek home station mainly using gravity. It was half-past eight o'clock, the morning was still and very cold. The horrible night was finally over.

The sound of the stagecoach coming in early on the morning of January 6th was most welcome. The Allphin household had been awake less than an hour when the stagecoach pulled up in their dooryard. Frank had already been down to the creek with a bucket for the household drinking water. Allen was fetching in more firewood for Allie Ann while she was building up the fire. Mulkey and Riddle were crowding the fire and getting in Allie Ann's way. "Shoo," she cried. "Shoo, give me some elbow room, or there ain't gonna be no breakfast." Mulkey and Riddle reluctantly got out of her way. Davis and Glover went outside with Frank and Allen to greet the arriving stagecoach.

"Good morning, John. Good morning, folks," said Frank. "Come on inside. My wife will have breakfast for you all right away. Go on in and warm up."

The four stranded passengers wanted badly to get back on the road. And the Allphin family would be glad to see their guests go on their way. Provisions were getting low. Usually, supplies could be brought from Dalles City by way of the new bridge crossing over the Deschutes River, located about forty miles upstream from the Columbia River. The recent high water had washed the new bridge out, making it impossible to cross the river anywhere near there. Now the only option for crossing the Deschutes was by taking the ferry at the mouth of the river.

———•+•+•———

Now you see, I told my nephew Tommy, this here is where I come into the picture. This is where we get to the meat of the story.

My brother Frank had been putting off his trip into Dalles City, hoping the weather would moderate. He knew I was probably already worried about him. My wife Mary, the children, and I were living in Dalles City. I'd been a farmer when we lived near Albany, but I had been hauling freight for a living since the summer.

During his last visit to Dalles City back in November, Frank had told me he would see us again sometime around the last week of December. That was when he had planned to make his routine supply run. Now with the high water, snow, and especially the washed-out bridge I knew he was forced to change his plans. But Mary and I knew they had to be running low on food.

———•+•+•———

Now supplies were indeed getting very short at the Willow Creek home station. Having to feed four extra men for a week had put an end to their fresh beef, potatoes, carrots, last season's apples, and the cone sugar. There was still some flour left and some cornmeal. There was about a quart of molasses remaining in the gallon tin and a little coffee. A side of bacon and a couple of pounds of dried lentils completed the store of food.

Frank and Allie Ann discussed their lack of supplies while she went about making breakfast. "Since the stagecoach had such a devil of a time getting here, I don't think I should try to get to town on my own. We've got to have some supplies, but going out by myself might be foolish. I think I might tag along with the stagecoach when they go," said Frank.

"I'd feel better about you going with them than you going alone," said Allie Ann. "I wish we wasn't scraping the bottom of the barrel for just everything. Jack and Mary are probably already fretting about us, too."

"I know. I hate to have them worrying. I'll get there as quick as I can, get our supplies and get back," said Frank. "Allen, you are going to have to look after your aunt Allie Ann and young William while I'm gone. I trust you to do a good job of it."

"You know I will, Uncle Frank. You can count on me," said Allen.

Even with the limited supplies, Allie Ann put on a plentiful and tasty breakfast for eighteen people.

There were enough tin plates for everyone, but only ten tin cups. Each man partnered up with another to share in the last pot of coffee.

"Hog meat and flapjacks ready to go. Step up and load your plates," called out Allie Ann.

She swept a huge iron skillet deftly off the fire and onto the bare wooden table. Chunks of seasoned meat sizzled in the full pan. While the men filed by and helped themselves, she came back to set down a platter full of pancakes. She then went back to the fireside to flip more golden cakes off the griddle and onto another platter.

"Let's hunker down here out of the way, back from the table," Moody suggested to Gay who was behind him in line. He and Gay sat on the dirt floor and leaned back against the log wall farthest from the fireplace. Jeffries, Niles, Glover, and Davis had taken seats on the floor near them. The men were hungry, and introductions were accomplished around full mouths as they demolished their food rapidly.

There were only two actual chairs in the building. Mulkey and Riddle occupied them as if they owned them. They also treated their new companions to a full recital of their laundry list of complaints against the Miller and Blackmore Stagecoach Company. Everyone listened politely, but no one else had anything to say.

Mulkey and Riddle finally tired of airing their grievances and ate their food.

Mulkey shifted around uncomfortably. His hand-made money belt was digging into his sides again. He would have to find somewhere private to adjust it, hopefully for good. He was tired of fiddling with the belt and frustrated that he could not seem to fix it so it rode comfortably. He had not realized how difficult it would be to haul over twenty pounds of gold home around his waist.

Jagger and Wellington had taken their full plates and gone to sit on the edge of Frank and Allie Ann's low pallet bed.

"What's with them two?" Wellington asked Glover, seated cross-legged on the floor nearby.

"I wish the frostbite had got to their tongues instead of their feet," Glover said. "Imagine listening to that for a week."

Wellington chuckled and centered his attention on his breakfast, and the room grew quiet as everyone ate heartily. Jeffries was especially impressed with the food. He would have come back for seconds if there had been any and he had to compliment Allie Ann. "Ma'am, that was the best breakfast I believe I ever ate," Jeffries said. "Your mother is sure one fine cook," he told young William.

William said, "You bet your bottom dollar she is." Everyone got a good laugh out of that, though William couldn't understand what was so funny.

Seeing young William made Jeffries miss his own small son. He would be glad to get back home, to see his wife and little Teddy. He was beginning to feel that he had been away from them for far too long. Jeffries searched through his poke of gold, finding a roughly round nugget about the size of a peewee marble.

"Here you go, William, have yourself a pretty," he said, tossing the nugget to the boy.

"Thank you, mister," said the serious youngster.

"And Allen, is that your name, Allen?" asked Jeffries.

"Yes, sir," said Allen.

"Well Allen, I'll give you a nugget, too, if you'll go out and fetch in the three buffalo robes out there in the stagecoach. I'd like to use them for sitting on while we're here," said Jeffries.

"Yes, sir!" cried Allen.

Allen rushed out to get the robes. They were very heavy and bulky. It took him three trips to bring them all in. Jeffries then tossed him a gold nugget.

"Thank you, sir," said Allen, bouncing the nugget in the palm of his hand.

"My boy's name is Theodore," said Jeffries. "We call him Teddy. He's just about your size, William."

"Mister, does Teddy have to wear his coat in the house?" asked young William.

"Generally not," said Jeffries. He saw the look in Allie Ann's eye and continued, "But if his Ma says he has to, then he sure will."

"I was afeared of that," said the boy.

Frank Allphin and John Stephens talked over their options. As employees of the stage company, they felt a responsibility for the welfare of their passengers. Together, they took stock of their situation. Just as there were no relief horses at Wells Springs, there were none at Willow Creek. There was, however, plenty of feed for the tired team. Frank and Allen had put up a lot of sweet hay this past fall. If they had to stay at Willow Creek, the horses would have food. But there was very little left for the people to eat. The stagecoach would have to go on to the home station at the John Day River, another twenty-five miles. Frank would go with them, walking behind the stagecoach. He would make a quick trip of it, get supplies at Dalles City, and come straight back.

After giving the horses a rest of two hours, the stagecoach left the Willow Creek home station a little after ten in the morning. Allie Ann kissed Frank good-bye and stood waving with Allen and William until the stagecoach was out of sight. She hated to see Frank go, especially out into the deep snow. She hurried the boys back inside as the stagecoach disappeared.

On her next birthday, Allie Ann would be nineteen years old. She had loved Frank Allphin her entire life.

CHAPTER EIGHT

Your Aunt Allie Ann, now she was born Alice Ann McClain in 1843 in Missouri. She was only two years old when her mother died. She was four years old when her father William McClain brought the family overland to Oregon in 1847. Allie Ann's brother Cary was the oldest of McClain's sons who made the journey. He was twenty-two.

In addition to numerous McClains, their wagon company had included the large family of my father, William Allphin. My brother Tom Allphin was the oldest of his sons to come on the trip. He was twenty. I was the next oldest at eighteen, and Frank was fourteen.

Allie Ann's nineteen-year-old sister Louisa soon was keeping company with my brother Tom. Now, Tom and Louisa, they married a few months after reaching Oregon. William McClain, his eldest son Cary McClain, my father William Allphin, and Tom Allphin with his new wife all took up land claims in the same area of Linn County.

Allie Ann's Daddy, William McClain, died in 1850. He had built a cabin on his land claim and had started farming. His three youngest children were still living at home. Allie Ann was nearly seven years old. Elvira was about fifteen, and Thomas McClain was almost seventeen. They did not know that their father had died before he could file papers on his land once he had "proved up." Although William

McClain had faithfully fulfilled all the conditions required in claiming land, this lack of paperwork left the title to his homestead legally in question.

One fine spring day some rough-looking, bearded men with guns came and told the McClain children they would have to leave. Knowing they were helpless against these armed adults, the children vacated the farm. They loaded up their possessions and drove the farm wagon over to their brother Cary's home. Cary was going to go get the sheriff and fight the claim jumpers for his father's land, but his brother Thomas stopped him. Thomas wanted to go to the gold fields in California. He did not think it was worth the trouble to fight for their farmland when there was still plenty to be had for free all over Oregon. Privately, Thomas felt that the claim jumpers must be awfully stupid men to have to steal from children.

Elvira didn't want to fight for their land, either. She had received a proposal of marriage and wanted to start her new life as Mrs. Titus Smith. Young Allie Ann went to live with their eldest sister Louisa, who had always been like a mother to her anyway.

The names of the claim jumpers were Byland and MacPherson. They split the McClain property between them. As the years passed, no one in the neighborhood forgot how these men had acquired their rich farms. Hard feelings persisted. The Byland and MacPherson families were never totally accepted. Their children were teased at school and never let to forget that they were low-down claim jumpers.

Allie Ann grew up in the household of Tom and Louisa Allphin. My brother Frank lived with our father on neighboring land. Frank ran the Springhill ferry on the Willamette River for Tom, and he was a frequent guest at Tom and Louisa's.

Frank was a bright and ambitious young man. He wanted a wife of similar temper. As Allie Ann grew into an attractive teenager, Frank started paying more attention to her. He had always known she was game and spunky. In footraces, she was fast on her feet. In school, she was bright and tricky with words. She loved a good pun, and she had lots of common sense. She had seen wild Indians and mean settlers with guns. She was not easily frightened. She was petite and pretty and cheerful by habit, though Frank knew she could be as sassy as a cupful of vinegar when she felt like it. The more time he spent with her, the more certain he became that she was the woman for him. He found himself grinning whenever he thought about her. He loved her so much it actually hurt to think about her. Frank proposed marriage during the summer when Allie Ann was fourteen.

Frank had been practicing what he wanted to say to his beloved for quite some time. Usually, he could talk with her all day long, but the thought of proposing to her made him nervous and tongue-tied. He decided the best way to go about proposing would be to take her out for a buggy ride and a picnic. He would ask father for the use of his nice black buggy. Sometime during their outing, he was sure he would find just the right time to ask for her hand.

Starting eastward from Tom and Louisa's house the single-horse buggy carried Frank and Allie Ann to the Santiam River ferry crossing at Syracuse. They would cross over using Milton Hale's ferry and enjoy their picnic in the shade of the big fir tree on the north, Santiam City side of the river. Pulling up at the crossing, Frank could see the ferry tied up, but no one was around to man it.

"I wonder where Milton's at," said Frank.

"Ain't no telling. He's a busy man," said Allie Ann.

"I'll bet he's not too busy to collect a crossing fee; if we can find him," said Frank.

Commotion upstream and upslope away from the river caught his eye and his ear. Someone was up at the cemetery, shouting about something.

"Let's see what's going on up there," said Frank, clucking to the horse as he directed the buggy around to circle back toward the little graveyard.

As the buggy got closer, Frank could see several people standing and seated on the ground outside the fence surrounding the cemetery. He recognized Milton Hale and several of the local Indians. And now he could plainly hear what Hale was shouting.

"No. No, you can't, not here, not now, not today," said Hale. "Get him up out of there, and I want you to fill that hole back in." He gestured down at what appeared to be an open grave. Hale looked up as the buggy approached.

"Howdy Frank, Allie Ann. How are you two this fine day?" asked Hale as he walked over to the pair in the buggy.

"We are just fine, thank you, Milton," answered Frank. "What are you and them Indians up to today?"

Hale laughed. "You won't believe it," he said. "I had to come up from the river and stop that bunch when I saw what they was playing at. I think I finally got it through their heads that they really shouldn't, they really oughtn't bury old Chief Santiam today."

"Why not, Milton?" asked Frank.

"Well, it ain't like I begrudge them the use of our burying ground. They are welcome here, like everyone else. They even made up their own rules about it. They tell me they will only bury their dead on the outside of the railings. They think we are crazy to try to coop up our dead people inside a fence. As a matter of fact, they think we are being real disrespectful," said Hale.

"So what's the problem with them burying the Chief today?" asked Frank.

"Just one little thing. Old Chief Santiam, he ain't dead yet," said Hale.

"In that case, I guess I can see your point," said Frank.

Two of the Indians were assisting Chief Santiam to rise from his grave. Reaching the level of the ground, he shook off their helping hands and stalked away with great dignity upstream, toward the Indian village.

"Matter of fact, he don't act like he's even half dead yet. I don't understand why he thought this would be a good time to go and get buried. Maybe he's mad at somebody. Maybe he's just bored. I don't know," said Hale. "Now, what brings you two down here?"

"We'd sure be pleased to pay you to cross over. Allie Ann packed us a picnic and Tom gave me the whole day off from running the ferry," said Frank.

"You two don't need to pay me. I'll take you over for free. We'll call it professional courtesy, us both being ferrymen and all. Besides, I ain't got a whole lot else to do now that I scotched them Indians' plan," said Hale. "Just give a whistle when you want to come back. I'll be going up to the house for some lunch myself, but I'll be back directly."

———•◦•◦•———

Frank and Allie Ann came back across the river later that day as an engaged couple. Milton Hale was the first to congratulate them. "I done told Susanna you two would be getting hitched soon. I seen it coming a ways off," he said.

"Say, Milton, there's something I've been studying on. I thought I'd ask you," said Frank.

"What's that?" asked Hale.

"Your brother Bill is married to my sister Rachel," said Frank. "So I'm the brother of your sister-in-law, and you're the brother of my brother-in-law. What does that make you and me?"

"Well, I don't know about you," said Hale, "But that makes me confused." Milton, Frank, and Allie Ann all laughed.

"I'll tell you what that really makes us, Milton," said Frank. "That makes us kin. I'm proud to say it makes us kin."

"Me too," said Hale. "Even if we are just some kind of shirttail relations. Congratulations again, you two. Give my regards to your brother Tom and his Louisa."

"We will," said Frank, clucking to the horse to set the buggy in motion again.

"Good-bye," called Allie Ann.

Arriving at Tom and Louisa's, they shared their news with Allie Ann's sister.

"I wish you all the happiness in the world," said Louisa. "But you know they won't let you get married in Linn County until you turn fifteen. You'll have to cross the Willamette River and go to Benton County," said Louisa.

"That don't make no sense," said Allie Ann. "Linn County sure has some dumb rules. When should we cross over on the ferry, Frank?"

"Hold your horses, my dear. We might not have to go to Benton County at all. Let's see how we make out with the folks in Albany first," said Frank, grinning widely. "It may not even occur to them to ask about your age. We sure won't suggest it."

Francis Marion Allphin and Alice Ann McClain got their marriage license and tied the knot on October 15, 1857, at Albany, Linn County, Oregon. No one thought to question the age of the bride.

Over the following winter, Frank and Allie Ann stayed with Tom and Louisa and made a plan. Come spring they would go back east on the Oregon Trail far enough to run a rest stop for the emigrants. There were still plenty of people arriving from back east every year. By the time they were nearing the end of their journey, they needed a lot of things. Frank thought it would be a good idea to go out there with a lot of goods and stock to sell. Also, Frank was a good mechanic and could fix damaged wagons. Allie Ann figured she could bake bread and cook meals for a profit, too. They headed east as soon as the spring mud dried enough to allow them to travel.

Upon reaching Dalles City, Frank had sought out the owner of the stagecoach company, Emmitt Miller. Frank had only wanted some advice, but after just a few minutes Miller had offered him the job of running the stagecoach home station at old Fort Henrietta on the Umatilla River. Frank accepted the job, sight unseen. It sounded perfect for his needs. It would yield a steady income and allow him to trade with the emigrants for himself. An abandoned barracks building and a lean-to barn came with the job.

Frank remembered the area and knew it was perfect as a rest stop. His own train of emigrant wagons had halted there ten years before.

Little William Allphin was just a few months old when they came to Fort Henrietta. Soon, William was joined by a sister. They named her Henrietta May. Little Henrietta was not strong and only lived a few weeks. Her parents buried her there at Fort Henrietta.

The fort was already abandoned when the Allphins arrived, and the Army never used it again. Miller evaluated the location and decided to turn it into an unmanned swing station. He asked Frank and Allie Ann to move to the home station on Willow Creek. The house and the barn were both bigger and better than the half-ruined ones at Fort Henrietta. The fireplace was better equipped for cooking. Frank, Allie Ann, and little William soon made the move. Allen McClain arrived for a long-term visit shortly thereafter.

CHAPTER NINE

The diversions were seasonal for the loafers hanging around on the wide porches of the Umatilla House Hotel in Dalles City. During the spring, summer, and fall, there was unceasing activity on the waterfront, situated almost on the steps of the big hotel. The loafers loved to speculate on this activity and on upcoming events. They would make wagers on all aspects of the steamboat traffic, everything from the running times up or down the river, to the nature of their cargoes. They would even bet upon the exact number of a ship's paying passengers. Similarly, the nature of cargo loaded onto canvas-covered wagons could also be a gambling topic.

During the seasonal fish runs, the head cook at the hotel would buy salmon from the local Indians. The porch loafers could be counted upon to bet on the weight of the fish. They might even bet upon the weight of the Indian fishermen.

In the winter, activities slowed down. After the river iced up, there was no more steamboat traffic for the season. There were far fewer wagons on the streets, and no Indians came to sell fresh fish at the hotel kitchen door.

However, there was still no lack of porch loafers, even in the current frigid weather. Some sat on benches against the hotel wall.

Some lounged against the upright supports, and some sat on the porch rails. One or two sat on the steps. Now and then a man would desert their ranks to enter the hotel, usually to renew his personal supply of whiskey. Men would drift in to laze around, have some conversation, maybe place a wager, or share a friendly drink.

On the cold morning of Monday, January 6th, the crowd was large and wagering on the porch of the Umatilla House was very brisk. Everyone seemed to want to put their money down on the outcome of the morning's drama. It was time again for a prime winter amusement, enacted every two weeks. Sometime this morning the mailman coming from the north would attempt to cross the frozen Columbia River.

Sometimes the mailman would be walking on gigantic snowshoes, and sometimes he would use impossibly long, skinny skis to better spread out his weight. Sometimes he had the mail in a large pack on his back. If there were too much, he would drag it behind on a small sled. Only during the coldest, longest freezes would he risk his horse in crossing the ice.

A cheer went up from the Umatilla House porch when the mailman was spotted on the far shore.

"He's down on the ice. Start timing him," said one man.

"He's on his horse!" cried another.

"That changes the odds!" yelled another man.

"You betcha, I'm offering three to five he makes it," said the first man.

"I'll take twenty of that!" declared another. "And I'm offering even money he makes it in less than ten minutes. Who'll take me up?"

"Who's holding the stakes?" asked a newcomer, rushing up, eager to get in on the action.

"What odds you offering that the horse don't make it?" asked another, running up the steps.

"You're very funny, neighbor. You know it's all or nothing with me. Horse and rider both got to make it to shore or both go down or all bets are off," the first man answered.

Gold, paper money, and IOUs were held, pending the results of the mailman's attempt. All eyes were on the small mounted figure just starting to cross over from Washington Territory. Swirling snow periodically obscured the view of the man and horse. Several bottles of whiskey were circulating among the watching men.

"The horse is stumblin'," cried an excited wagerer.

"No, he ain't," disagreed another. "Don't you try to hoodoo him. Don't you say that! Don't you even think it!"

A man with a spyglass had his own little audience as he told them what he could see. "He's a comin' along right steady. Yeah, right steady. He's takin' it slow. The ice looks good to me. I don't see no cracks, nothin's movin'. Gentlemen, I think he's gonna make it. Him and the horse, just like that," he said, closing up his spyglass and snapping his fingers.

"Fourteen minutes and thirty seconds, gentlemen," yelled the timekeeper.

Money, gold, and IOUs changed hands as the mailman urged his horse up the embankment from the frozen river. He received a rousing cheer as he neared the Umatilla House steps. The mailman's broad-brimmed hat and the shoulders of his coat were covered with snow. He spat tobacco juice before addressing his audience. He was well aware of their recent gambling frenzy. He thought they were welcome to lay bets on his abilities. After all, he certainly was betting on himself each time he attempted to cross the frozen river. It still amused him to make them all feel just a little ashamed of themselves.

"Your faith is touching," he told the porch loafers. "Especially since there ain't a man Jack of you yahoos who would even try what I just done."

Not one man answered him. Certainly, none would disagree. He stared them down; no one would look him in the eye.

The mailman spat into the snow again.

"Let's go, Percival," he told his horse. "We got mail to deliver."

———•••••———

Later that morning, I stopped by the Umatilla House porch to get the latest news.

"Jack Allphin, what do you know?" asked one of the regulars.

"Oh, I don't know much," I said. "How's the river? Did the mailman show up this morning?"

"That he did, Jack. That he did, he rode his horse over just as pretty as you please. He made me twenty dollars. Have a drink," he said, offering a bottle from an inside coat pocket.

"No thanks, friend, I got no time. I got things to do and places to be," I said, already striding away, thinking hard about the state of my personal world.

While Mary, the children, and I were safe in Dalles City, some of our dearest relatives were possibly in danger. Frank, Allie Ann, Allen, and little William were way out east there at Willow Creek. Frank was late in making his regular supply run. I knew the weather was to blame. Everyone thought the rotten weather couldn't possibly last, but it had, and now a lot of time had slipped by. Supplies had to be getting low out at Willow Creek.

I had other people to think about, too. Mary's sister Catherine, her husband Merrill Short, and their little daughter were living at Columbus Landing, twenty-two miles upstream from Dalles City on the north side of the Columbia River. Merrill had been making good money supplying firewood to the steamboats at the landing. The frigid weather had put an end to that activity.

A number of people had come into town from around Columbus Landing in the last couple of weeks. I suspected that Merrill and his little family might be about the only folks left out there. Supplies had to be getting low for them, too.

In the summer, Columbus Landing was a busy place. The steamboats tied up there to take on wood, cargo, and passengers. Passengers left the steamers at this point to access the interior of central Washington Territory. At this time of year, no more steamboats would come. With the river iced over, there would be no boat traffic of any kind for at least two months or maybe longer.

I made up my mind as I walked through town. I would have to go out there and see what I could do for my people. For Mary's peace of mind, I thought I would go to check on her sister's family at Columbus Landing first.

I went by the Miller stables before going home. I wanted to talk to Emmitt and any of the drivers who happened to be around. I hoped they might have some useful information on conditions outside of town.

Over a foot of snow and ice had fallen in Dalles City over the last several weeks. Little of it had melted. It mostly lay where it fell and froze. The streets were more treacherous than usual. The frozen, rutted mud was covered with a layer of sharp, crusty ice. Walking was hazardous, and I was careful to watch my footing as I made my way around town.

I stepped off the street as I arrived at Miller's stagecoach barn. I rolled open the big barn door just a bit and slipped inside. Emmitt Miller himself sat on a barrel in the far corner close to the woodstove, whittling and talking with Rafe Garrity. A.J. Kane, Miller's newest hosteler and general flunky stood to one side, leaning on his broom.

Kane was a single man, about thirty years old. He had come west several years previously from his native New York in search of his fortune. So far, he had been too late for every opportunity he heard about. The job at Miller's stable was now keeping him from starvation. Kane was grateful to Emmitt Miller and willingly handled the dirtiest tasks around the stable. He also seemed to spend a lot of time leaning on his broom.

"Close the door, Jack! Were you born in a barn?" yelled Miller.

"Why Emmitt, how did you know?" I asked, easing the big door closed again.

"Oh, I heard tell," laughed Miller.

"Rafe, A.J., what do you know?" I asked.

"Not much," said Garrity. "It's too cold to know much."

Kane just grinned and said nothing. He went back to sweeping the stable floor.

"No. I mean it. What do you know, I mean about the trails, and the weather," I said.

"Oh," said Garrity. "You ain't thinking of going somewhere?"

"I am," I said. "Good Lord willing, and the creeks don't rise much more."

"You sure do pick the times to go gallivanting off. I never seen the trails worse and I never seen the weather here colder. Makes me feel like I'm back in that nasty old Dakota country again," said Garrity.

"I'm not doing the choosing. I got people to check up on. I guess I already sort of knew what you were going to say," I said.

"If you're set on going," said Miller, "More power to you. Stop by when you get back. Are you heading out to Frank's?"

"Yeah, but first I think I'll check on Merrill Short and his little family out to Columbus Landing. Mary's getting worried about them," I said.

"Keep your wits about you out there. I almost didn't make it in from Walla Walla. It's vicious cold, 'specially when you get moving," said Garrity. "And it's tricky. Unless you know 'zactly where you are, you can lose the trail pretty easy. Don't underestimate how bad it is out there. It took me two days to get back here from the John Day crossing. We cover that in under eight hours in the summer."

"Thanks, Rafe, I'll keep that in mind. Don't work too hard there, A.J., Emmitt, I'll be seeing you," I said, rolling the door closed as I went out again.

"You forgot to tell him you lost most of your passengers on the way," Miller said to Garrity.

"Don't you start on me, Emmitt," grumbled Garrity. "You know I'll be the first man back out there as soon as conditions will allow."

I found Mary up to her elbows in flour and bread dough when I got back home.

"The mailman made it across the river on his horse this morning," I said.

"I didn't think it had been quite that cold," said Mary, shaping the dough into loaves.

"That makes it a lot easier for me to go check on Merrill, Catherine, and the baby," I said.

"Oh, Jack, thank you so much!" exclaimed Mary. "You know I've been worried."

"I know, and I'll go out to Frank and Allie Ann's, too, as soon as I get back from Columbus Landing," I said. "Frank may be a grown man, but he's still my little brother. I got every right to worry about him. I asked around Miller's stable, and I guess the trails are pretty bad."

"You be real careful," warned Mary.

"You know I will. I'll take Napoleon 'cause he's stout in the body and got feet bigger than frying pans," I said. "I'll get set to go before first light tomorrow. The ice will be hard, and that will be the best traveling conditions. I sure don't want to get into no soft snow or anything melty or slushy. We'd get stuck for sure."

"I'll fix you a bunch of grub to take. They might be out of food. I'll fix it into a pack with some blankets," said Mary.

"I'll take all I can. If things are as bad out there as I think they might be, I'll bring Merrill, Catherine, and the baby back with me. They would be more than welcome here until spring," I said.

"You are the best husband a woman could ever have, Jack Allphin," said Mary, giving me a big, floury hug.

"Why, thank you, Mrs. Allphin. I take that very kindly," I said, returning her hug wholeheartedly.

CHAPTER TEN

Even though Emmitt Miller knew very well how bad the weather had been, he still couldn't help thinking about attempting to run a stagecoach east. There were paying customers waiting impatiently to go to Walla Walla. If he followed the usual schedule, he would send a coach outbound for Walla Walla on Friday, January 10th. The trails were packed down hard, and it had not snowed much for over a day. There was over an inch of ice on top of the snow. Even so, the footing didn't seem too bad. Taking everything into consideration, Miller thought he might just put Rafe Garrity back on the road. He'd give him a span of six horses, turn him loose and see what happened. He might even make it there with all the passengers this time, Miller sourly reflected.

I left home around four in the morning. Mary briefly considered waking the children so they could see me off. Little Mary was almost eight years old, and Olive was four. I stopped her from disturbing them.

I said, "I'll be home tomorrow. Don't bother waking up the

young'uns. They will hardly know I've been gone before I get back."

"Alright. You promise not to take no chances. Come home safe to us," said Mary.

"I promise," I said.

I guided Napoleon down to the river and crossed using the trail broken by the mailman. The snow and the wind had both stopped. It was very quiet; the only sound was the crunch of Napoleon's big hooves on the icy snow.

I let Napoleon set his own pace, and we made slow, sure progress, eventually getting to the north side of the frozen river. Gaining the north shore, I kept the big horse moving north beyond the embankment. We continued to follow the trail left by the mailman for about two miles. This took us over the first bench of land and up to the second bench above the river. We would travel east on the level of this second bench for several miles, thus avoiding the water at Big Eddy and again further upstream at the cliffs, which the local Indians had covered in curious line drawings.

I had been afraid we would have to break a lot of trail. I was glad to see I was mistaken. Several horses, I estimated maybe six or seven of them had used this trail on the second bench level within the last two days. The tracks showed that these horses were going west, toward Fort Vancouver. The crust was broken on the snow, and the trail was somewhat beaten down, making travel for us much easier.

I ate some of the bread Mary had packed for me as the day grew light. Napoleon kept up a slow but steady pace. It did not snow, and it stayed a frigid cold, never getting any warmer. The sky was a uniform, featureless white. The miles felt very long as monotonous, bitterly cold hours passed.

When I ate again, it was late in the afternoon. I had come within sight of the big waterfall at the mouth of the Deschutes River and took a break. I dismounted and staggered around, kicking down each leg of my pants, working the cramps out of my legs. I could see the forty-foot high waterfall plainly from across the Columbia, looking over the big island where the two rivers meet. I knew Emmitt Miller had a home station over there on the other side, but it was not visible from where I stood. I couldn't see Graham's hotel, either, but I knew it was there. I could see the smoke from their chimney.

I estimated that we probably had another six or eight miles to go to get to Columbus Landing. I mounted up again, and Napoleon plodded on.

———•••••———

It was just after dark when Merrill Short heard the horse. He opened the door and shone the lantern out into the dooryard. There was enough light to see Jack Allphin and his big bay horse coming up between the house and the stable shed.

"Jack, let me help you," said Merrill, hurrying to open the stable door.

I slid down off Napoleon's back and shook hands with my brother-in-law.

"You are a sight for sore eyes. It's real good to see you," said Merrill.

"Good to see you, too. Are you alright? Your family alright?" I asked.

"Fine, everyone's fine. I been worried, though, never seen nothing like this weather. We're running out of everything, and it just won't warm up," Merrill said. "Come in and thaw out, Jack. We still got plenty of wood for the fire. I'll see to your horse."

"Just this once," I said, "I'll let you. I'm about frozen through."

I went inside the little house. Catherine insisted I take the chair by the fire. The warmth felt wonderful. Catherine handed me a steaming mug of coffee. That felt wonderful, too. Soon, Merrill came back inside the house. "You don't know how worried we've been, Jack," he said. "We need to go back to Dalles City, but I'm not sure we could make it on our own. We only have the one horse. And it's been so cold."

"I guess I won't have to persuade you much then to let me help you. And please accept our hospitality until spring," I said.

"We can't thank you enough," said Merrill, greatly relieved.

<hr />

The Short family and I got ready to travel early in the morning on January 8th. We ate the rest of the bread I had carried along and used the last of their flour to make pancakes. I saddled Napoleon while Merrill saddled Sadie, their old white horse. While Sadie was old and not in the best condition, she was spunky and willing to travel. Merrill loaded the old horse with blankets and helped his wife and little girl settle in. He strapped the blankets securely around Catherine and the child. Merrill and I would take turns riding Napoleon and walking, leading Sadie.

It started to snow again before we left Columbus Landing. While we kept moving all day, our progress was slow. Snow continued to fall. By nightfall, we had only covered about half the distance back to Dalles City. The wind started to pick up, and it got colder and colder. Merrill and I talked about what we should do. We would have to find some kind of shelter for the night. We couldn't stay out in this storm.

I remembered passing an abandoned shack during my ride the day before. I hadn't paid much attention and didn't recall exactly where it was located. I thought we should be coming to it soon.

It was fully dark and snowing hard when we finally came to the abandoned shack. It was not only deserted; half of the walls had collapsed. But the roof was intact, and the place would offer us shelter from the wind and snow.

Merrill got his wife and daughter settled into a nest of blankets in the most intact corner of the shack. I busied myself with starting a fire, using the floorboards from the ruined little building.

Merrill and I stayed up all that night feeding the fire and talking. We had picketed the horses in the lea of the little building. Every now and then one or the other of us would go out to check on the two horses. The frigid night passed slowly, and we were relieved when it eventually gave way to dawn.

We got moving west down the trail again at daylight. The snow continued to fall. We traveled slowly, steadily, all day long. We had nothing left to eat, and as darkness fell, we were still several miles from home. It had been dark for over three hours when we finally arrived at my snug little house in Dalles City.

Mary and the girls had been anxiously expecting us. There was a large pot of beef stew ready. Warm, dry clothing was on hand for everyone to change into. My two little daughters proudly pointed out the comfortable pallet bed on the floor, which they had helped their mother make for their guests.

I was relieved to get back home safely. Conditions outside really were bad. The trip to Columbus Landing and back had taken far longer than I had expected. Now, I told myself, we'll just see how I do getting out to Willow Creek.

⸺◆◇◆⸺

Survival at the Florence mining camp was getting to be a challenge. Three hundred men had elected to stay on the mountainside for the winter, not knowing what kind of conditions to expect. They had hoped to get some mining done, or at the least, to be the first to recommence work in the spring. But the temperature had not risen above freezing since late November. Over ten feet of snow had fallen, burying cabins and wiping out landmarks. The creeks were frozen solid; the rockers stood idle, no mining could be done. The trail out along Slate Creek was considered impassable. The men on the mountain would be staying put right there until the spring thaw.

The erstwhile miners now spent most of their time trying to stay warm. Firewood became harder and harder to find. Every tree and bush in the area had already been hacked down and burned. A walk to get firewood now entailed a round trip hike of over two miles. Tempers were short, and bloody fistfights erupted over a few sticks of burnable wood.

Food supplies were already getting scarce. Three-fingered Smith had to post an armed guard at his store. His prices skyrocketed. Smith was charging five dollars a pound for sugar. Tobacco was going for ten dollars a pound. Wheat flour was thirteen dollars a pound. Coffee was not to be had at any price. And the winter had barely begun.

The well-known outlaw and murderer Boone Helm, "The Kentucky Cannibal," had gotten himself stranded in Florence for the winter. He spent most of his time drinking whiskey, playing cards, and picking fights. He let it be known that he would gladly kill any man for a price.

One December evening a very drunken Boone Helm had murdered the German prospector known as Dutch Fred. Seeing unarmed Dutch Fred at one of the local saloons, Helm calmly walked up to him, drew his handgun, and fired. Being very drunk, Helm missed. He then took more careful aim and fired again, killing Dutch Fred. Helm was immediately apprehended. A meeting was then held among all the snowed-in miners where lynching Helm was narrowly voted down.

It was decided that the murderer would be taken to the Canyon City jail as soon as travel was possible again. Until that time, a cell was improvised to hold Helm. It consisted of a pair of handcuffs chained to the log wall of one of merchant Smith's locked storage rooms. The storage room was chilly and uncomfortable, but no one felt sorry for Helm. At least Smith would be feeding the prisoner.

Helm managed to escape almost immediately. He and an accomplice fled the area using snowshoes. When their tracks were found, the men placed bets on the likelihood of finding their frozen bodies along the trail or at the bottom of the icy Slate Creek gorge in the spring.

In later months Helm would claim that the man who helped him escape had also become the chief item in his diet while hiking out of the mountains and back to Lewiston.

John Stephens set the team moving at walking pace as they left the Willow Creek home station just after ten in the morning on January 6th. Refreshed from the short break and fueled by a hearty breakfast, the nine stagecoach passengers were ready to load back into the stagecoach for the next station. The four men who had spent the week at Willow Creek were anxious to perhaps find an inside seat on the full coach and finally get moving. It was lightly snowing as they headed west toward the John Day River, twenty-five miles distant. The stagecoach was carrying its original passengers and baggage plus the additional bags of Mulkey, Riddle, Davis, and Glover. Moody and Gay rode on top with the baggage, having from the goodness of their hearts given up their inside seats to Mulkey and Riddle. Glover, Davis, and Frank Allphin all walked behind the stagecoach.

During that twenty-five mile stretch, Stephens took every opportunity to make things easier for the horses. He never urged them to go faster than a walk. He stopped and made the passengers, even Mulkey and Riddle walk at each uphill section of the trail. Both men complained loudly, but they did as Stephens directed.

Gay and Moody observed and approved of how Stephens was handling the situation. Gay said, "Our driver is a right square man. He treats his horses better than he treats his passengers."

"That's just as it should be," agreed Moody, nodding his head. "If anyone can get us all to Dalles City, Stephens is the man."

Everyone was hungry and tired by the time the stagecoach got close to the John Day River home station. It was just getting dark. Though he couldn't yet see the buildings, Stephens recognized where he was and brought the stagecoach to a halt just over the top of the last rise. The passengers straggled up on foot.

"This here is the last downhill stretch, gentlemen," said Stephens. "Pile in, and you can ride for the last mile down to the station. Frank and you other two fellas hop on where you can, and you can ride, too."

The seats in the stagecoach were rapidly occupied. Allphin, Davis, and Glover found places among the baggage, joining Gay and Moody.

"Hang on, everyone. Here we go," yelled Stephens. "Hup, boys, hup, there. Shake a leg! Let's go." The team started the stagecoach moving, slowly at first, but gaining speed rapidly despite the snow on this downhill stretch. There wasn't a sign of the trail in the blanket of white, but Stephens and the horses knew right where it was. Unfailingly, they headed for the gap; a notch cut into the hillside. The snow had drifted deeper here. In some places, it was over four feet deep. The stocky black horses dragged the stagecoach, plowing, skidding, and slipping down the incline. The body of the stagecoach cut a wide furrow, sliding through the snow cover, more sledlike than anything else.

The horses might have foundered if it had not been so steep. As it was, the tired horses were putting a lot of effort into staying in front of the hurtling stagecoach. They managed to stay ahead of the stagecoach, swinging a wide turn south as they reached the flat next to the John Day River. The snow was only about two feet deep on the flat. Tom Scott's little house and huge barn were just ahead. The horses were familiar with that barn and moved out briskly to get to its shelter.

Driver John Stephens halted the stagecoach at Scott's house first, letting his passengers out, and unloading bedrolls and baggage to go into the little building. Tracy Express agent James unloaded the bag of mail and had Stephens give him a hand with the strongbox. There was smoke coming out of the house chimney, but no one came out to help or even to greet them.

Stephens then crossed the yard with the team and the stagecoach. Seeing that they were going to get no help from the house, Frank Allphin stayed with him, knowing the driver would appreciate a little assistance with the horses after this long, cold day.

Opening the barn doors wide, Frank said, "John, you done yourself a job of work today. Let me give you a hand here."

Stephens pulled the stagecoach into the big barn, halting the team for the last time that day.

"It's the horses what done the job of work," said Stephens. "For a stagecoach, she makes a pretty good sleigh, huh? Too bad we ain't got no runners to put on her. I bet she'd go slick like greased lightning if we did."

"Probably would," agreed Frank.

"Where do you suppose Tom Scott's at? Or, now that I think of it, where in tarnation is that old coot Miller hired to help out around here?" wondered Stephens.

"Old coot?" asked Frank.

"Yeah," Stephens said. "Some old drunk Emmitt took pity on and hired. From what I've seen, he ain't worth much."

"I hope it ain't who I think it is," said Frank. "If it is, Emmitt sent him out to me first. And he ain't just worthless; he's poison. He's not just a drunk. He's lazy. And what's worse, he's a bully, too. He had Allen doing his chores by threatening to thrash him. I run the old codger off after I heard about it, maybe four or five months ago. As a goodbye gift, he left the stable doors open in the wind and got them ripped off the building for me."

The two men took care of the unhitching, unharnessing, rubbing down, and feeding of the team of horses. It took Frank some time searching through the feed bins in the barn to find enough oats to give to the exhausted team. He didn't see any sweet hay at all.

"I'm scraping the bottom of the barrel here to get a little something for our four-footed friends," Frank said.

Stephens said, "Somebody's been slacking around here, leaving everything undone and a mess. These stalls ain't been cleaned out anytime recently. And there ain't no straw bedding down here on the main floor. I'm gonna have to go up to the loft and toss some down. I hope there's some up there."

"Say," said Frank, "There should be a haystack out back. I'll go out and get a big armful to feed these fellas while you finish up in here."

Stephens found straw to drop into the stalls and was coming back down the ladder from the haymow when Frank came back in, empty-handed.

"You wouldn't believe it," Frank said. "There's no haystack out there at all."

"That can't be. Unless my eyes were playing tricks, a couple of weeks ago there were two big haystacks, not fifty yards from this here barn," said Stephens.

"Well, they ain't there now. Ain't nothing but snow and back-wash from the river out there now," said Frank.

The sound of several angry voices back at the house reached the men in the barn. Frank Allphin and John Stephens exchanged a disgusted look.

"What do you suppose that is all about?" asked Frank.

"I guess we better go see," said Stephens.

CHAPTER ELEVEN

Miller and Blackmore Stagecoach Company employee William Halberth, age sixty-two, had spent the day dozing in a wooden chair by the kitchen fire at the John Day River home station. He was enjoying the warmth of the blaze and a sweet feeling of power. He had blustered and bullied and bluffed the two passengers Garrity had deserted here. He made them stay in the big, chilly main room of the house with the unreliable wood-burning stove which drafted poorly and liked to smoke back into the building. He made them cut and haul their own firewood for that cranky stove. To do this, they had to go down to the grove of willows near the flooded, ice-choked John Day River. He also charged them for meager rations, which should have been theirs for free. He would not let them into the kitchen for fear they might find out what good food he really had back there. He had cowed them into obedience, listening to nothing they said, and giving orders in a loud, bossy voice.

Halberth was getting away with taking advantage of the abandoned passengers only because Tom Scott, the actual owner of the house, farmer, ferry operator, and manager of the stagecoach home station, was not at home. If Scott had been present, Halberth would never have attempted to pass himself off as the man in charge of this home station and ferry crossing. Halberth was well aware that Scott could come home at any time. He was actually grateful to the raw weather for delaying the man for as long as it had. Halberth knew it was possible that Scott would fire him, or at least send him back to Emmitt Miller when he found out how the stranded passengers had been treated. But Halberth had been drinking and did not care what happened. He had been drunk since shortly after Scott had left, several days previously.

Halberth woke from his nap with a start. He heard voices, several unfamiliar voices out in the main room. He quickly got to his feet, tipping over his chair. He came through the canvas curtain that served as a kitchen door into the main room, ready to defend his domain. "Here, now," said Halberth, "Who are you people, and what are you doing in my house?"

Jagger and Wellington came forward to represent the group.

"My good man," said Jagger, "We are from the Miller and Blackmore stagecoach and need to get food for ourselves and fodder for the team of horses. Further, we require accommodations for the night. Where should we leave our bags?"

Halberth opened and closed his mouth several times, at first unsure of how to handle these pesky new passengers. He did not want to do anything for them and so, with drunken logic attempted to get rid of them.

"There ain't nothing here for you," Halberth lied. "There ain't no provisions here at all, at all. You can't stay here, no, no. You had better go camp down in the willow grove down by the river. Yes, down by the river in that lot of willows. I cannot entertain you here."

Wellington said, "That is absurd. We are paying passengers of the stagecoach company. We are cold and tired. We don't have any tents. We don't even have an ax! We won't go!"

Everyone shouted their agreement at once.

"We have come as far as we are going to go tonight," said Jagger, pointing a finger at Halberth. "We are stopping right here, right where we are. And furthermore, we are willing to pay top dollar to partake of whatever you have in this house to eat. Bring it out."

"You stay put here," said Halberth, turning on his heel and disappearing into the little kitchen, twitching the curtain closed behind himself.

Upon entering the kitchen he first took his open bottle of whiskey, corked it and hid it behind the sack of cornmeal. He grabbed the side of bacon and hid it under an empty barrel on the floor. He took the large pot of simmering beans off the stove and hid it in the oven. Three cold biscuits sat on a tin pie plate on top of a barrel full of crackers, and satisfied with himself, Halberth grabbed the pie plate with the biscuits and stomped back out into the main room.

"Here," he said, "That is all I have in the whole building."

"He's lying," said one of the men who had been inside when they arrived. Pat Davis recognized him as fellow passenger Slim Nichols. He was one of the two men who had been left behind by Garrity here. Nichols had already experienced more than enough of Halberth's hospitality and was thoroughly fed up with him.

"Oh, is that so? Let's just go have a look for ourselves," said Jeffries.

"Yes," said Moody, "Let's just take a little inventory of what there really is back in that kitchen."

"You got no right to go back there," said Halberth, trying to block the doorway.

Moody, Gay, and Jeffries ignored his protests and pushed their way past him and into the kitchen. They found all that Halberth had hidden and took note of a large quantity of other supplies. There was an entire wheel of cheese, a sack of unmilled wheat and at least two dozen cooking apples.

Jagger intercepted Stephens and Allphin as they came in the door.

"It seems our landlord claims he can't entertain us and he's got nothing to offer us to eat, neither for men nor for beasts. It also seems that he is most certainly lying. He is some kind of highfalutin old Irish codger," said Jagger.

"Old Irish codger, eh?" asked Allphin. "Where is he?"

"I believe he's back in the kitchen trying to keep Mr. Gay, Mr. Moody, and Mr. Jeffries from taking stock," said Jagger.

Allphin strode briskly over to the kitchen doorway. Pulling back the curtain and peering inside, his worst suspicions were confirmed. Standing before him was that worthless William Halberth. Allphin exploded.

"I do not believe my eyes. Cuss your ornery hide, Halberth. I thought I'd seen the last of you. But here you are, shirking your duties and drinking on the job again. If you won't get to work, then get out of the way. And don't give me any of your sass about being just a poor old man. I don't want to hear about your rheumatiz' or your bunions or your lumbago. My dear Daddy is twice the man you are, and he's got a good twenty years on you. Bring in some more wood for both these stoves. And you better get out any other supplies you got hid from the paying passengers. You are a worthless scarecrow and I ought to thump you up some. Now get moving," Allphin ordered.

He dropped the canvas curtain back down. Shaking his head, he turned and addressed the company of passengers. "Gentlemen, I must apologize. That man is a disgrace to the Miller and Blackmore Stagecoach Company, and he has no authority to deny you anything. I have the misfortune to have known him from before. He is the kind of lazy, shiftless flunky who would pretend to be sick, or even throw away his tools to get out of his work. Now he's impersonating his betters. His helpful ways have caused him to be sent packing in the past. I'll sure be talking with Emmitt Miller about our Mr. Halberth's ideas on hospitality. I am sorry."

"I told you all he was lying," said Nichols.

Allphin said, "I got to thank you. I admire a man who will call a skunk a skunk. Sorry you had to be his guest. My name is Frank Allphin," he said, extending his right hand.

"Pleased to meet you. My name is Slim Nichols. I'm trying to get home from the mines at Florence, but the other stagecoach driver left me here because I'm not sure how much walking in the snow I could do. I'm from the mining camps around Nevada City, Yuba County, California," he said, shaking hands.

Frank turned to the other men. "Gentlemen, we will be staying here tonight, if you would like to get comfortable, maybe roll out your beds. I sent that old liar out after more firewood. I wish I knew where Tom Scott went. This is his house, and he's the man in charge around here. Anyone want to volunteer for cook duty?"

"Moody and me already got that covered," said Gay from behind Allphin. "We found a big pot of beans about ready to eat, and we got the makings for more biscuits. It won't take us but a minute, or maybe two."

Tom Jeffries thought he had seen a face from home over on the other side of the room. "David?" Jeffries asked, walking over. "Aren't you David McDonald from Polk County?"

The seated man looked up at Jeffries.

"Who wants to know?" he asked.

"It's me, Tom Jeffries," he said, extending his right hand for a handshake.

"By golly, it is, and still on this side of the dirt, too," said McDonald, rising and happily shaking Jeffries' hand.

"Sure, you bet," said Jeffries. "You never heard I done expired, did you?"

"Naw, I never did," said McDonald. "But I sure ain't seen you in about a month of Sundays. Where you been keeping yourself? How have you been?"

"Fair to middling, all things considered. I'm on my way home from the mines. What about you? What in tarnation are you doing here?" asked Jeffries.

"I'm on my way home, too. I did alright operating a rocker for the summer. Now I'll be happy to go back to farming. That last stage-coach left me here. I told the driver I'd had enough hiking in the snow, so here I am," said McDonald.

The two men proceeded to get caught up on their recent activities and to talk about old times. They had each taken up land claims in the Bethel District of Polk County. McDonald was forty-two years old, a farmer usually, with a wife and three nearly adult children. He had gone to the Salmon River mines like Jeffries, but they had never run into each other while they were there.

Bolton engaged Nichols in conversation about the California mines, reminiscing about his own time there. "I done alright in California, but I done even better in Florence," said Nichols with a smile.

"Oh, I must agree with you there," said Bolton. "California gold kept me in groceries, but Florence did much better."

Halberth had come back from his foray to get firewood with precious little. Allphin took the ax away from him and went out and cut a generous armload to bring back. Coming back in the rear door of the kitchen, Allphin addressed Halberth, who was huddled up next to the stove, trying his best to look misused.

"I'd just as soon shoot you and feed you to them brave horses out in the barn. I'd do it, too, but they wouldn't get no nourishment from your stringy carcass," said Allphin. "Where's Tom Scott, anyway?"

"I don't know," mumbled Halberth.

Although Halberth stood a head taller than Frank Allphin, he sidled away from the angry younger man.

"Stand still, you skunk," said Allphin. "I got another bone to pick with you. What happened to Tom Scott's haystacks, you old bog-trotter?"

Halberth would only look at his feet and repeat, "I don't know."

Allphin finally gave up on him.

The evening meal, consisting of coffee, beans, bacon, biscuits, crackers, and cheese, was served within the hour. Various groups fell into conversation as they ate. Gay, Moody, Glover, and Niles made up one of these groups.

"Why would that old coot want to pull a stunt like that?" asked nineteen-year-old Glover. "Did he really think he could get away with turning us all out to freeze and starve?"

Niles was quick to answer. "He's a drunk. Just smell him. He's addled himself with drink, so he can't think. I got no time for drunks. And I've sure had my fill of them over the years."

"I done signed the pledge last spring," said Glover. "Me, my brother, and my Daddy all signed. It made my Ma real proud. You know, I would never go back on what I signed. It would be like breaking my word, both to God and to my Ma."

"That's good to hear, friend, good to hear. You know about how many men in the mining camps are real abstainers. You been there," said Niles.

"Yes, sir, I do know. I seen some real poor behavior while I was out at the diggings," said Glover. "But I still don't understand how he thought he could get away with it."

"You might be surprised at what people think they can get away with," said Gay. "Human nature can be awful contrary. Why, I had me an example in my own dear wife, Frances. Now, don't mistake me, I love my Frances just fine, shared hard times with her, got a passel of young'uns with her. I would trust her with my life or my fortune. But there was a time," Gay shook his head, then continued, "When I asked her to be my wife we made an agreement that we would be going to the Oregon country right away. All my folks, my parents and my brothers and sisters, we all were going. I thought she was happy about our plan. I thought she was with me all the way. So we got married, and I thought everything was alright with the world."

Gay paused and smiled sadly at the men around him.

He said, "Then she set her heels like a Missouri mule and would not budge an inch. She claimed she was not going anywhere. I didn't know it then, but her parents had got to her, playing on her sympathies, telling her that if she would not go, then her new husband would be persuaded to stay. When I found out, I was about fit to be tied, ready to blow straight up and then turn left. I felt ambushed. It was so unexpected."

"What did you do?" asked Glover.

"I kept on getting ready to travel. I didn't know what else to do, and it turned out alright in the end," said Gay. "Her Daddy saw that I was serious about going to Oregon. When he saw me getting ready to put whip to my team, he done gave up. He told me he was sorry and he didn't ever mean to keep his daughter and me apart. He said it just hurt him and his wife so bad to see her leave, probably never to return. So, it wasn't my Frances's fault that she was acting so contrary. She just hadn't been a wife very long and was still trying to be a good daughter."

Conversations continued around the room while the men settled down for the night. Express agent James sat in the far corner with the strongbox for a seat and the mailbag for a backrest. He took his ease, listening to Mulkey and Riddle trade plain and fancy lies about raising horses. Neither man had ever actually owned a horse as intelligent or as fast as they claimed.

Jagger and Wellington were comparing notes about the various big cities each of them had visited.

"There is nothing to compare with New York City," said Jagger.

"But have you ever visited Philadelphia? Or what about New Orleans? Now there is a city," said Wellington.

Wilson and Bolton were explaining to Nichols and Stephens about a crooked Faro layout they had the misfortune to participate in back at the mining camps.

"Right then and there," said Swede Wilson, "I figgered I better stop trying to buck the tiger. I ain't got the knack for it. Serious gambling just is not for me."

"I would have felt a lot better about losing if the game had been square," said Bolton.

Pat Davis gave in to exhaustion and fell asleep on top of his blankets. A whoop of laughter from Nichols woke him again with a start.

"Doggone it," Davis complained. "I was dreaming I was back at home. Not just back at home, but in the summertime, too. Air all warm and soft, the smell of fresh bread and fried chicken cooking in my mother's kitchen. Then I wake up, and where am I? Here, with you bunch of smelly miners. That is what I call a big disappointment."

"Don't feel too bad, friend. At least we are out of the snow and that cruel wind. Got to pity anyone who is out in the weather tonight," said Nichols. "I'll try to be quieter if you want to get back to sleep again."

Frank Allphin had rolled out his bedroll against the farthest wall. He was asleep almost before he hit the blankets. Nothing was going to disturb him. The long walk in the cold and the snow, plus dealing with Halberth, had worn him out.

CHAPTER TWELVE

Tom Scott finally came home around midnight. Scott was forty-one years old. Originally from Indiana, he had taken up his land on the John Day River in 1858. There had never been a ferry where the Oregon Trail crossed the John Day before Scott built one and started running it that same year.

Scott walked through the door, accompanied by a burst of frigid, snow-laden wind. Having already been to the barn to stable his own horse, he had seen the stagecoach and the horses. He knew there would be people bedded down in his house, but he was surprised by how many people were actually there. He was careful not to step on anyone as he came in out of the weather.

John Stephens rose up immediately from among the sleeping men.

"Say, Mr. Scott, can I have a word with you?" he quietly asked.

"Sure," answered Scott. "Come on back to the kitchen. I'm about starved. I went up to Rock Creek a few days ago to get a load of hay and got my stubby little horse stuck in every drift we came to. We had to hunker down once we got there, the weather took such a foul turn. Might have froze to death if we hadn't stayed at the dug-out barn for two nasty nights. Then I only made it back to my neighbor's upriver. Had to stay there another couple of days. Good, there's biscuits."

Scott had lit the lantern in the kitchen. He stirred up the cookfire, adding more wood. He put the pot of beans back on the stove and lifted the coffee pot to see if there was any left. He poured himself a cup of lukewarm coffee and ate two biscuits while he waited for the beans to reheat.

"I've got to say I'm relieved to hear you went for hay since I couldn't find any for my team out in your nice, big, empty barn," said Stephens. "What happened to your haystacks? Or did I just imagine two big haystacks last time I had the run through here?"

"No, you didn't imagine them haystacks," said Scott, mouth half-full of biscuit. He washed the biscuit down with coffee and continued. "There was two of them, alright. Had us a fine hay crop this summer, you know. I had Halberth put the haystacks up on the first bench of land above the river. Never had no trouble, put them there for the last four years. Well, this here year the water just come up and took them. Happened in the middle of the night and I never got a chance to salvage one bit. My good hay all washed down to the Columbia River, and on out to sea, it was raining so hard. I maybe wouldn't believe it if I hadn't been here."

"How much feed were you able to bring in with you tonight?" asked Stephens.

Scott swallowed a mouthful of beans. "I rigged me some runners onto half of a wagon box. I filled that short box, filled it, and tamped it down to get as much in as I could. I heaped it up and tied a canvas tarp over the top. My Little Joe, he's a chunky little horse, but it was all he could do to get us back here with that one, big load."

"I'm right glad you did it," said Stephens. "We've had nothing but trouble since we left Umatilla Landing. It's a pure wonder we made it here, now that I get a chance to think about it."

"Pray, tell," said Scott, chewing steadily.

"For starters, nobody was manning the Wells Springs station. No relief stock there, either, and not much feed. No food at all for the passengers. What was really kind of strange, though, is somebody took the stove pipes from both stoves, and we found them in the pool at the Springs," said Stephens.

"What?" asked Scott. "I wonder what that was all about."

"I surely don't know," said Stephens. "We had to put a stove back together in order to get a little heat. Then we had some real rough going to get to the Willow Creek home station. I had the passengers walking, and even pushing part of the way. When we got to Willow Creek, we found that Allphin's about out of everything. By the way, Frank come along with me. He's pounding his ear out in the main room with the rest of our passengers. He about wore himself out wading through the snow all day behind the stagecoach. He's going to come along for the run into Dalles City to get supplies. Food is getting awful low for them."

"At least we got some food here for your passengers," said Scott.

"I'm glad," said Stephens. "You know, there was no relief stock at Willow Creek, either. I was right pleased to see that Frank has a lot of good hay put up in his stable barn. No oats for the team, but plenty of good, dry hay. He's a good man."

Stephens located a cup and poured himself some of the reheated coffee. Scott held out his cup for a refill. William Halberth snored loudly from his bedroll behind the kitchen stove, oblivious to Stephens and Scott.

"Frank's furious with that old drunk," said Stephens, motioning toward Halberth. "I thought he was gonna knock the daylights out of him."

"Ha!" scoffed Scott. "I feel like punching him almost every day. It's hard to be anything but angry with him. He's lazy. And he's drunk a lot of the time. There ain't much he can do right, even when he puts his mind to it. I'd send him back to Emmitt, but he's such a pitiful creature. If Emmitt fires him, he'll starve, and that would make me feel responsible."

"Hasn't Emmitt sent anyone out to bring us some replacement stock, or maybe some groceries?" asked Stephens.

"No, he hasn't," said Scott. "We haven't had anyone out from Dalles City in more than a week, maybe ten days. You know, I was watching, and Garrity almost didn't make it out of the canyon, even with no passengers on board. The three men who went with him had to hike behind the stagecoach up the switchbacks to the top of the rise. That's why we ended up with our two guests out there. Them two thought they couldn't make it to the top of the plateau on foot. So they decided to stay here and wait for you."

"Wait for me?" asked Stephens. "Why, I already got five extra men with me now. I got the four passengers Garrity dumped at Wells Springs and Frank Allphin. Conditions ain't been no better today, neither. As a matter of fact, they are probably worse than when Garrity came through. Come morning I'll be having the passengers walk to the top of the rise myself."

"I hate to tell you," said Scott, "But you may not be getting to the other side of the river in the morning. The ice has been very bad, very unpredictable. It's not solid enough for a man to walk on. It keeps shifting, cracking and piling up, making ice dams and then breaking them. That makes it too dangerous to try to run the ferry. It could be crushed like an egg."

"Seriously?" asked Stephens, "You think it's too dangerous to float the ferry across?"

"I wouldn't have let Fred bring her over anytime since Garrity came through. We'll have to see how things are in the morning. Just don't be too surprised if we can't get your stagecoach across," said Scott.

"Now don't that beat all? Ain't that just the icing on the cake?" asked Stephens.

"Maybe I said it before, but I'll tell you again that I never seen the like," said Scott. "Say, you remember young Wilcox, Fred Wilcox? I got him over on the west side, running the ferry when we can and staying in a wall tent. Him and his big old hound dog. For almost a week I can't even get supplies over to them. We got a two-inch rope running over the river with a pulley and a box slung on below. But the pulley froze in place, and the ice has built up on it so bad the rope is now about twice the size it should be. "

Stephens had been thinking about what all this meant. He said, "One short wagon-box full of hay ain't gonna last my team of blacks very long. What am I supposed to do if we can't cross?"

"You might just have to get shed of your passengers and go back east, back to Walla Walla," said Scott.

"Hoo boy," said Stephens. "Wouldn't that be a kick in the teeth?"

Allie Ann's eyes popped open. While it was still dark, she felt that it must be near dawn. Young William was snuggled up next to her, head under the quilt, serenely sleeping. She could just barely identify the lump on the far side of the room, near the fire as the slumbering form of Allen. She wondered how Frank was doing and if he and the stagecoach had made it to the John Day River safely.

She whispered, "My thanks for the new day. Please give me strength and bless William and Allen, Louisa and Tom. Bless Frank and keep him safe. In Jesus' name, I pray, amen." It was basically the same simple, sincere, prayer she said each morning.

The room had taken on a definite chill, and Allie Ann moved quickly to stir up the banked fire and add more wood. Soon there was enough heat for her to cook breakfast. Having slept in her clothing, she only had to put on her long-sleeved wool jacket to be comfortable in the house. She let the boys sleep and completed her morning chores.

Pulling on her long canvas coat over her wool jacket, she got ready to make the journey outside to the outhouse. The wind was gusting, flinging down waves of tiny ice pellets from the sky.

Allie Ann was careful to make sure the door to the house was latched before she walked away. A new crust of ice covered the fallen snow, and her steps crunched like she was walking in deep gravel. She completed her business outdoors and rushed back to the house, stopping to grab an armload of ice-sprinkled firewood from the pile near the door on her way back inside the house. It was so cold outside her face stung, and her hands hurt. She was glad there were no animals to feed in the barn.

Once inside, she set down her armload of wood and picked up the almost empty water bucket. There was an inch of solid ice in the bottom of the bucket. It had been liquid water the evening before. Steeling herself for another trip outside, she left the house again to get some water. A few steps outside the door, a blast of icy air hit her, staggering her, and she decided not to go all the way to the creek for water. She stopped, bent down and scooped up a bucket full of clean, white snow, complete with a thick, icy crust. While it would not yield her a full bucket of water, she knew it would soon melt on the fire, giving her perhaps a short half of a bucketful. She knew it would be enough for now, and she could always come back for more.

Allie Ann decided she did not want to chance going down to the creek. Willow Creek had frozen from the banks out into the shallow main channel. There were still a few open areas of moving water where one could dip a bucket, but walking on the ice would be risky. It was slick, and she might slip and fall in. She might only get her feet wet, but then they might freeze before she could get back inside the house. She did not dare risk getting hurt, Allen and young William were counting on her to take care of them. She didn't want to be the cause of any disasters, and she certainly did not want Frank coming home to any problems she had caused.

Allen was awake and up, putting on his boots when she came back in with the bucket full of ice and snow.

"Aunty Allie, how you 'spose Uncle Frank is doing?" he asked.

"Oh, I expect he's doing just fine, him and all that crowd of fellers he went with. They all appeared to be capable, grown men," said Allie Ann. "I'd think they made it to the John Day home station before dark yesterday. And that means they are getting ready to cross the river pretty soon now; after they have had a bite to eat. Frank should be putting his boots under Aunt Mary Allphin's kitchen table before dark tonight."

"Really?" asked Allen.

"Yes, really," said Allie Ann. "Now, I got some water heating. How about you wash your hands and face, and we have some breakfast for our own selves?"

"I like breakfas', Mama," said young William, round face peeking out from under the quilt.

"Well, good morning, there. I know you like your breakfast, honey," said Allie Ann. "Rise and shine. And let Allen help you wash up. Breakfast will be served in two shakes of a lamb's tail, my young gentlemen."

Allie Ann faced few decisions regarding the menu. She could count all her supplies on one hand. She had about a quart of molasses remaining in the big tin, and roughly fifteen pounds of wheat flour left in the sack. There was about the same amount of cornmeal, but she hadn't been using it. Kerosene had been spilled on the bag and, while she had not thrown it away, she hesitated to cook with it.

She had given it some consideration and thought perhaps she would try to leach the kerosene out by rinsing and soaking the cornmeal in water. Maybe she would try that later today. Of course, she had plenty of saleratus to make dough rise and salt and a big stone jar of bacon grease to fry things in. Her last couple of pounds of dried lentils she had soaked overnight in water in a covered kettle next to the fire, and those would be made into soup for dinner.

"Who wants pancakes with sweet molasses?" asked Allie Ann.

"I sure do," said Allen.

"Me, too," chimed young William.

———◆•◆•◆———

Tom Scott and John Stephens were down by the John Day River before daylight on the morning of January 7th.

"It's no good," said Scott. "Look at that."

He pointed downstream, where a huge chunk of ice had just broken loose and started moving, grinding along beside a wide, flat plate of the frozen river. As the men watched a jagged hunk of ice as big as a wagon bed flew up in the air and came crashing back down onto the partially frozen surface of the water. Both men stood silently watching the river while their frozen breath hung in the still air.

"Alright," said Stephens breaking the silence. "I wouldn't have believed it if I hadn't seen it. I guess I can't buck that. But I sure hate to leave a job half done. It plumb goes agin my grain."

Scott delivered the bad news to the stagecoach passengers and Frank Allphin. The moaning and complaining were quite bad. He also told them that Stephens was going to have to take the stagecoach back to Walla Walla.

"Miller is sure going to hear about this," said Mulkey. "I'm going to fill his ear up with a funnel."

"At this rate, I'll die of old age before I can get home," moaned Riddle.

"Snakes of purgatory!" exclaimed Niles, fed-up and disgusted.

"Where?" cried Halberth, suddenly full of panic and scrutinizing the floor.

Niles looked over at Halberth.

"What?" Niles asked. "Why, you old geezer, you're afeared of snakes!"

"Where?" demanded Halberth again, mistrustfully scanning the floor.

"In your head, you drunk old coot," said Niles.

Allphin and James went out to the barn to help Stephens with the team of horses. They ransacked the barn, but there was no more horse feed to be found. Stephens was thankful for the hay Scott had managed to bring back from Rock Creek. He fed each horse lightly, knowing there was plenty of feed for the horses at Willow Creek. He was planning on leaving before noon, and he figured with an empty coach, they should make it back to the Willow Creek home station by dark.

Stephens was pleased to see no new snow had fallen overnight and the deep trench made by the stagecoach was still plainly visible from across the flat.

The three men came back from the barn to Scott's house to thaw out and get some breakfast. Wellington came forward to talk to Stephens and shake his hand.

"You're a game one, Mr. Stephens, and that's for sure," said Wellington.

"Thank you kindly," said Stephens.

"I been observing, and I can't help but admire the way you done handled the team," said Gay. "I appreciate a good man on the reins."

"We're all mighty grateful it was you handling the ribbons," said Moody.

"We gotta thank you. We know you done your best to get us there," said Niles.

"Wish I could have done better," said Stephens. "I hate to leave a job half done."

"You done all you could. No one could have done better," said James. "I'll ride with you again any day, John. You're a square man, and I have never seen a better captain of a coach."

"I thank you for that, sir, indeed I do," said Stephens.

"You are all man, Stephens, all man. Let me give you my hand," said Jagger.

"Me, too," said Jeffries.

Each man had to shake Stephens' hand. They found that they had gotten quite attached to their trusty driver.

"There's a lot of bark on that old boy," Gay remarked to Moody.

"Sure is," agreed Moody. "That there is a fine man."

Allphin and James helped Stephens bring the stagecoach and team out of the barn. "Could you give my wife a message for me?" Allphin asked.

"Of course, Frank," said Stephens.

"Just tell her for me that she is not to worry. I'm doing fine. I'll be getting to Dalles City and back to her just as soon as I can. Tell her I'm thinking of her and the boys," said Allphin.

"I'll do that, Frank. I'll tell her, for sure," said Stephens.

Just before noon, Stephens mounted the box and strapped down his lap apron. He let off the handbrake, gave a flick to the reins and a single crack to the whip. The stagecoach started moving, heading back east.

"Come on, let's go, pick it up," he spoke to his team and popped the cracker on his hickory whip again.

Stephens swung the coach wide across the flat to gain a little speed. He would need some momentum to get to the top of the grade above the river. The horses dug in and got good traction for the uphill pull.

"Steady there, fellas, we're making it now, yes, we're making it," he encouraged them.

The going got easier after they reached the top. Stephens breathed a sigh of relief. They should do fine back to Willow Creek now. It was twenty-five miles, but the coach was empty, and the horses were rested. There were a few hills between here and there, but nothing like this first pull out of the John Day Canyon. The air was brutally cold, but the horses didn't seem to mind. He hoped the snow would hold off until they got back to Allphin's.

CHAPTER THIRTEEN

"You don't know how long we might be stuck here now, do you?" Jeffries asked Tom Scott.

"Miller was supposed to have another coach out here from Dalles City to meet the Walla Walla stagecoach days ago. If he don't send nobody, or if we still can't get across the river, then right here is where you all will be staying," said Scott.

Jeffries sought out Moody and Gay, telling them what Scott said.

"If we are going to be here for a while, I think we should get organized and take stock of what all we got to work with," said Jeffries.

"It might be a good idea to have a little meeting and make us into a company. From what I've seen, we got ourselves at least two natural born work shirkers among us. If we elect everyone to a job, we might get some good out of them," said Moody.

"I think everybody is inside the house now. Let's just call everyone to order," said Gay.

The sixteen stranded men were all present in the main room of the house. Jeffries called for everyone's attention. "It looks like we are gonna be here for a couple of days. It would probably be for the best if we were to get organized. If we form a company, we can assign duties to keep busy, so no one gets bored or feels like he's doing more than his share of the work."

Moody said, "We need to look around and see what we got to work with, then we should elect some officers to take charge. The food in this house is about gone. I say we search through the freight out in the barn and see if there is anything out there we can use." His plan met with general approval.

Halberth poked his head into the room from the kitchen. "You got no right to mess with any of that freight out in the barn. It don't belong to you."

Several voices immediately raised in protest. Halberth again retired to the kitchen.

A delegation was selected to go out and search the barn. Pat Davis, J.E. Glover, Doc Gay, and W.A. Moody put on their coats and went out to see what they could find.

Tom Scott had retired to the tack room in the barn the night before. There was a small Franklin stove there, and Scott was much more comfortable alone in the barn than he would have been in his overcrowded house. The tack room would be his headquarters while he had so many guests. He heard the searchers come in by way of the barn door.

"How are you, gentlemen?" Scott asked. "What can I do for you?"

Gay said, "We are fine, sir, but the food in the house is about to run out. We thought we would look through the freight out here and see if there is anything to eat."

"I know for a fact there is quite a bit here," said Scott. "The wheel of cheese we got in the house came from out here. That whole lot of stuff stacked on the far side of the stalls is hardware and food supplies going out to Cyrus Jacobs in Walla Walla."

"Say, I know Jacobs," said Moody.

"Me, too," said Davis. "Seeing the fix we are in, I don't think

Cyrus Jacobs would begrudge us some food. We'll keep an account of what gets used so we can settle up with him later."

The men opened crates, barrels, and burlap sacks to find out what was inside. Cornmeal, wheat flour, whole sides of bacon and more wheels of cheese came to light. Davis whistled in surprise as he opened a stout wooden crate. "Oh my," he said, "Looks like some real fine forty-rod to me." He held a liquor bottle with a fancy label up for general inspection.

"Keep that away from Halberth, or it will disappear, and he'll be even more useless than he already is," said Scott.

"Why do you put up with that old drunk, anyway? Why don't you get rid of him?" asked Moody.

"Sometimes, I think maybe I should," said Scott. "But then I remember what my old Granny used to say. She used to get so mad at folks she'd turn purple in the face. But then she'd just settle down a bit and tell me that the devil can kill his own meat. She said she wasn't about to give him a hand. I didn't know what she meant for the longest time. I think I do now. Say, what's in that big gunny sack over to your left?"

Moody tugged the gunny sack out of the tangle of supplies. "Here we have fifty pounds of rolled oats. Dang it! The horses could have used this," he said.

"Shall we save it for your pony, Mr. Scott?" asked Davis.

"I think we should. We got a lot more people food here than horse food," said Scott.

"I guess we ain't gonna starve, not with all these provisions," said Gay. "I'll bring this burlap bag of dry beans."

"I can manage a wheel of cheese under each arm," said Davis.

Glover asked, "Should I lug in one of these sacks of cornmeal?"

"Sure," said Moody. "I'll bring in a side of bacon. We'll make a list of what we took when we get back in the kitchen."

The men in the house were glad to see food coming in from outside. They greeted the laden Glover, Gay, Moody, and Davis with relief.

"We don't have to worry about food now, anyway. There seems to be plenty out there in the barn that got stuck here, kind of like us," said Gay.

"Anybody got a piece of paper?" asked Moody. "We got to keep track of what we use out of the barn so we can pay Cyrus Jacobs back."

"Cyrus Jacobs from Walla Walla?" asked Wellington. "I think I've met him."

"Hey, I know I met Cyrus Jacobs, too," said Niles. "Now don't that beat all?"

"I got paper and a quill and ink in my assay chest. Let me get them out," said James.

"I call a meeting. Now that we ain't got starvation staring us in the face, we should get organized. Everyone needs a job," said Gay.

"I would like to make a motion. I nominate Mr. Jagger for president of our company," said Wellington.

A chorus of voices immediately agreed, seconding Wellington's motion. Jagger was accepted as president by acclamation.

"Alright, then," said Gay, "Mr. Jagger, as president, will you take over this meeting?"

"Thank you, sir. That I will," said Jagger, rising to his feet. "Mr. James, do you have enough paper with you so that we could write the names of all the jobs on little pieces? Then we could draw them out of a hat."

"Yes, sir, I do," said James.

"Say, since James has the paper and the ink already, I nominate him for secretary of our company," said Niles. General approval was voiced, and James was installed as secretary by acclamation also.

"What all jobs are we going to draw for?" asked James as he ripped up several small squares of paper. "I'm ready to mark them down," he said.

"I make a motion to have the jobs be cook, wood man, dishwasher, commissary supply man, water tender, and a stoker to make sure neither of the fires goes out," said Niles.

"I think we need two men for cooks. It's a big job," said Allphin.

"We should have a head cook and an assistant, just to head off any disagreements in the kitchen," suggested Jeffries.

"We need two men for bringing in wood, too," said Bolton.

"I think we need two for washing dishes, too," said Gay. "You got to haul and heat the water before you can even start the job. That's a lot of work."

"We could use somebody to generally tidy things up, like a steward. And a slush-lamp man would be good. That lamp went out in the middle of the night because nobody thought that refilling it was any of their business," said Wilson. The slush-lamp consisted of a tin pie plate full of bacon grease with a piece of rag for a wick. It worked surprisingly well, giving enough light to walk around the room without stumbling over sleepers in the night.

"I make a motion that the man who is steward should also be in charge of the slush-lamp. Neither of those jobs takes much time or effort. Maybe that same fellow could also act as stoker," suggested Bolton.

"That's a good idea," said Jagger. "Who all is in favor of having one job be the combined steward, slush-lamp tender, and stoker? All in favor, say aye."

"Aye," was the unanimous response.

"Let me get all these jobs written down. Who has a hat we can use?" asked James.

Davis offered up his big, flat-brimmed hat.

Mulkey spoke up. "I ain't drawing. My feet done got froze and I ain't doing any of those jobs."

"Me neither," said Riddle, folding his arms across his chest and looking defiant.

"Don't you gentlemen worry about it," said Jagger. "It appears to me that we only have nine jobs to fill. Being that there are sixteen of us, not everyone is going to be employed. I am asking for volunteers first to draw for jobs."

Moody, Gay, Bolton, and Allphin immediately stepped up to take turns drawing from the hat. Moody unfolded his piece of paper and said, "I am your commissary man." Gay pulled the job of assistant wood man. Bolton became the head cook. Allphin drew out the paper which made him Bolton's assistant in the kitchen. Bolton and Allphin immediately shook hands, agreeing to help each other in good faith.

Wilson and Wellington stepped up next to draw for their jobs. Wilson looked at his slip of paper and said, "Meet your new assistant dishwasher, Swede Wilson, Esquire, of the Willamette Valley, Oregon, and at your service." He bowed to the assembled company. There was a little scattered laughter. Wellington drew out his slip of paper "I'm your water tender," he announced.

Jeffries stepped up and drew the job of head wood man.

James reached into the hat next and then offered it to Jagger. James said, "Looks like I'm the head dishwasher. What does that leave you with, Mr. President?"

"I am pleased to say that I will be the finest steward, stoker, and slush-lamp man you ever did see," said Jagger. "Is there any other business we need to take care of? If not, can I get a motion to close this meeting?"

"There ain't no more jobs?" asked Glover.

"No, son, we done got everything covered, I think," said James.

Glover said, "If anyone can't do their job or needs some help, let me know. I want to do my part."

Niles, McDonald, Nichols, and Davis all indicated that they would be willing to help, too, if they were needed.

A motion to close the meeting was made and seconded. The stranded passengers were now a stranded company.

———————

John Stephens followed his own tracks back east to Willow Creek. The little bit of ice and snow which had fallen since he passed made no difference. The horses were handling the trip well. They were even able to break out into a slow trot on some of the flat, exposed portions of the trail.

About two miles short of the Willow Creek home station Stephens spotted what he thought he had remembered. On his way west he had noted several dead cows in a snowdrift near the trail. They had frozen to death on their feet, just where they stood. Their heads and backs were sticking out of the snow. Stephens knew Allie Ann, and the boys were short on food. He decided he would bring them one of these cattle.

"Whoa, whoa now boys," he spoke to the horses. He brought the team to a halt on level ground just beyond the frozen cattle. He set the brake, wrapped the reins around it and hopped down from the box. He reached under the seat and brought out a length of coiled rope. Stephens waded over to the nearest frozen animal. He formed a loop with the rope and put it over the horns, head, and the stiff neck. He kicked the frozen snow away from the body and legs, estimating how the animal would fall once enough force was put on the rope. He kept the rope taut as he brought it back to the rear of the stagecoach, where he secured it using several knots.

Mounting the box again, he took off the brake. "Hi-yup there, hi-yup," he cried. "Come on, fellas, give a pull, we're gonna be a meat wagon until we get to Willow Creek." The horses responded, and the stagecoach started off again, skidding the frozen carcass along behind.

The stagecoach, Stephens, and the frozen steer arrived at the Willow Creek home station around four in the cold, white afternoon. Stephens halted the stagecoach in the dooryard, bringing the frozen carcass close to the door of the station building. Allie Ann heard the stagecoach arrive and sent Allen out to open the barn doors. Stephens was unhitching the steer when Allen came outside. "I never saw any frozen stiff cattle before," said Allen. "Where did you come by that, Mr. Stephens?" he asked.

"Oh, it just followed me home," said Stephens, coiling his rope up and stowing it back under the driver's seat. "Get the barn doors for me, son. We'll just take care of these fine horses, and then I'll see about hacking a few choice cuts off that there frozen animal."

Allie Ann came out of the house to inspect the frozen steer. Young William insisted on coming out to see this unusual sight for himself. "Mama, how did that cow get so froze?' he asked. "Did you ever see a froze cow before, Mama?"

"No, William, I surely never have seen a cow frozen like that before," she said.

Allen and Stephens finished with the horses and started walking back to the station house. "What do you think of that, Miz Allphin?" asked Stephens. "There was six or seven of them back there by the side of the trail, froze stiff, dead as doornails, standing up to their necks in the drifted snow. I done brought you the prettiest one."

"We must thank you for that. You know how low on food we are here," said Allie Ann. "You and that animal are sure a welcome sight. But, if you don't mind my asking, what are you doing back here with no passengers? Wasn't there anyone on the eastbound stage for Walla Walla?"

"Well, it's kind of a long story. What it comes down to is this. No stagecoach came to meet us at Tom Scott's. I couldn't go on west because Scott wouldn't run the ferry. He's scared of the ice on the river crushing the boat. And Halberth stacked the hay where the flood water could wash it away, so there ain't no food for the horses at the John Day station," said Stephens.

"Halberth!" exclaimed Allie Ann, horrified. "Late last summer Frank had to run off that horrible, worthless old man. What is he doing at Tom Scott's?"

"From what I could see, he's doing as little as possible," said Stephens. "Emmitt Miller's heart is too soft. He hates to fire anyone. Halberth is spending his time at Scott's hiding in the kitchen near the fire, evading his chores, getting underfoot, and trying to cheat the passengers. He ain't high on anybody's list of favorites."

"What did Frank do when he saw Halberth was there?" Allie Ann asked.

"It did not make him very happy, that's for sure," said Stephens. "He took Halberth to task, and he read him out proper. Not that it did much good. From what I could see there ain't no remedy for that lazy old man."

"I feel sorry for Tom Scott, getting stuck with him," said Allie Ann.

"Say, Frank wanted me to tell you not to worry. It may take some time for him to get to town and back what with the high water, the ice, and the snow. But he will get it done and get back here, even if it takes a while. I wish there was some way to let him know that you three have enough vittles now. Ain't nobody gonna starve to death around here. Not with this nice big frozen steer here. What does Frank use for cutting up meat, anyhow?" asked Stephens.

"We got a bow saw in the house. Allen, run fetch that saw for Mr. Stephens," said Allie Ann. Shortly, John Stephens, Allen Mc-Clain, William, and Allie Ann Allphin enjoyed a fine dinner of beef steaks, beef broth and sliced beef tongue at the Willow Creek home station.

———◆◆◆◆———

Stephens had Allen help him bring in the buffalo robes from the stagecoach. Stephens never brought a bedroll when driving the stagecoach in the winter. He preferred to bed down with the buffalo robes used by the passengers. They were warmer than most bedrolls, and they always carried them until warm weather. Two were placed near the fire for Stephens.

Allen was curious about sleeping under a buffalo robe. Stephens told him to go ahead and wrap up in the third robe for the night and see how he liked it. "I'll have to take it with me when I go, so enjoy it for tonight. Me and the horses will be on our way again first thing tomorrow," said Stephens.

"Say, Miz Allphin, there ain't much feed for the horses at the Wells Springs swing station," said Stephens. "Would it be alright with you if I was to haul along a load of that sweet hay Frank put up?"

"Acourse it's alright. Take all you can carry. Make sure you take some beef, too. We would have sure been on slim rations without it. Got to thank you again," she said.

Early on the morning of Wednesday, January 8th John Stephens stuffed the stagecoach with armloads of hay, covering the floor and seats. He didn't want to take too much and make the team's work more difficult. But he wanted the horses to have enough to eat when they reached Wells Springs. Allen helped him with the hay and then loaded the buffalo robes aboard. "I slept real warm in that robe, Mr. Stephens. Thank you. I might have to get me one of them someday, myself," said the boy.

Stephens was ready to get moving again at daylight. "When I get back to Walla Walla I'll put a bug in Blackmore's ear. Maybe I can get him to send out some relief animals and some grub from that end. Miller sure ain't getting it done from his end. Say hello to Frank for me when he gets back," he said.

"Thank you for everything," said Allie Ann. "Good-bye and good luck."

"Bye-bye Mr. Stephens," said young William.

"Take care. Good-bye, and thank you, sir," said Allen.

"Bye, folks. Could be I'll see you in about a week. Hi-yup, let's go, boys," said Stephens, guiding the team and stagecoach out of the dooryard, headed east. The remainder of his trip would be uneventful. Stephens brought the stagecoach back safely to Walla Walla from Willow Creek in two long days.

⸻◆⬩◆⸻

Emmitt Miller sent Garrity's stagecoach east out of Dalles City an hour before daylight on Friday, January 10th. It hadn't snowed in Dalles City for about a day and a half. But tiny ice crystals had fallen overnight, lightly dusting the existing frozen snow with icy sparkles.

Garrity had taken a hitch of six. Miller thought they looked good as they left town. They looked strong and sure going down the rutted, frozen street. Garrity was hauling a full load of nine passengers plus the mail. Miller hoped they would have no trouble on their way to Walla Walla. He had intended to send A.J. Kane out following Garrity with relief stock for the stations at the mouth of the Deschutes River, Scott's at the John Day River, and Willow Creek, and to retrieve the six men Garrity had left behind, but Mr. Kane had not yet reported for work this chilly morning.

Kane had been sleeping in the haymow of Miller's stable barn since he had been hired in September. Occasionally, he would disappear, only to return after a few days, stinking of booze and hung over. This appeared to be another one of those times.

Emmitt Miller was irritated. Sometimes he thought he was doomed to hire competent professionals and sorry nincompoops in about equal numbers. He told himself that he would have to be more careful when he hired people in the future.

———◆◆◆◆———

Garrity was careful bringing his stagecoach east from Dalles City. He took it easy on his way to the Deschutes River crossing, getting there at noon. Once across, he had a decision to make. It was twenty-eight miles to the John Day River. If he continued on, he might not make it to the ferry at the John Day until after dark. He knew that Scott would never run the ferry in the ice at night. It was too dangerous, and Scott was a careful man. That would strand Garrity and his passengers on the west side of the river for the night. Garrity knew that the only shelter on that side of the river was the wall tent occupied by Fred Wilcox and his dog. Staying there would make for a miserable night for everyone.

On the other hand, if Garrity stopped at the mouth of the Deschutes, there was a hotel for the passengers and a home station for the stagecoach and team. William Graham was running the hotel, and wagon-maker C.B. Poole was doing a good job with Miller's Deschutes River home station. Graham's wife Harriet was an excellent cook who set a lavish table. Rafe Garrity was no fool, and it didn't take long for him to decide to stay.

Garrity had the loaded stagecoach back on the trail early the next morning. They met with no trouble and came skidding and sliding down the switchbacks into the John Day Canyon around noon on Saturday, January 11th.

Fred Wilcox heard them arrive and came out of his tent on the run. "Don't drive up on the ferry boat yet!" he yelled, loping down the incline to the ferry landing. His dog wisely elected to stay inside by the fire.

"Whoa, whoa there, boys," said Garrity, halting the team short of the ferry itself.

"Hang on here," said Wilcox. "The ice has been right tricky. I'm supposed to be real careful not to wreck the ferry. I've got to signal Mr. Scott to see if I got his permission to take you across." Wilcox hauled a long-barreled handgun out of one of his coat pockets. Pointing his artillery at the sky, he shut his eyes and winced as he fired. The handgun went off with a very loud "boom." Wilcox lowered the gun and grinned. "That is the goldarndest noisiest gun I ever did fire."

"Makes a fine signal," observed Garrity. "Look there." He pointed across the river, where he could see several men coming out of the little house. One figure dressed in red and black came out of the barn.

"That's Mr. Scott with the red hat and in the red and black blanket coat. If he fires his gun, too, then I can take you across. If he don't, well then, I'm afraid you ain't going nowhere," said Wilcox.

Garrity and Wilcox could plainly see Scott, only about a hundred yards distant. Scott walked down to the edge of the river. He looked up and down the river. It was full of chunks of ice but seemed to be moving smoothly. He hesitated for a few moments, making up his mind. Then he reached in his coat pocket for a tiny pistol known as a "pepper-box." He raised his arm in the air and fired off an answering shot. With the noise of the wind and the ice-filled river, it could barely be heard.

"Alright," said Wilcox. "I guess we're in business."

Garrity's stagecoach crossed the river on the ferry in good order. Drawing up in front of Scott's overstuffed house, Garrity was greeted by cheering men.

"We're saved!" cried Mulkey.

"I never thought a stagecoach could look so good," said Riddle.

"Whoa, whoa boys," Garrity said to the horses. He next addressed his passengers. "We will take a little break here, gentlemen. We will be back on the trail in a half-hour."

The nine passengers got out of the stagecoach to stretch their legs and warm up in the little station house.

Scott came forward to talk to Garrity. "Why do I get the feeling that your arrival here ain't gonna do me no good?" he asked.

"That's because you are an observant man," said Garrity. "You can see I got a full load, so I sure can't take nobody else along. Besides, I'm going east, heading out to Walla Walla. I don't expect any of the men here want to go back there. Emmitt was set on sending A.J. Kane out with some relief stock for you, but he couldn't find him this morning."

"You are just full of good news," said Scott.

"You sure do got a full house," Garrity said, looking around the room. With Garrity and his current nine passengers in the house, it was standing room only.

"I'll say. I been keepin' to myself out in the barn." Scott replied.

"How long these men been waitin' here?"

"The two of 'em you left behind already been here almost two weeks. And the rest, about five days. Sure would like to see them on their way." answered Scott.

Cringing, Garrity looked around the room and recognized his six stranded passengers. He was glad to see the four men he left at Wells Springs had at least made it this far.

"Old A.J. Kane ought to show up in a day or so and he can take these men off your hands," assured Garrity.

Word passed swiftly among the stranded men that this east-bound stagecoach would be of no use to them. Garrity would only take a thirty-minute break before going on to Willow Creek.

Frank Allphin sought out Garrity before he left again. "How are you doing, Rafe?" asked Allphin.

"Why fine, Frank, just fine. How are you? And what in blazes are you doing here?" asked Garrity.

"I ain't real happy, but I'm alright," said Allphin. "I had to make a little run in to Dalles City for some supplies. Let Allie Ann know I'm fine if you would. Tell her not to worry. It's gonna take me a little longer than I first figured, but I'll get to Dalles City and back as soon as I can. Tell her I'm thinking about her and the boys."

"I sure will," promised Garrity.

CHAPTER FOURTEEN

——————— ✳ ———————

Rafe Garrity and his stagecoach full of passengers approached the home station at Willow Creek two hours after dark on Saturday, January 11th. It had been a simple run from Scott's at the John Day River crossing. Stephens had beaten down the trail coming and going, four and five days before. It had snowed about six inches since then. When Garrity arrived, Allen came out to open the barn doors and help with the team. "Hello, son," said Garrity. "Who graded the roadway into here, and what did he use?"

"Graded, sir?" asked Allen.

"Yeah, graded," said Garrity. "The trail is so bare the ground is almost showing. Something scraped all the snow off the trail back there for a good couple of miles, at least."

"Oh, I think I know what that was," said Allen, "Mr. Stephens brought us a frozen beef animal. He roped it and drug it here behind the stagecoach. That must be what cleared the snow off the trail. There it is, too." Allen pointed out the frozen steer over near the station building, now minus its hindquarters and head.

"Say, that's a pretty good trick. I might have to ask old John how he managed it," said Garrity.

Allie Ann briefly left her cookfire to come out of the station house to greet Garrity and his nine passengers. The men climbed down out of the stagecoach, stretching and yawning.

"Welcome gentlemen," Allie Ann said, holding open the door to the house. "We are short on a lot of things around here, but we do have beef. Matter of fact, about all we got is beef. We got plenty of beef steaks, beef broth, some tongue, and some heart. We got roasted marrow bones if you like them. If anyone is partial to sweetbreads, we got a steer's head, but it ain't been cracked yet. You'd be welcome to it if you want to go to the trouble. Come on in and make yourselves to home. There's only two chairs, so you'll want to bring in your bedrolls to sit on. This here is my son young William, and that's my nephew Allen out there helping Mr. Garrity with the horses. I'm Mrs. Frank Allphin. Food will be ready in two shakes."

After feeding the newcomers, Allie Ann gathered up young William and retired for the night. Allen would stay up and see to anything the passengers or the driver might want. They could sort themselves out and make their beds on the floor.

Garrity finally remembered the next morning to tell Allie Ann that Frank had sent her word not to worry.

"Thank you, Mr. Garrity. It's good to hear from Frank. I'm afraid I still might worry just a little," she said.

———————◆•:•◆———————

It was just before midnight on Saturday, January 11th when Pat Davis awoke with a start. Someone had opened the door of the house and come in along with a big gust of icy wind. It had been snowing steadily in the twelve hours since Garrity had left and it seemed colder than ever.

"Hidy," croaked Davis, sitting up and clearing his throat. He realized he did not recognize the man standing near the door. "How do you be, stranger?" he asked, blinking the sleep out of his eyes to focus on the newcomer.

The man stood leaning against the closed door. The warmth of the room felt very good to him. But the accumulated odors from so many men living in close quarters for the past several days hit his nose like a sledgehammer. "Smells worse than a cave full of bears in here," he quietly said. The slush-lamp gave enough light for him to see the large number of sleepers in the room.

"Maybe so," said Davis, "But we're in out of the cold. You hungry, stranger?"

"I'm about starved," he admitted. "I'd be right grateful for anything you could spare for me to eat."

Davis led the way into the kitchen, lighting the lantern as he entered. "There's cheese, and there's biscuits left from dinner. I can poke up the fire if you want your coffee hotter than lukewarm." Halberth snored fitfully from his bedroll behind the stove.

"You got people stuffed into every corner, don't you?" asked the stranger. "Thank you kindly for the cheese and biscuits. Hot coffee sure would be nice if it's not too much bother. What is going on here, anyway?"

Davis stirred up the fire and added more wood. "Well sir, a bunch of us, we was coming west from out of Walla Walla. The going was so bad we had to walk a lot of the way behind the stagecoach. We got left here when the stagecoach couldn't cross the river on the ferry because of the ice. Then that stagecoach had to go back to Walla Walla, 'cause there ain't no food for the horses here."

"That sounds like a mess," said the man, speaking with his mouth full.

"It sure is," admitted Davis. "By the way, the name is Pat Davis," he said, extending his right hand.

"I'm J.W. Knight. Pleased to meet you. I'm trying to get to Dalles

City myself," said Knight, shaking Davis's hand. "Me and my cousin got a ranch at the mouth of Willow Creek right near the Columbia. We sold some cattle to the government, and one of us had to go to Dalles City to get paid. I won the coin toss." He grinned. "Would it be alright if I was to bed down here next to the back door?"

"Fine by me," said Davis, moving back toward the main room. "I'm going back to bed. Blow out the light when you're done eating."

Tired as he was, Knight had a hard time getting to sleep. At least four of the men in the main room were snorting, snoring, or mumbling in their sleep. Halberth snored, wheezed, and muttered from behind the stove. Someone kept coughing and clearing his throat. Knight even heard somebody vigorously breaking wind. He dozed off several times, only to be awakened by noises made by the sleeping men. He finally gave up and decided to get going again. The food and the warmth had done him a lot of good, and he was eager to be on his way, away from this stinking, stuffy house.

Knight left Scott's station house using the rear door and headed down to the ferry landing. He could see that there were several trails broken in the snow down to the water's edge. Knight followed Garrity's tracks to get down to the river. The sky was clear, and it was incredibly cold. The wind gusted from the west, making Knight duck his chin into the collar of his coat. Daylight was still several hours away. But he could see pretty well with the light from the moon. The ice on the river was crashing and crunching, swiftly drifting and unstable. The ferry boat had been taken back across the river to the west side by Wilcox.

Knight turned his attention to the rope with the pulley contraption hanging over the river. The thick rope sagged from the weight of all the ice adhering to it. The pulley was stuck out in the middle of the span, frozen in place. Knight got out his hatchet. Experimentally, he hit the iced-over rope with the flat of the blade. To his surprise, about ten feet of the line immediately dropped its load of ice. When the falling ice hit the river's frozen surface, it sounded like breaking china. "Now that's some punkins!" exclaimed Knight. He slapped the rope with the hatchet again. More ice fell. Next, he took a good grip on the rope and tried shaking it. That freed up more of the line, getting rid of the worst of the sag. Knight shook the rope again, putting his weight and strength into it. That got rid of the rest of the ice remaining on the rope.

Knight tried the smaller line attached to the box and pulley. At first, it still seemed stuck. He gave it a good tug, and it broke free. He brought the pulley with the box attached over to the shore and climbed in. "All aboard for Dalles City," Knight said to himself.

It only took a couple of minutes for Knight to pull himself across the river and be on his way again. Hitching up his trousers and belting his greatcoat tight, Knight was soon making tracks up the switchbacks to exit the canyon. Since he followed Garrity's route, he did not have to break through the crust of ice on the snow. But the wind had formed snowdrifts where the trail switched back on the steep grade. Knight plowed on, nearly swimming in the deepest snow.

───•✦•───

Davis awoke in the morning and went out to the kitchen to look for the man who had arrived in the night. He was surprised to find that the man had gone. Davis almost doubted that he had ever been there until Jagger enquired about him. "Didn't I hear someone come in late last night?" asked Jagger.

"You sure did," said Davis. "Big older fellow, hungry, and about frozen. He introduced himself, but I was so sleepy, I can't hardly recall. What was his name anyway? Wright? Was that it? J.W. Wright, I think he said. I wonder why he left."

CHAPTER FIFTEEN

Garrity's loaded stagecoach departed the Willow Creek home station at daylight on Sunday, January 12th. The temperature was below zero the entire way, but aside from the cold and some light snow, the rest of their journey was uneventful. The passengers passed the time being thankful they were not stuck at a stage stop like those poor fellas at Tom Scott's. Garrity and his passengers pulled up in front of Blackmore's barn in Walla Walla during the late afternoon on Monday, January 13th. John Stephens was on hand to greet Rafe Garrity as the hostelers took over his team. "There's the good-for-nothing horse thief now," accused Stephens.

"Good to see you, too," said Garrity. "You broke me some right pretty trail back there between the John Day and Fort Henrietta."

"I'm glad to see you appreciate it," said Stephens. "I about polished myself off going out there and then having to turn around and come right back."

"Want to go have a drink? I'm buying," said Garrity.

"In a minute," Stephens said. "First, come on in the office with me. I'd like it fine if you would add your voice to mine about getting some grub, some fodder, and some relief animals out to Wells Springs, Willow Creek, and to Tom Scott on the John Day. Old Blackmore claims he's already tired of hearing me talk about it. He claims that it's Miller's responsibility. Maybe you can help me wear him down some."

◆━◆◆◆◆━◆

J.W. Knight cleared the top of the west side of the John Day Canyon before daylight on Sunday, January 12th. He kept to the Oregon Trail and made steady progress all day. He holed up in a depression sheltered by a rock formation at nightfall. He found enough dry sagebrush to make a fire, even though there was no larger wood. He spent the frigid night getting very little rest, constantly feeding the fire, and not freezing to death.

He started out again early on Monday, January 13th. It started to snow sometime before noon. The west wind picked up and became gusty. Soon the snow was falling so thickly that Knight could barely follow the trail. He continued to walk, seeing no shelter anywhere. The snow swiftly accumulated, and then drifted, finally obliterating the stagecoach tracks on the trail.

Knight was unaware of exactly when he lost his way. He continued to walk vaguely westward across the plateau, occasionally stumbling over hidden rocks and low brush. He was also not aware of the loss of feeling in his feet. He was increasingly confused, and he found it hard to concentrate. Strangely, his head felt hot. He took off his hat and dropped it in the snow as he trudged on. Still too hot he unbuttoned his thick wool greatcoat. The icy wind felt good on the exposed skin of his throat and face. Pushing through a hip-deep snowdrift, Knight lost his balance and fell. Somehow, falling did not bother him. He briefly wondered about that. He decided to take a little break, lie quietly in the snow, and try to think things over. Then, he told himself, he would get up and go on.

J.W. Knight did not rise again. His leather purse and the government payment vouchers remained in the pocket of his greatcoat.

———◆◆◆◆———

The men stranded at Scott's house on the John Day River tried to think of ways to pass the time until another stagecoach would arrive. Stories were told, some true and many with very little truth in them. Speculation upon the future was popular. Plans were made, discarded, and then made again for the next mining season. Schemes and options for leaving Scott's hospitality were discussed. Once or twice the war back in the eastern states was mentioned. Every man had an opinion, but no one had any news, and the subject soon was dropped.

Each evening Niles spent about a half-hour playing his harmonica. Most of the men found themselves looking forward to the melodies.

There were two decks of cards among the group, and there was usually a game of some kind in progress. Moody, Gay, Wilson, and Bolton favored poker. Davis, Wellington, Jagger, and Niles played whist.

Glover spent more spare leather and time working on his boots. Jeffries was a whittler, and he occupied himself making wood shavings from kindling sticks.

Mulkey, Riddle, Nichols, and McDonald had discovered the crate of whiskey in the barn. They dedicated a fair portion of their time to making it disappear. However, they were not greedy. They would offer a drink to anyone who cared to have one. "Glover, my friend," said McDonald, "You may be young, but you're full a man. This here whiskey is real fine. You're more than welcome to a snort."

Glover held up one hand to ward off McDonald's offer of the bottle. He held one of his much-mended boots in his other hand. "No, thank you sir, but I can't. I done took the temperance oath, and I won't be going back on it. I done signed it, and that's all there is to it. Not that I got nothing against you fellas having a drink. I won't. You had better handle my share for me."

"That's fine by me, son. Sounds like you know your mind," said Mulkey. "Pass that bottle back over my way. I'm an old man, and I feel the need of a nip. Yessir, I do. It's medicinal, you know. It'll do my old bones a world of good. Ain't that right, Doc Gay?"

From across the room, and deep in his card game, Gay answered, "You know I already told you I ain't no real doctor. That there, "Doc" is just a nickname. Swede, I raise you ten."

"Why Doc, from what I seen, I'd trust your judgment a lot better than most of them quacks up at the mining camps. I don't think very many of them were real doctors, neither. And they claimed to be. I seen that old thief who called himself Doctor Farber sell a sick man three little bitty bottles of medicine for a hundred and fifty dollars in gold. I wonder what they'd have to say about that back in town, any town," said Mulkey.

Glover gave up on his boot repair job and decided to take a nap. As he settled down and drifted off to sleep, he thought about his family back in the Willamette Valley. He knew his parents were getting on in years and had worked hard their entire lives. They had provided a good, loving home for their children, even if they were not rich. He looked forward to seeing them again, and he knew the gold he brought with him would make their lives easier from now on.

Glover missed his brothers and sisters, too. He found himself thinking especially about his brother James, four years his senior. James had always been his nemesis and his partner, his detractor, and his biggest champion. Once, when they were both small, James had saved him from drowning in an eddy in the Willamette River. It would be good to see him and tell him all about everything at the mines. Glover drifted off to sleep, mentally reviewing some of his silly antics and dumb tricks from childhood. He sighed and started to snore, remembering the feeling of the peak of the barn roof under his feet, right before he fell off and busted his arm at the age of ten.

Tom Jeffries took a walk down to the river early on the morning of Sunday, January 12th. He could plainly see the tracks left in the snow by J.W. Knight. Following those tracks, he came to the rope across the river which supported the pulley and wooden box. Jeffries used the pulley line to bring the mechanism back across the river. Little new ice or snow had fallen to stick to the rope since Knight had passed through and the pulley operated smoothly.

Jeffries hurried back up to Scott's house, stamping his boots free of snow as he reached the back porch. "The pulley at the river is free of ice," he announced, stepping through the rear door into the kitchen.

"How'd you do that?" asked Davis.

"I didn't do a thing," said Jeffries. "I think your mysterious Mr. Wright freed it up and used it to cross the river. I just now brought it back from the other side."

Davis said, "If it don't snow more, I just may follow that Mr. Wright. If he made it across the river and is going to walk to Dalles City, I can too. Do you want to come along, Tom?"

"I don't know. I been thinking I'd wait a couple more days and see what happens," said Jeffries.

Frank Allphin spoke up. "We're so close to Dalles City I can almost taste it. It's twenty-eight miles from here to the crossing at the mouth of the Deschutes River. From the Deschutes to my brother's doorstep in Dalles City is another fourteen miles. I'm only forty-two miles from my own kin and good home cooking. What's more important, then I can get supplies and use Jack's freight wagon and those big bruisers of workhorses he owns to get back to my wife with supplies as soon as I can."

"If you think you want to chance it, I'll go with you," said Gay. "I'm getting mighty tired of people and their smelly feet. I'm tired of sitting around here playing cards and doing nothing, too."

"If you boys are serious, I want to come along. It may not seem like much, but it purely rubs me the wrong way to have to stand in line of a morning just to use the outhouse," said Moody. "I got things to do back at home, and I'll go crazier than a bedbug if I have to stay here much longer."

"I say, let's do it. The weather don't look too bad. Let's do it now. Could you fellas be ready to go in an hour or so?" asked Davis. Allphin, Moody, and Gay agreed and said they could.

———◆◈◆———

Going back into the main room Moody approached the Tracy Express agent, James. "Say there, Mr. James," said Moody, "You have your assay outfit there in your luggage, don't you?"

"Why sure. I never go anywhere without it," answered James.

"Alright," said Moody, "I'd like for you to take my gold. I'm carrying at least twenty pounds, and I'm figuring on heading out on foot here in just a bit. I'd rather not carry my gold, you understand."

"I do understand," said James. "Company policy is to charge five percent of the weight for the carry. Does that sound alright to you?"

"You got a deal," said Moody. "Here's my poke. Let's test 'er and weigh 'er up."

James set up his assay equipment, tested Moody's gold for content, and weighed it. He filled out an official Tracy Express Company receipt, good for redemption in gold or paper currency at any of the company's offices in the major cities of the west coast. Given the absence of banks, an express company's receipt was respected everywhere as legal tender. In many areas, it was more readily acceptable than paper money.

"Your Tracy receipt guarantees the safety of your deposit, no matter what happens," said James. "If I lose the treasure box crossing the river, you get paid. If the company offices in Portland burn down, you still get paid. Just hang on to your receipt."

Gay stepped up next. "If you would be so kind," he said, "I'd like to leave my gold with you, too."

"Sure thing," said James. "It won't take me but a minute."

Davis spoke up. "A man would have to be a fool not to take a deal like that. Mr. James takes on all the worry and the heavy lifting, too. Five percent ain't nothing at all considering what I took out of them mountains. When you get done with Doc, will you weigh mine up next?"

"I sure will," said James. "I got plenty of room. Anyone else who wants to entrust their gold to the Tracy Express can leave it with me. Like I told Mr. Moody, we charge five percent for the safe carry, guaranteed." At that time, no one else came forward to turn their gold over to James. But several men were seriously thinking it over.

Allphin, Gay, Davis, and Moody stepped out on the tiny front porch to get some fresh air.

"The wind is picking up out of the west," observed Allphin.

"The only wind I'm worried about is the wind coming from Riddle's rear end," said Gay. "I sure picked the wrong neighbor to bed down next to."

"It don't make much difference whether you're right next to him or clear across the room," said Moody. "Believe me."

"At least you haven't ended up trying to sleep smack-dab in the middle of the four worst snorers in the bunch," said Davis.

"There again," said Moody, "It don't make much difference whether they are right in your ear or clear across the room. We all get to enjoy them."

"It'll be good to get moving. I've about had my fill of this fancy tea party," said Allphin.

While the other men were organizing their affairs, Moody took a few minutes to empty out and repack his canvas traveling kit. It was the same kind of pouch his father had carried, calling it his "possibles bag." Moody remembered his father's smile as he explained the meaning of the term. "You see, son, just about anything possible might come out of that there bag," he said.

Now Moody had his own possibles bag. He carried it whenever he was in rough country. The contents included a mirror, a magnifying glass, a flint and steel, a fist-sized lump of crystallized pine pitch, a deck of cards, a plug of tobacco, a small ball of twine, a bone-handled knife with a sharp, three-inch blade, a stub of a candle, a small, corked jar of lard, a needle and thread stuck into a piece of leather, and a leaking paper package of headache powder. He thought about throwing away the headache powder, but packed it back in with everything else. A little headache powder wouldn't hurt anything else in the bag.

Moody, Gay, Allphin, and Davis left Tom Scott's house at about ten in the morning on Sunday, January 12th. They left their baggage and bedrolls in Scott's care. He agreed to send their effects along when a stagecoach finally could make the trip west to Dalles City.

Preparing as best they could for the long hike, the men wore their warmest clothing. Allphin had a heavy, knee-length wool coat, an oiled felt hat, and good boots. Moody wore a long wool overcoat and a hat with a wool liner and a chin-strap. His boots were worn but serviceable. His possibles bag was strapped to his back, over his coat. Davis wore his flat, low-crowned hat and a canvas poncho covered in gutta-percha over his jacket. The poncho was heavy and stiff, but it was waterproof and windproof. His boots were fairly new, with thick soles. He was confident that they could handle a twenty-eight mile hike. Gay wore his canvas trousers and vest with a heavy topcoat over long woolen underwear. Over his topcoat, he wore a piece of a canvas wagon cover that he had found in the barn. It reached to his knees and was covered in India rubber. He had cut a hole for his head in the middle and used a length of twine for a belt. He had waterproofed his felt hat by coating it with hot bacon fat.

"I got me a hankerin' to make tracks," said Davis.

"I almost wish I was going with you," said Wellington.

"Good-bye and good luck to you all," said Allphin. "We'll send back a team and a wagon from Dalles City for you men and all your gear."

"Don't eat up all the best steaks at the Umatilla House before we get there," said Nichols.

"Look me up if you are ever in Eugene City," said Gay.

"Until we meet again, gentlemen," said Moody. Hands were shaken all around.

"If you find that it's too bad out there, turn right around and come back," said Jeffries.

More cries of good-bye and good luck were exchanged between the four who were going and the twelve stranded men who were staying. The room seemed very quiet when the four walking men had gone.

———◆◆◆◆———

The nearest thermometer was located in Dalles City at the Fort Dalles Army hospital. It was a spirit thermometer, more accurate than a mercury thermometer for determining minimum temperatures. At noon on Sunday, January 12th, this instrument read twenty degrees below zero.

———◆◆◆◆———

Gay, Moody, Davis, and Allphin made short work of crossing the river, one after the other, using the box and pulley. Their trail then ran almost level for a quarter of a mile before passing Wilcox's tent and starting the gradual climb up to the steeper switchbacks marking the path out of the canyon.

Fred Wilcox emerged from the wall tent and hailed the group. "Good morning. What are you gentlemen up to this fine, crisp, raw day?" His dog had again opted to remain inside next to the fire.

"We're fixing to walk in to Dalles City," said Allphin. "Did you see a man go by heading west real early this morning?"

"Can't say as I did," said Wilcox. "And old J.D. hasn't barked or caused no fuss since Garrity came through with the stagecoach going east."

"Say, there's more than one way out of this here canyon, ain't there, Fred?" asked Allphin, scanning the canyon walls.

"You know dang well there is," said Wilcox.

"Yeah," agreed Allphin. "I do. Let's take a minute to think about this, fellas. I can see by his tracks that our mysterious Mr. Wright went right straight up through the drifts and climbed the switchbacks. I'm not sure that's the easiest way. You got to do all your climbing all at once. If we were to walk up the big canyon there to the left instead, it might be a little further, but it wouldn't be so steep. I know that canyon. I rode up it last summer when the wagon trains had the trail all dusty and clogged up. It comes out on top on the flat almost next to the trail, not more than a half-mile south of it."

"Then I say let's try it," said Davis.

"I'm game," said Moody.

"Lead off," said Gay.

"See you on my way back, Fred," said Allphin, waving as he turned to go.

Allphin did indeed lead off, breaking trail uphill through snow from two to four feet deep with an inch of icy crust on the top. It was difficult, exhausting, damaging work. The ice on top of the snow broke into pieces as sharp as a knife. Allphin gave up his place to Moody after a few hundred yards of progress. Moody broke trail for as long as he could and then gave up his place to Gay. Gay tired himself out at the front of the group and then turned his position over to Davis. Davis did his turn in the lead, and then it was Allphin's turn again.

The west wind picked up, and it started to snow, swirling the flakes into the faces of the struggling men. They stopped to take a short break every few minutes. They knew they could not stop for long or they might freeze.

After about six hours, Allphin tried to estimate how far they had come. They had to have covered at least six or eight miles. The top of the big canyon had to be almost in sight. The falling snow made it impossible to see very far.

Frank Allphin knew he was in trouble, but he did his best to ignore the fact. His legs were numb from the knees down to his feet. His feet felt like blocks of wood, making it difficult to keep his balance. He was stumbling and had almost fallen several times. He said nothing to the other men and kept going as well as he could. He felt obligated and responsible for his companions. After all, he was their guide, being the only man who had ever come this way before. He knew they were counting on him to show them the way to Dalles City.

His companions were not the only people Allphin felt a responsibility for. Allie Ann, and the boys were counting on him too. He kept going. He could see no other option. He was sure they had come too far to turn back. The snow kept pelting down, carried on the bitter west wind. Darkness fell shortly after four in the afternoon.

The four walking men were each slowly freezing. While their icy feet were their main concern, any exposed skin on their faces or hands was also in jeopardy. They helped each other over rough spots in their climb, but each man was also occupied with his own problems. The others failed to notice Allphin's growing lack of coordination, and they were stunned when he fell, face down on the snowy hillside. Moody knelt next to Allphin and turned him over. Allphin was trying to speak.

"What's that again, Frank?" asked Moody, bending close to Allphin to hear what he had to say.

"I could die more contentedly if I only knew that my wife on Willow Creek had a sack of flour," sighed Allphin. He closed his eyes. Nothing the others could do would rouse him again. They knew they could not carry him. They were shocked.

"I can't believe it," said Moody. "What can we do?" he asked the others.

Davis just shook his head.

Gay said, "I don't know, but we can't stay here, and we can't bring him along. I just don't know. I sure hate to leave him. He ain't dead. He can't be dead."

"I know," said Moody. "The best we can do is this." Moody unstrapped his possibles bag, unbuttoned his heavy wool coat, took it off and tucked it around Frank Allphin. "I won't need that coat, and it might make the difference for Frank. It's an awful warm coat," he said, strapping on his canvas bag again.

Davis crossed himself, being a lapsed, but sincere Catholic.

"You rest now, Frank," said Moody. We'll come back with help as soon as we can. We'll get some grub to your wife and them youngsters, too. Don't worry about a thing, Frank. We'll see to it." Walking single file, the three remaining men again trudged up the snow-filled canyon. Gay, Moody, and Davis took turns breaking trail for the next half hour.

Davis was in the lead when he stopped and turned to the others. "Fellas," he said, puffing from exertion, "I gotta stop here for a bit. I'm plumb tuckered out."

"You gonna be alright?" asked Moody.

"Oh yeah, I guess I will, maybe," said Davis. "How far do you reckon we've come?"

"Got to be five or six miles, maybe more," said Gay.

"Well," said Davis, "It might just be that I know when I'm licked. I'm sorry, fellas, but I'm going to have to turn around and go back. I sure can't go forward no more. I'll tell the boys back at Scott's about Allphin. I'll see that they get him brought in before he perishes."

"Are you sure?" asked Moody.

"Yes, I believe I am," said Davis. "And don't you worry about me. It's downhill the whole way. I'll make it back in half the time it took us to get here." Davis shook frozen hands with Moody and Gay. He then hurried off, back the way they had come.

"Good luck," shouted Moody.

"Take care," shouted Gay.

Davis raised one arm in farewell but did not look back as he hurried away. He was relieved to find that the trail down the canyon was indeed much easier to traverse than it had been on the way up. He stumbled a little but did not fall. He made good progress and soon came back to where Frank Allphin lay in the snow. A shallow dusting of new snow already covered his body. Davis tipped his hat and mumbled, "Pardon me, Frank," as he skirted past the form in the trail.

Davis staggered on for almost another mile before his frozen legs betrayed him, dumping him face down in the snow. He struggled and got to his knees. He thought about getting to his feet. He thought about it for a long time. He then tried to get up and failed, falling with his face in the snow again. He decided to rest for a minute, but not for too long, he warned himself. He nodded in agreement with his wisdom. He turned over on his side and stared at the snowflakes landing on the fallen snow surrounding him. He told himself he would only rest here for a minute. Then he would get up and go back to the little house on the far side of the John Day River. Or maybe he would just stop at the tent on this side of the river. Either place he went, it would be warm. There would be a fire.

Davis drifted away, thinking about comfort, warmth, and safety. He would never get any closer to them than in his thoughts. Within an hour the snow had covered him, disguising him as just another lump in the unending drifts of white.

CHAPTER SIXTEEN

———— ❈ ————

I spent Sunday, January 12th watching the weather. My intention was to start out for Willow Creek early the next morning. I would take Napoleon again, along with a large pack containing food and blankets. I hoped I was wrong about how the weather looked. The wind had been increasing all day, and I thought it sure looked like more snow coming. It looked like it was going to be ugly weather to travel in. The temperature stood at about twenty degrees below zero in Dalles City. Emmitt Miller claimed it was at least five to ten degrees colder up on the plateau between the Deschutes and John Day Rivers. Miller had told me that he doubted whether he would send a stagecoach east this week. No stagecoach from Walla Walla had managed to arrive in Dalles City since Garrity had struggled in with his three passengers. Conditions were, if anything, getting worse. Regardless, I had made up my mind. I would be going.

———— ❖ ————

Eliza Jagger sought out many small tasks to keep her mind, and her hands occupied while her husband was away. One of these tasks entailed the organization of his desk and correspondence. While doing this, she found an ink-spattered first draft of the letter he had written to his father on the occasion of little Hattie's birth. She reread the letter, remembering how proud he had been to show it to her on the day it had been written.

Most Esteemed Pater,

Mister Ira Eugene Jagger and his lovely wife Eliza are most Pleased to announce that Carrie and Henry no longer have the Market cornered on providing you with darling grandchildren. Please welcome to our family circle Miss Henrietta Jagger. We call her Hattie. She is most lovely and perfect. With every best wish for your continued good health, sir.

I remain your obedient son,

Finding the letter made Eliza miss John worse than ever. His playful wording brought tears to her eyes. "Please come home soon. Oh, please," she whispered, clutching the announcement tightly.

———◆◆◆◆———

In Portland on Monday, January 13th Captain John C. Ainsworth received an official written report from Lawrence W. Coe, the Dalles City agent for the Oregon Steam Navigation Company. Coe's report stated that the Columbia River was now blocked by ice from Dalles City to Portland.

A separate report detailed the situation downriver from Portland to Astoria, at the mouth of the Columbia. It stated that the Columbia River at its junction with the Cowlitz River would soon be impassable. Steam navigation from Portland to Astoria was now also suspended.

Ainsworth dropped the reports back on his desk. He shook his head, remembering conditions on the Mississippi River during the years when he had been a riverboat captain there. He had never had the misfortune to be blockaded by ice. But then, he thought, winter was a bit warmer in Louisiana and Mississippi than it was here in Oregon.

The men at Scott's house continued to cook, wash dishes, bring in firewood, stoke the stoves, bring in supplies from the barn, haul in water, and mind the slush-lamp. Glover, Niles, and Nichols had taken over the jobs left vacant by Gay, Allphin, and Moody.

Jeffries almost expected the four walking men to return. The weather had gotten steadily worse. But none of them came back. Jeffries hoped they had reached someplace safe. The weather closed down, and it stormed in earnest. The temperature dropped to thirty degrees below zero.

The faulty wood stove in the main room was a constant source of irritation. It didn't draw well and would smoke back into the room if given half a chance. Jagger was stoking the fire when a particularly noxious cloud of smoke puffed back into his face. "Gahk," he choked, "This stove is the poorest excuse for a heating unit I have ever seen. My father makes the best stoves in the whole country, and I wish I had even one of his rejects right now. This thing is an abomination!" he said, slamming shut the stove door.

"I'm all for walking out of here. Them four that left had the right idea. We should have gone with them, Riddle," said Mulkey.

"We'd be sitting next to the fire and eating steak in Dalles City at the Umatilla House Hotel tonight instead of sitting here eating beans and sucking wood smoke," said Riddle.

"If you gentlemen are getting together another party to leave, count me in," said Wellington.

"I don't trust the stagecoach company at all no more. I'd trust my own two legs to get me out of here just fine," said Mulkey.

Several other voices spoke up in agreement.

"I think we all would like to get out of here," said James. "I've been thinking about asking Mr. Scott if there is a wagon and team anywhere near here that I could make use of. With the mail and the express box, I've got to have a wagon or a stagecoach to carry it all. And frankly, I don't think we're gonna see another stagecoach for quite some time. Matter of fact, I think I'll just take a walk out to the barn and see what Mr. Scott has to say."

James told Scott what he would like to attempt and what he would need. Tom Scott had already been thinking about ways to send the stranded men on to the home station and hotel at the Deschutes River. His neighbor upriver to the south, just below Rock Creek had a wagon and a team of six horses that he probably would be willing to lend. Scott volunteered to go talk to his neighbor and try to bring back the wagon and team.

James came back to the little house. "If Mr. Scott can bring us back a wagon and team, we'll all get out of here in a couple of days, lock, stock, and barrel."

"Now you're talking," said Mulkey. "Riding out of here in a wagon would sure beat walking."

"I heard Allphin say it's only twenty-eight miles over to the Deschutes River from here," said Riddle. "Even if we got to walk part of the way, we ought to be able to make it."

"First let's see if Scott can come back with that wagon and team. I certainly won't be going anywhere without them," said James.

Doc Gay and W.A. Moody continued to walk uphill through the drifted snow and directly into the increasing storm. Davis had been gone less than thirty minutes when they reached the top of the canyon and came out on the nearly level Columbia Plateau. The walking was easier there. While the snow was still over two feet deep, there were few large obstacles to form deep snowdrifts.

The two men angled their path to the north of west, hoping to intersect with the Oregon Trail. With the storm and in the dark, they almost missed the Trail when they came to it. The snow had nearly obscured the track, but it showed up as a long, even depression.

"There's the way," said Gay, pointing as he recognized the long sunken area for what it was.

"You're right," said Moody. "You got a good eye. I wouldn't have seen it."

The two men stuck with the Trail when they found it. They walked all night. They stumbled more frequently as the long hours passed. Finally, near dawn, Gay called a halt. "I think I see some trees in that gully ahead. We got to stop and make a fire or I'm gonna freeze clear through," he said.

"I'm with you," said Moody. "I never been so cold in all my life."

Upon reaching the gully, Moody asked Doc Gay to kick the snow cover away from several large, close-growing sagebrush clumps. While Gay cleared the area, Moody broke small branches from the nearby juniper trees. Stacking up an armload around the most sheltered clump of sagebrush, Moody knelt and opened his traveling kit. Bringing out the short candle, the flint and steel, the knife, and the wad of crystallized pine pitch, he said, "Right lucky to have the moon come out for us. I can see good enough to get something done if I can just get my fingers to work."

Moody made a little nest in the bottom of the sage plant, keeping dead, dry branches and leaves under, over, and on three sides of the compact hollow. He used the knife to shave the candle stub into tiny bits. He lined the hollow with the bits of wax. He broke the crystallized pitch into several pieces, laying them on the wax bits. He put small branches and dried grass over that. Getting out the flint and steel, his frozen hands fumbled, flinging the steel up in the air, only to land in the adjacent clump of sagebrush. "Noooo," moaned Moody, sitting back on his heels.

Gay spoke up. "I saw where it landed! Sit tight, and I'll fetch it," he said.

With the steel firmly in hand, Moody soon had a tiny flame, then a blazing fire going. More branches and dead, oily vegetation kept it flaming strongly.

Two hours later, both men had warmed themselves sufficiently to think about going on. "This fire is a lifesaver," said Moody.

"I don't know how much further I could have gone without it," said Gay. "I hate to leave it now, but we've got to get someone back out here for Allphin. I hope Davis made it back to the John Day alright."

"I do, too," said Moody. "I don't know that a man could survive last night out here without shelter or a fire. I got my doubts."

Moody and Gay staggered into Poole's house next to the hotel on the Deschutes River at ten in the morning, Monday, January 13th. Their arrival and the news they brought caused an uproar. Harriet Graham rushed over and quickly hustled the two freezing men next door and into the large hotel kitchen, seating them next to the fire. Moody and Gay were cold to the point of numbness, so exhausted once they sat down, they couldn't get back up. But what was most pressing on their minds was Frank Allphin and the hope that he was still alive. William Graham and C.B. Poole heard their story with horror and decided to send Graham's seventeen-year-old son Robert to

Dalles City for help. Robert was mounted on a shaggy pony and was riding west by noon. He had instructions to spread the news at the stagecoach office, the Umatilla House Hotel, and the Oregon Steam Navigation Company office. He also had instructions to stay put in town once he got there. His mother didn't want to risk having him out in the cold weather for longer than was necessary.

"If you can find Jack Allphin, tell him the news, too. Once he hears, he'll be the first man out here, I know," William Graham instructed his son.

———◆◦◆◦◆———

I left our house in Dalles City before daylight. I was again mounted on Napoleon. A pack full of food and blankets was tied behind the saddle. The temperature hung at twenty degrees below zero, almost as if it was stuck there.

I urged Napoleon into an easy walk east out of town. The wind was at our backs. It continued to snow, sometimes less, sometimes more. The wind drove the flakes ahead of us. I could see them pass me and slant down to land on the white landscape. I hoped to reach the hotel and stagecoach station on the far side of the Deschutes River before noon. I had no idea whether the Deschutes ferry would still be operating. If it got too dangerous, or the river froze totally, there would be no ferry. Crossing on the new ice on the Deschutes would be very chancy, so I considered having to go out on the Columbia to get where I was going. I thought it might be my best option.

———◆◦◆◦◆———

Allie Ann Allphin would be out of firewood very soon. She knew she did not dare let the fire go out. It would be difficult to get it kindled again. She remembered how much trouble it had caused ten years before when her sister Louisa had let the fire go out while their father was away from home on a trip to Oregon City. Teenaged Louisa tried but failed to kindle a new fire. She did not have flint or any gunpowder to use. She and Allie Ann finally walked about a mile to a neighbor's house and borrowed some glowing coals which they brought home in an iron kettle covered with a lid. It had been embarrassing to admit they had been so careless as to let their fire go out. All the way home they fed the red coals bits of wood, bark and dry moss from fence posts and tree trunks.

On Willow Creek, the nearest neighbor was over three miles away. Borrowing fire would not be an option in this weather. And if there were no fire, they would all shortly freeze to death.

Allie Ann thought about what she could do. She could get some poor wood from the willow grove down by the creek. It was green and small, and it wouldn't burn well, she knew. It would give little heat and require constant attention. She also knew there were some juniper trees about a half a mile upstream, but they were too far away. She was afraid she might freeze before she could even get to them. She was also afraid to get out of sight of the station buildings. She might lose her bearings in the storm and not be able to find her way back to the boys and the safety of the house.

She wondered how much wood she could get to burn from the barn. She thought she probably could dismantle the stalls, but it would take tools and quite a bit of effort. Then Allie Ann remembered the fence rails. Frank and Allen had spent a good deal of time that past autumn building a rail fence around the pasture north of the station. As a matter of fact, the job stood incomplete. Other chores and then the bad weather had halted progress on the rail fence. There were a few of the cedar and juniper rails left, still stacked behind the house.

"Allen, could you go out and fetch me in one of those fence rails you and Frank were using for the pasture fence? I'm afraid we're gonna be needing them for the fire. You'll have to cut more come spring to finish your fence. I'm sorry," said Allie Ann.

"Sure thing, Aunt Allie," said Allen. He put on his long coat, his woolen hat, and leather gloves. He grabbed the ax. He might have to hit the icy, snow-covered wooden rails with the ax to get them free. "I'll see if I can bring two."

Allie Ann watched from the half-open door as Allen disappeared around the corner of the building. Soon he came back dragging two fence rails.

"That's it, Allen," said Allie Ann. "Good job. How many more of them rails are left back there?"

Allen set the ax and the rails on the floor. He took off his gloves and shucked out of his heavy coat. "I think there's about a dozen in the pile. But you know what?" asked the boy.

"What?" asked Allie Ann. She had the bow saw in hand and started to make the first cut in the first rail. If she cut each rail four times, they would fit into the fire.

"We got us a supply when those are gone, too. All I got to do is go out and take apart the fence Uncle Frank and me built. It wouldn't be that hard to do. There's plenty of wood out there, and like you said, we can cut more rails and build more fence in the spring," said Allen.

Allie Ann set the saw aside and gave the boy a big hug. "You are a thinking man, Allen. I'm real glad you're here."

"I'm glad you're here too, Allen," said young William. "Or Mama might send me out after the rails. I wouldn't like that."

"Don't you worry none, William. I'm here to fetch in rails and take good care of you and Aunt Allie. You remember how I promised Uncle Frank?" asked Allen.

"Yup, I done heard you. You're a good cousin, Allen. And you give the best piggy-back rides," suggested young William.

"You think so?" asked Allen. "Then come here and hop on."

Allen and young William spent the next half hour playing "Ride 'Em, Cowboy" with Allen as the horse and young William as the daring, heroic rider. Allie Ann sawed up the first of the fence rails and stayed out of their way as they circled the little room, leading cavalry charges, winning battles and saving whole towns from disasters. Young William even got a medal, as did his horse.

* * *

Tom Scott rode his pony to the neighbor's house on Monday, January 13th. He stayed overnight and came back to his house around noon on Tuesday, January 14th. He had succeeded in borrowing a wagon and team of six horses from his neighbor upriver. The wagon was full of hay also borrowed from his neighbor. It was snowing hard as he came back and drove the loaded wagon into the big barn. His pony followed, tied to the back of the wagon.

Scott was glad to be home. It had been another difficult trip. The snow was getting deeper by the hour. He knew the men at the house were anxious to leave, but they would have to wait at least until morning. Maybe the storm would pass before then.

Scott stabled, fed, and tended to all the horses, then fought his way back to his house, leaning against the force of the wind. Entering the main room, he saw express agent James hard at work.

After giving the matter some thought, Tom Jeffries and David Mc-Donald had asked James to carry their gold. The agent assayed and weighed the contents of each man's poke. Each man received an official, signed Tracy Express Company receipt.

Bolton and Wilson came forward next to transact the same business. Glover decided it was a good idea, too. He had already hiked his fair share weighed down by his gold, and his parents wouldn't begrudge him the five percent fee to lay down his burden. Niles followed Glover. Jagger spoke up while Niles was collecting his receipt. "I'd leave my gold with you, too, Mr. James. But I'm carrying so little there would be no point in it. You know, I'm not a miner. I never have been one at all. I only came out to the camps to get the straight story for my father-in-law."

"I would have gladly carried your gold, too, sir," said James. "Anyone else?"

Nichols and Wellington came next. Riddle stepped up after Wellington saying, "If there's any chance I'll be walking again, I don't want to have to carry this." He emptied the contents of his custom-made money belt onto the table.

While James was busy with his gold, Riddle turned to speak with Mulkey. "It would make the hike easier if you was to let Mr. James here take your load," he said.

"I ain't gonna do it," said Mulkey.

"How come?" asked Riddle.

"Well, I'll tell you. For my whole life, everything I have, I have got by my own industry," said Mulkey. "I'll not trust it to another now." He nodded in agreement with himself. "Besides, there may not be that much hiking involved."

"You're sure?" asked Riddle.

"I'm telling you, ain't I?" Mulkey challenged.

"That you are, my friend. That you are," said Riddle, accepting his receipt from James.

———•◦•◦•———

I intercepted Robert Graham about four miles west of the Deschutes River crossing. The wind had picked up to about thirty miles per hour. It was snowing so hard we almost missed each other in the storm.

"What are you doing out here?" I shouted at the teenager.

"Mr. Allphin! Pa sent me. We need help. Some of the passengers from the Walla Walla stage came walking into Mr. Poole's house this morning. They were about frozen and got terrible news about people getting lost out in the snow. One of them being your brother Frank. I'm supposed to tell the folks at the Umatilla House, Mr. Miller at the stagecoach office, Mr. Coe at Oregon Steam Navigation, and you," said Graham.

"That's bad, son. I've been afraid of something like this. But, I tell you what. This here storm is getting worse, and I really don't think you should try to make it to Dalles City today. If you do, we might have to send out a search party for you, too," I said.

"You really think so?" asked Graham.

"I do. No use in risking you freezing. It's a long ten miles to Dalles City from here. Your Ma would have my hide if I let you go on, and anything happened to you. You done told me now, and I'll be able to start searching a lot quicker than you could even get to anyone in Dalles City. Let's go talk to your Pa, and I'm sure he'll see the sense in what I'm saying," I said.

"Yes, sir," said Graham, turning his pony.

"Did you get to this side of the Deschutes on the ferry?" I thought to ask.

"Yes, I did, but it might not be safe to run it soon. Pa brought me over, but then he probably went back to the hotel. We might have to go out on the big river to get back home," Graham said.

CHAPTER SEVENTEEN

The complaints and urgings of Stephens and Garrity had their effect on Blackmore. Early on the morning of January 13th, he sent driver Marv Knowles out of Walla Walla with an unscheduled stagecoach pulled by a hitch of six, loaded with food supplies for horses and people. There was enough room left inside for only four paying passengers.

They made it to Umatilla Landing with little trouble but the trail ahead was deeply drifted with snow. The hostelers told him when he arrived that the stagecoach would be unable to go on. Consequently, being detained at Umatilla Landing was not Knowles' fault.

The four passengers settled in to wait at the big, drafty warehouse owned by the stagecoach company. There were the typical beans to eat, plus a sack of flour and one of potatoes, so they would get a decent meal without having to break into the supply food.

Two of the passengers, Daniel Welch and Isaac Kaufman, went to ask Joe the hosteler if there was any other way to get to Dalles City.

Welch was a single man, fifty-two years old. He was a professional miner based in Amador, California. He had done well at the Salmon River mines and was on his way back home.

Kaufman was a single man also, and forty-eight years of age. He had been born in Baden, Germany. He was a merchant and an excellent tailor. He had been among a party of German tailors who were assaulted and robbed in their canvas shack back at Lewiston. He had had a profitable season and was trying to get home to Dalles City where he ran a mercantile and haberdashery. He was grateful that he had not lost his money like his friend Emil, nor had he lost his life like Emil's brother Hans. Taking everything into consideration, he felt very fortunate. He considered it another stroke of good luck that Welch was anxious to be on his way to Dalles City again just as he himself was.

Joe said, "If I was of a mind to get to Dalles City right now, I'd put on my pair of snowshoes and shoe it on down the edge of the Columbia. Everything is froze solid. Wouldn't be no trick at all. There's shelter before you get to Dalles City, too. There's a nice hotel just this side of the Deschutes River. You might be able to make it in two-three days, maybe less.

Kaufman and Welch briefly talked it over and decided to take Joe's advice. Joe even had two pairs of snowshoes he could sell to them. They haggled him down to two dollars per pair. Kaufman insisted on paying for both pairs of snowshoes, telling Welch he was grateful for his company. They decided to leave early the next morning, Tuesday, January 14th.

The twelve men remaining at Tom Scott's house decided to make their attempt to get out of the canyon at eight in the morning on Wednesday, January 15th. Scott let Wilcox cross the ferry to bring over Tracy Express agent James, the loaded wagon, and team of six horses. He made a second trip to get the rest of the men. The temperature still stood at about twenty degrees below zero. The wind had died, and it had stopped snowing. The conditions appeared to be somewhat better than they had been for several days.

The men tried to dress for the weather. Some of them wore virtually every piece of clothing they had. Jagger did not have any rough miner's clothing, but he wore both of the two town suits he had brought along. Over the suits, he had his wool topcoat, with the matching wool scarf, and his hard derby hat. He tried not to think about his shoes. They had never been made for walking in any kind of heavy weather. The leather soles were not thick and, the stylish, shiny black uppers were made of varnished, processed cardboard glued to a thin silk lining. They were not warm or durable or waterproof. In bad weather, shoes like that might be the death of a man. He reasoned they had gotten him through the long on-and-off hike from Willow Creek so they could get him through the next twenty-eight miles to the Deschutes River station.

Wellington was better off, having kept his rough miner's clothing in his baggage. He put away the fancy shoes he had purchased in Walla Walla and resumed wearing his heavy, sturdy boots. He still wore his fancy new suit, but now it was covered with canvas trousers and a canvas shirt. A heavy coat went over everything else. He also wore his new black top hat and his white kid gloves.

Jeffries wore his bulky wool topcoat over his heavy gear. With wool socks, heavy boots and his wide-brimmed oiled felt hat he considered himself pretty well prepared. Still, he wished he had some gloves.

Glover had done all he could do for his poor boots. With all his repairs, he hoped it would be enough. His trousers, shirt, and coat were worn and patched. His oiled felt hat was the best piece of foul-weather gear he owned.

Riddle was worried about his boots, too. While they had seemed perfectly adequate back at the mining camp, they weren't offering his feet much protection in the snow. He could feel worn spots in the soles where the leather was getting thin. He wished he had bought some new boots in Walla Walla.

Mulkey was in a sour mood. It was mighty cold, and his money belt was digging into his sides again. He wore all of his clothing, and under the several layers of fabric, he couldn't easily get at the belt to adjust it. He decided he would just have to endure it until he could get to Dalles City.

Niles, McDonald, and Nichols all had decent coats and boots, and they felt prepared for the long cold walk out of the John Day Canyon.

William Halberth had watched the twelve men pack their baggage and cross the river with glee. "Good riddance, good riddance to bad trash," he said. "I thought I'd never get shed of the lot of them. Now, let's get back to important business." Halberth hurried into the kitchen and located his bottle of whiskey, hidden behind the pile of firewood in the corner. Cradling the bottle in the crook of one arm, he dragged the wooden chair over near the stove. "They about worked poor me to death, waiting on them hand and foot. I need me some rest and the benefits of this here bottle," he mumbled. "It's medicinal and no mistake."

Just then, Tom Scott came back into his house, grateful to finally be able to peacefully enjoy his own home again. "Halberth!" shouted Scott. "Get your lazy bones out here and clean up this main room. Fetch in some wood and build up this poor excuse for a fire."

Halberth sighed and hid his bottle again. The poor working man never gets no rest, he thought.

The twelve men with the team and wagon would be forced to use the main trail. It was a steep climb out of the canyon, and the snow had drifted badly. It covered the trail to a depth of over four feet in some places.

After pulling the wagon off the ferry, the team couldn't move it another inch. The men would have to break trail for the six horses and the wagon in the three to four-foot-deep snow.

They tried pushing the snow out of the way. That didn't work very well. They tried kicking and stomping down the snow, working in pairs to flatten the snow cover. They made some progress but it was slow and exhausting work. James checked his watch after the team and wagon had finally reached the base of the switchbacks. It had taken over an hour to come about two hundred gently sloping yards. Now the real climbing would begin. Taking everything into consideration, James decided to abandon the wagon. He told the men they would have to carry anything they wanted to bring along now. Any baggage they left behind would be sent on by the stagecoach company eventually. He loaded the mail and the heavy express onto the six horses. He had to open the treasure box and split up the now four-hundred-pound load. Still, it didn't take long to transfer the mail and the gold.

The men continued to take turns breaking trail for the horses. The four-foot deep snowdrifts made progress difficult. As the morning went on, the wind started to blow from the west, gusting down into the group's faces, making everyone miserable. Even the horses didn't like it. One of them finally shied, slipped, and fell to his knees. It took some time to get him back on his feet, and then he refused to go on. James privately sympathized with the horse. He thought perhaps the horse was smarter than any of the men were. He took the load from the balky horse and distributed it among the other five. He let the unloaded horse go back down the hill, to where Fred Wilcox waited, alternately watching the proceedings and going back inside the wall tent to warm up. As usual, his dog stayed inside, right next to the fire.

It was only a matter of minutes before another horse slipped, lost his footing, and refused to go further. When the third horse gave out, James started distributing the express among the men. In this fashion, the mail, the express, three horses and twelve men got to the top of the hill coming out of the John Day Canyon. It was noon.

Express agent James was a practical man. He wasn't one to be influenced by wishful thinking. He looked at their current situation with a critical eye and considered his actual position and the possibilities for the near future. It had just taken four hours to travel about a mile from the river. It was twenty-seven miles further to shelter at the Deschutes River Crossing. It would be dark in less than five hours. The wind was blowing harder, and it looked like it could snow again, any minute now. He no longer had the wagon, and he had only three unwilling horses. James made up his mind. "Gentlemen," James spoke up, "We need to have us a little consultation before we go on. Or, I should say, before any of you go on. I'm turning back. There's no way I can get the mail or the express through to the Deschutes River today. I know when I'm beat."

"I'm with you," said Bolton. "If I stay out much longer I'll turn into a block of ice."

"Me too," said Wilson. "I bet the horses are with us, too."

"Well, I ain't," said Mulkey. "I ain't come all the way up that there booger of a hill just to go back down. I'm walking to that hotel on the Deschutes River, just see if I ain't."

"I'm walking on, too. We'll do a lot better now that we're up here on the flat," said Wellington.

"I'm with you, boys," said Riddle.

"I'm not licked yet," stated Niles.

"I've got my face set for it, and I can make it," said Jagger. "I've always been a dare-the-devil kind of man."

"Are you fellas sure?" asked James. "It'll be dark before five o'clock, and it's already past noon. I may be turning back now, but I'll be getting out of here just as soon as it's possible. I'll be trying again tomorrow or the next day. Anybody who wants to go back with me and then try again is more than welcome."

"Thank you, Mr. James, but no. Where others have gone, I can follow," said Jeffries.

"We can do it," said Nichols.

"I'm all for going," added McDonald.

Glover nodded his agreement. He knew it was a risk to keep going since he was already half-frozen, but Glover agreed with Mulkey. They had made it out of the canyon. He was set on going.

"Alright," said James. "I can see there ain't no use in trying to stop you. I guess you all have your hats on. Good luck."

Jeffries shook hands with James and gave him back his share of the express and mail. "Take good care of my gold Mr. James, and I hope to see you in Dalles City shortly," Jeffries joked.

James, Bolton, and Wilson were the only men going back down to Scott's. The mail and the express packages were all given back to them. "Farewells" were exchanged, and nine men walked west together, into the freezing wind and snow.

Bolton and Wilson followed James and the horses back down the grade. They left the wagon where it sat as they passed it, only taking their own bedrolls and tucking in the canvas tarp covering the load as they passed. They collected the three exhausted horses from Wilcox and asked him to ferry them back across the river.

When Wilcox signaled for permission to bring the ferry across, Scott was not at all surprised to see the men coming back to his house. What did surprise him was how few had turned back.

"I'm sticking with that expressman like a leach," said Bolton as he and Wilson hiked back up the slope toward Scott's barn.

"I'm with you. He's got a level head on his shoulders. If anyone gets out of here in one piece, it'll be him," agreed Wilson.

———————

James, Wilson, and Bolton brought the six horses back to the barn, the three men fed and tended to the exhausted horses. Exhausted themselves, they carried their bedrolls, the express, and the mail back to the house. By the time they came back inside, James was limping on frozen feet.

Tom Scott knew what to do for mild frostbite. He made James sit down by the kitchen fire and take off his boots and socks. Scott heated some water and had James soak his feet in a lukewarm bath. After drying off, James stayed by the fire, drinking hot coffee with his feet wrapped in a blanket. He would suffer no permanent damage.

———————

Jagger, Wellington, Jeffries, Glover, Niles, Nichols, McDonald, Riddle, and Mulkey walked west into the wind. The snow was anywhere from two to three feet deep. They walked single-file, taking turns breaking trail. No one had any energy for conversation.

As darkness fell, they continued to walk. They had no choice, it was too cold to stop moving, and there was nowhere to stop for shelter. The sporadic snowfall had stopped, and the gusting wind ripped holes in the cloud cover. Much of the time the full moon could be seen, giving a surprising amount of light. The trail ahead was easily identified as a long, sunken area in the surrounding snow. The nine men quietly walked on all night across the barren flat plateau.

They continued to walk the next morning, taking short breaks.

As the new day dawned, the line of men spread out more and more. Glover, Niles, and Jeffries were leading, breaking trail between the three of them. Jeffries tried not to think about the cold. Focusing all his energy on putting one frozen foot in front of the other, he trudged across the long flat plateau. Glover and Niles, on the other hand, frequently wondered just how cold it was.

The temperature that day, January 16th, read thirty degrees below zero at the Army hospital in Dalles City. On the Columbia Plateau, it was perhaps five or ten degrees colder.

Nichols, McDonald, Riddle, and Mulkey walked in a group behind the first three men. They were sharing a bottle of whiskey in the mistaken belief that it would help them keep warm. Instead, it was cooling their body temperatures dramatically, and putting their lives in danger. The temperature of the alcohol in the bottle was at least thirty, and perhaps as much as sixty degrees colder than the freezing point of water.

Mulkey's money belt had been digging in his side since late last night. He couldn't seem to get it to sit right, and now he felt a shooting pain with every step. Even though he knew it was a bad sign, he couldn't stop and try to adjust it. He was glad he brought that bottle of whiskey to keep him warm and distract him from his discomfort. It did seem to be helping. Riddle passed Mulkey the whiskey and watched as Mulkey took a nip and recapped the bottle. Mulkey had stopped complaining a few hours back, but he was starting to limp. Riddle was worried, and he was keeping a close watch on his friend.

Jagger and Wellington walked together, bringing up the rear. Both were feeling the effects of the cold. Jagger was suffering, especially due to his thin, stylish shoes. He was almost glad when his feet went completely numb. At least then they no longer hurt.

As he walked, Jagger found his mind wandering. He considered how nice it would be to take Eliza and Hattie for a tour back east. He would show them New York City. He would be so proud to introduce them to his father in Albany. He would take them to see Niagara Falls. It would be so wonderful, and how Eliza's eyes would shine, oh how Hattie would laugh. It made him feel so good to think about it.

It was just fully light when Jagger started to stumble, and he had a great deal of trouble trying to control his legs. Noticing Jagger's wobbly steps, Wellington wrapped an arm around his friend's shoulder and helped him to walk further. "It's no good," said Jagger. "I have to sit and rest."

Wellington stopped and reluctantly helped Jagger to sit in the snow. "You can't stay there," said Wellington. "You'll freeze."

"It's only for a minute," said Jagger. "I'll get up again in a moment. I'm so tired. I must rest."

Wellington saw Jagger close his eyes. "No, no, you don't," he said, pulling on Jagger's hand, trying to get him to rise.

"Leave me alone," said Jagger, trying to shake off Wellington's grip, "Leave me alone. I'll catch up. Leave me alone."

Wellington continued to tug on Jagger, trying to get him to move. It was hopeless. Jagger sagged down further and stretched out on his back. When his hat fell off, he did not even notice. He just laid in the snow and refused to make any effort to get up again.

"I can't carry you. You have to try to get up," said Wellington.

"Go on," said Jagger. "I'll be coming directly."

Wellington finally had to walk away, eventually catching up to Nichols, McDonald, Riddle, and Mulkey. He fell in line behind the four men. He could see the figures of Jeffries, Glover, and Niles a hundred yards ahead. He kept checking behind him, hoping to see Jagger, but after a while, he knew he wouldn't be coming. He muttered a prayer for his friend and kept his focus on the trail ahead. The eight men continued to walk west.

———•◦•◦•◦•———

Jagger truly had intended to get up and continue on after a brief rest. Lying in the snow, he didn't feel cold, but exhaustion and his inadequate clothing conspired against him. As he lay there, he thought about his dear Eliza. Suddenly, she was there, right in front of him. She looked so lovely. She was sitting on a low chair with her full, wide, white skirts spread out around her. Her face, her hands, her skin was so perfect, so pale. She smiled. Her teeth were so white and perfect. "Eliza," he said, looking up, lost in admiration for her. "Eliza," he whispered, letting his head fall back into the snow again.

CHAPTER EIGHTEEN

Robert Graham and I made it back to the hotel on the Deschutes River a couple of hours after meeting on the trail. Harriet and William Graham were grateful that I had made their son come back with me. The weather was too bitter for the boy to be out, but now at least one of the men he had been sent to notify, me, knew about the tragedy still unfolding just a few miles to the east. When the weather moderated, his parents would send Robert back out to Dalles City.

I was anxious to talk to Moody and Gay. They were relieved to have the chance to tell me what had happened. "I left him wrapped in my long wool overcoat. It reaches below the knees, and it's awful warm," said Moody. "It might make the difference for him. I hope so."

"That was more than good of you," I said. "Not many men would have done that. No matter what happens now, whether I can find him or not, I've got to thank you. That was a right noble thing to do."

"I'm praying for the best," said Moody.

"Frank's a fine man. I hope you find him safe," said Gay. "I trust Davis made it back to Scott's. Then they would have sent men out to fetch in your brother. He's probably back at Scott's house now."

"I'm heading that direction next. Thank you both for all you done and for telling me about it. It helps a lot to know what happened," I said, shaking hands with each man.

My best hope was that Pat Davis had made it back to Wilcox at the tent and had then summoned help for Frank from across the river. But I didn't put a lot of faith in Frank being back at Scott's. I knew that once a man exhausted himself and then fell in the snow, he seldom rose again. And it sounded like Davis himself had been at the point of exhaustion when he turned back. I would have to go look for Frank myself.

I took Napoleon back out into the storm, heading east. When darkness fell, we holed up in a gully. I cleared the snow out a little, arranged canvas tarps as windbreaks and kindled a fire from some scrubby trees, sagebrush and an accumulation of wind-blown debris. We were on our way again at first light. It continued to snow, though the wind had died down.

We continued on eastward, seeing no sign of life. I located another gully at nightfall, and we endured another sub-zero night with only a weak fire. We were both tired and getting more chilled by the hour.

I turned Napoleon back to the west on the morning of Wednesday, January 15th. We had found nothing. We would go back to Graham's hotel and try again once we had a chance to thaw out properly and get something decent to eat. I hoped the weather would let up. It would help in the search if visibility improved. As it was, I sometimes couldn't see further than a few yards. I hated to have to give up, but Napoleon and I had both reached our limits. It would do no good to stay out any longer.

We traveled all that day, and most of the night, afraid to stop before we reached shelter. Walking Napoleon into the big barn at the Deschutes River station, I silently vowed to be out searching again just as soon as I could.

Thursday, January 16th dawned with snow flurries and wind gusts of thirty miles per hour. I got about six hours of sleep and a good meal. I was restless and decided to go out searching some more.

I was in the process of getting Napoleon saddled about noon when I heard shouting from up the hill behind the hotel and barn. The Deschutes River home station hosteler, John Irvin, and I ran out and around the barn to see what the commotion was about. We saw three men staggering down the slope from the east. These men held on to each other to keep from falling. And they were shouting for help as they tottered down the incline. We ran to help them, practically dragging them the last several yards across the flat into the hotel kitchen. Jeffries, Glover, and Niles had arrived. Within minutes Nichols, McDonald, Wellington, and Riddle followed. All seven men were dehydrated and frozen to the bone. Any exposed skin was showing varying degrees of frostbite and they had all lost feeling in their frozen feet. The men were alive but they were in pretty bad shape.

Riddle clutched me by the arm as he came in the door. "My friend Mulkey, he's still out there. Someone has to go back out for him. He's all tuckered out, but he's alive. I left him sitting in the snow. It wasn't more than three or four miles back where he gave out. Please! Someone has to go fetch him," he pleaded.

"Calm down, mister," I said. "I got my horse all saddled up and ready to go. I'll bring your friend back directly, don't fret. I'll just follow your back trail. What was his name again?"

"His name is Mulkey, Johnson Mulkey. Thank you so much. Thank you kindly," said Riddle.

"Let me come with you. I'll haul the stoneboat behind my mule," said Irvin. "We can bring Mulkey back on it. If he's froze bad he probably can't sit a horse."

We left within minutes in search of Mulkey. We thought it would be fairly simple to follow the trail left by the seven walking men. For the first mile or two, the trail was plain, but once we got out of the Deschutes River Canyon and up onto the Columbia Plateau, the trail got more difficult to follow. The wind had drifted the snow in the short time since the walking men had passed. We completely lost the trail twice, having to circle around to find it again. We were glad it was only noon. It just might take all the daylight we had left to find Mulkey.

———•◦••◦•———

Daniel Welch and Isaac Kaufman spent four long days snowshoeing west and then south. They picked up J.W. Knight's tracks west of Willow Creek and used the trail he had broken. They encountered the same hazards and made the same decisions Knight had made, even when they lost his trail. They safely shoed up to Tom Scott's house late in the evening on Friday, January 17th.

James, Wilson, Bolton, Scott, and Halberth were about ready to turn in for the night when thumping and bumping out on the front porch alerted them to the new arrivals. Scott greeted Welch and Kaufman as they came in the door. "Come on in and sit down by the stove. It ain't a fit night to be out there, not one bit it ain't," he said.

The new arrivals came inside, and introductions followed.

"We're trying to get to Dalles City," said Kaufman. "I got a business there to run."

"What are the prospects for getting there from here, anyhow?" asked Welch.

"You got here at just the right time," said James. "First thing in the morning we're packing up and getting out of this canyon. We got six horses and a wagon. We got broken trail up the switchbacks on the other side clear to the top. We tried it before and had to turn back. This time we are going to make a go of it. You, gentlemen, are welcome to come along if you want."

————•+•+•————

Johnson Mulkey sat huddled in the middle of the snowy trail. He was disgusted with himself. He wished he could find the gumption to get up and go on. He would try but, he couldn't feel his feet or his legs at all. His sides hurt horribly every time he moved, even when he breathed. He was angry to have been so weak. He was angry to have been left behind. He knew it was very possible that he would die right on this spot, sitting in the snow. He was thinking about death when John Irvin and I found him. Mulkey was groggy and didn't hear us come up to him.

Looking up, he couldn't speak at first.

"You two don't look much like angels," he whispered, confused.

"What did he say?" asked John.

"He thinks we're here to take him home, but he don't think we look much like Saint Peter's helpers," I said.

"No use in being abusive, Mr. Mulkey. Let's just get you comfortable on this here stoneboat, and we'll have you sipping coffee by the fire directly," said John.

Mulkey could not get up on his own, he would push his hands down into the snow at his sides and mutter to himself, but his legs didn't move.

"Mr. Mulkey," I said, "John and me are gonna pull you up real careful and lay you on this stoneboat. Then we will get you outta this weather and someplace warm."

Mulkey nodded his approval.

————•+•+•————

Allie Ann did not want to have to tie a rope onto Allen when he went out after more fence rails, but she did not see any other way.

The last time he had gone out, he had walked away into the snow-storm and completely disappeared from view. Watching from the half-open doorway, she had felt her heart leap up in her throat. She could not allow Allen to get lost. So she got out all the rope she could find, even making a trip out to the barn to get a couple of short halter ropes. Every foot of rope would help.

Visibility was, if anything, getting worse. Right now, at high noon, she could barely distinguish the barn from the storm. It was irritating. She knew the barn was out there, and right big, too, but every now and then it would disappear. "I wouldn't send you out after more rails at all if the floor were puncheon instead of dirt," said Allie Ann. "Then we could just pry up the flooring, saw it up, and burn it."

"I don't mind, Aunt Allie," said Allen, picking up the ax. "Throw a loop over me, and I'll bring us back another couple of rails." Over the next two weeks, they would burn up the entire string of fence bordering the pasture on the east side.

———————•❖•———————

While John Irvin and I were bringing in Mulkey, Robert Graham was again dispatched to Dalles City. This time he made it safely to town in less than three hours. By late afternoon virtually everyone in Dalles City had heard about the tragedy. With nine frostbitten men in various states, four men left out in the snow, three men stranded at the John Day River station, and the Willow Creek station almost out of supplies and snowed in, people jumped into action.

My wife Mary correctly assumed that I would not be home anytime soon. She knew I would be searching for Frank and any other men lost in the snow. And with this weather she knew I would have a heck of a time getting to Allie Ann and the boys at Willow Creek.

Emmitt Miller and A.J. Kane recruited a couple of volunteers,

Thomas O'Brien and Frank Shelton. The four men left immediately for the Deschutes River home station. O'Brien and Shelton were friends of John Irvin, and as soon as they heard the news, they volunteered to go out and search for those men still missing in the storm.

The local doctors held a meeting at the Umatilla House Hotel and prepared to receive the injured men. Four medical practitioners were living in Dalles City, and Doctor J.W. Hunter happened to be passing through town. He had spent the past season at the Salmon River mines and was on his way home to the Willamette Valley. Doctor Hunter immediately volunteered to care for the injured as they arrived. After learning the men were also from the west side of the Cascade Mountains, he thought he might already be acquainted with some of his patients.

Doctor Dennison was a friend of Doc Gay and a brother Mason. He had his modern medical office downtown, and he donated the use of his office to Doctor Hunter, a more experienced man. Together they prepared this space to act as an operating theater. The report they had heard about the victims of the storm was very bad. Doctors Dennison and Hunter figured they might have to treat up to twelve men. Doctor Dennison had some experience treating frostbite, and the subzero temperature these men were out in was sure to cause damage to any wet feet and exposed skin. Frozen limbs could very well mean amputations, and they prepared for the worst.

Doctor Andrew J. Hogg was a single man and thirty-one-years old. Originally from Virginia, Doctor Hogg was a formally trained surgeon. Deciding the space would be too cramped in his Dalles City office, Doctor Hogg set up a temporary office in the Umatilla House Hotel. Given the use of a suite of interconnecting rooms on the second floor, he prepared to examine, treat, and shelter any casualties brought to him there.

Doctor J.S. McAteeney also thought it was possible that he would know some of the injured men. McAteeney had first come to Benton County, Oregon around 1854. Now living in Dalles City, he was thirty-eight-years old, and newly married with a baby daughter. He let Doctor Hunter and Doctor Hogg know he could be called on to help if needed.

The most junior member of the Dalles City medical community was Doctor J.C. Shields, age twenty-five and also newly married. Doctor Shields voiced his willingness to help, but he certainly did not want to appear to encroach on the territory of the more senior medical men.

⁂

Emmitt Miller and A.J. Kane set out early on the morning of Friday, January 17th from the Deschutes River home station. John Irvin would have come with them, but he had badly frozen one foot the day before while bringing in Johnson Mulkey with me. Miller and Kane were going out to try to find Jagger's body and bring it back. They had a horse and a mule and a wide board to tie the body to. It was snowing hard as they left the hotel. They promised to return by nightfall.

On that morning I had breakfast at Graham's hotel and left the dooryard just behind Miller and Kane. I would spend the day searching on my own, covering ground to the south and east of the other two men. I wasn't specifically looking for Jagger's body. I was hoping to find some trace of Frank.

Miller and Kane did not return to the Deschutes River home station by dark as they had promised. I brought Napoleon into the dooryard at sunset and was surprised that they were not there ahead of me. John Irvin met me at the barn door.

"I'm glad somebody decided to come back in out of the weather.

You see anything of Miller or Kane out there, Jack?" Irvin asked.

"I sure haven't," I admitted. "I hope they haven't gone and got lost, too. It's no picnic out there. I'm near frozen."

"I won't go out tonight, but if they aren't back early tomorrow, I'll go out after them. O'Brien and Shelton are here, too, getting some dinner. They said they'll be ready to join the search in the morning," Irvin said.

Just before noon the next day Irvin, O'Brien, and Shelton went after Miller and Kane. It was a great relief when they met the two men about a mile from the Deschutes River, bringing back Jagger's body on the board drawn by the mule. Miller, Kane, and Shelton would return to Dalles City on Sunday, January 19th, bringing Jagger's body with them.

James, Bolton, Wilson, Kaufman, and Welch left Scott's house at eight in the morning on Saturday, January 18th. They had the mail, the express, and a large amount of baggage loaded in the wagon. It was a still morning. Very little snow had fallen since the men had made their previous escape attempt and the snow continued to hold off. The trail remained fairly clear, with only a little drifted snow on their tracks The six horses were rested and seemed willing to pull. Welch and Kaufman led the way on their snowshoes, mashing down the remaining snow somewhat with their passing. Bolton and Wilson walked behind James as he drove the wagon slowly to the top of the John Day Canyon. They only had to help by pushing the wagon once or twice. After they reached the Columbia Plateau, everyone could ride. The wagon and five men reached the hotel at the Deschutes River just at dark.

CHAPTER NINETEEN

———————— ❖ ————————

On January 17th Lawrence Coe of the Oregon Steam Navigation Company was organizing men to assist with the rescue mission. Fred M. Stocking and C.H. Johnson, two local Dalles City farmers, volunteered to help. They were hardy, resourceful men accustomed to working outside in all kinds of weather. Lawrence Coe had met them at the warehouse of the Oregon Steam Navigation Company in Dalles City to outfit them for their rescue mission. Coe had given them two hand-sleighs loaded with blankets and provisions intended for the relief of the victims of the storm. The sun was setting as they finished loading the sleighs. They decided it was best to wait and leave early the next morning.

Stocking and Johnson were leaving the warehouse at the same time James and his four companions were making their way out of the John Day Canyon, forty-two miles away. Stocking and Johnson made good time to the Deschutes River, despite the icy wind and snow flurries. Once there, they faced a severe disappointment. The solid ice on the surface of the river had broken up overnight. The river was full of crashing chunks of floating ice, making walking impossible and rendering the ferry boat useless, too.

After evaluating the situation, they decided to cross north on the Columbia River, where the ice was solid. Stocking and Johnson pulled their hand-sleighs out onto the ice of the Columbia River. They made a wide detour around the waterfall at the mouth of the Deschutes River and came back onto land east of Poole's house, the barn, and the hotel. They arrived at about the same time as James and his party with the wagon.

Stocking and Johnson were in the process of dragging their loaded sleighs up the embankment from the Columbia River when they saw the wagon loaded with men come from the east into the hotel dooryard. The men piled out of the wagon and stood talking with Poole and Graham as the rescuers came up with their sleighs. It was just getting dark.

"Hello," said Johnson. "We've been told you folks need some help out here."

"We have men missing in the snow, and we have some who are hurt and need to get to Dalles City," explained Graham. "And you probably seen the ferry is just useless."

"That's why we come in off the Columbia. The ice is good and thick out there. We'll take your injured men and go back the same way, but not in the dark," said Stocking.

"We got blankets, wool clothing, and bread. Can I get some help unloading?" asked Johnson.

Welch and Kaufman helped unload the hand-sleighs while James, Wilson, and Bolton brought the mail and the express box into the hotel. Glover, Nichols, and Niles sat around the woodstove in the small lobby. They all got up and started talking at once. Hands were shaken all around.

"Moody and Gay are here," said Glover.

"And Frank Allphin and Pat Davis are out lost in the snow somewhere," said Niles.

"No, that's awful," Wilson lamented, looking around. "What happened and where's everybody else?"

"Moody and Gay are back in the kitchen with the others. They say Allphin fell in the snow and couldn't be roused. Then Davis turned back. He didn't make it back to Scott's since we left, did he?" asked Glover.

Wilson and Bolton both shook their heads.

"McDonald, Jeffries, Riddle, and Wellington are staying close to that kitchen stove. Mulkey is here, too. Got a little frost-bit. We lost Mr. Jagger," said Nichols.

"What? Lost Jagger? How?" asked James.

"Him and Wellington was bringing up the rear of our line. Jagger just sat down, then laid down in the snow, saying he needed to rest. Wellington did his best to get him up and get him moving, but it was no use. He feels real bad about it now, but there wasn't nothing he could have done," said Glover.

"We almost lost Mulkey, too. Sent the hosteler here and Frank Allphin's brother out to bring him in off the trail a couple of miles east of here. He's upstairs, sleeping now," said Nichols.

"He's in pretty rough shape," said Glover.

"That's not good," said James.

"Frank Allphin's brother is here?" asked Wilson.

"He was the first man out here from Dalles City to help. He's out now, searching for Frank and Davis," said Niles.

"Come on back to the kitchen. Everyone will be glad to see you. Mrs. Graham says dinner will be ready pretty soon. She's a darn good cook," said Nichols.

Round, motherly Harriet Graham ran her household and hotel with precision. Meals were served exactly at six in the morning, noon, and six at night. Some leeway was allowed when stagecoaches were not on time, but Harriet preferred a steady schedule.

Having so many guests at once she found both good and bad. There was little she could do for the injured men beyond keeping them warm and giving them hot food and drinks. But there was an extra quantity of food to prepare and more beds to make. There were also lots of willing hands to pump water, bring vegetables from the root cellar, fetch firewood, or run messages out to the barn. She would be both happy and sad when her guests all left.

———◆•••◆———

Stocking and Johnson spent the night at Graham's hotel and started early on Sunday, January 19th to transport the injured men back to Dalles City. They wanted to take those who were most injured first. Mulkey raved and cursed at them when they attempted to touch him, so they left him in bed. Riddle was anxious to go and even held off from voicing threats against the stagecoach company for the duration of the trip. Wellington went with Riddle for Johnson's first run to town.

Johnson delivered the men to Doctor Hogg at Umatilla House and made good time back to the Deschutes River station. He took Jeffries and McDonald on his next trip over the ice and west. It snowed very little, and everyone was grateful the wind had died down. While none of the frostbitten men relished the idea of going out in the cold again, they were consoled by the idea of getting some qualified medical help. It was fourteen miles to Dalles City, and took over three hours using the hand-sleighs. By six in the evening, Johnson had made his two trips, bringing four men in to the Umatilla House Hotel.

Doctor Hogg went to work right away, taking each man's vitals, getting them properly re-warmed and hydrated, and assessing the damage to their face, hands, and feet. Of these four men, Riddle and Jeffries were in the worst condition. Both men were generally frozen all over, but their feet were especially bad. Their feet were a bluish-gray color, and large blisters had formed on the sides and soles of their feet. Each would definitely lose some toes. McDonald and Wellington fared better but would have to be watched. Doctor Hogg was hopeful that they might recover without the loss of any of their fingers or toes. He asked Doctor McAteeney to help with monitoring McDonald and Wellington so he could focus on Riddle and Jeffries.

Fred Stocking came back to Dalles City a little after seven that evening, bringing Moody and Gay. They were lodged at the Western Hotel and attended by Doctor J.W. Hunter.

Moody and Gay each had badly frozen feet and were still experiencing some numbness in their toes. Doctor Hunter would have to observe them carefully over the next few days to see if any amputations would be necessary.

Stocking wished them well as he left. "Doc Hunter will take good care of you both. I've been glad to help," he said.

"Thank you for the ride. I've never been more relieved to get moving," said Gay.

"You're a fine man, Mr. Stocking. Thank you. Real good to make your acquaintance," said Moody, reaching out to shake hands.

Niles and Glover had by some miracle come through unhurt. At Graham's hotel, they attached themselves to the group led by express agent James. Whenever James would be bringing the wagon to Dalles City, they would be with him.

Lawrence Coe was busy making arrangements for Jagger's remains. He located a metal coffin and arranged to have it filled with alcohol to preserve the body. The coffin would be stored in the Oregon Steam Navigation Company warehouse until the ice left the Columbia River and it could be shipped back to Portland.

Coe sent a full written report to R.R. Thompson. It would fall to Thompson to find some way to tell Eliza what had happened.

———◆◆◆◆◆———

Nichols and Mulkey were the only two injured men left at the hotel on the Deschutes River. Nichols had been quick to take a place by the fire when he was first brought in from the cold. The situation was different with Mulkey.

"Come sit by me Mulkey, you ought to sit by the fire and warm up a bit," Riddle had coaxed.

Mulkey, however, did not want to sit by the fire with the other men. He said he wanted to go to bed. He didn't want to get undressed, either. It was all Harriet Graham could do to persuade him to remove his coat and boots before getting under the covers.

Mulkey fell into a fitful sleep which turned into delirium as night came. He ran a high fever and thrashed around in his bed, tangling the covers. Only toward morning did he settle down and get some rest.

Harriet Graham wanted to attend to the injured man, but he would not let her. He shouted whenever anyone came near him and wouldn't allow anyone to touch him. She took Mulkey a bowl of soup a few hours after Johnson had tried to rouse him, but he refused to eat.

Late on the night of January 19th Mulkey passed away. Harriet Graham discovered his body when she came to try to interest him in some breakfast the next morning.

When William and Robert Graham were loading Mulkey's body onto the wagon, they found that Mulkey was still wearing his heavy money belt under his shirt. All the skin around his midsection had turned black with gangrene. The money belt had constricted, chafed, and ultimately froze the flesh of his stomach, sides, and back.

Expressman James took charge of the contents of the money belt, assaying, weighing, and filling out a receipt for the family of the dead man. They would receive full value on his treasure, minus the five percent delivery fee.

On Monday, January 20th Moody and Gay were moved from the Western Hotel to a private residence. Doctor J.W. Hunter amputated each of Doc Gay's little toes, though he was able to save the rest of his toes and his feet. Fortunately, Moody would recover without surgery.

Gay trusted Hunter, and knew that gangrene could be the end of him. He made no protest over the loss of toes which would certainly otherwise kill him.

Doctor Hogg had his four patients removed from the Umatilla House Hotel and brought to the Army hospital at Fort Dalles. He would have to observe them for a few more days to see if amputations were in order.

The ice broke up enough so the ferry on the Deschutes River could safely run by Monday, January 20th. James, Bolton, Wilson, Kaufman, Welch, Niles, and Glover arrived in Dalles City with the wagon shortly after noon that day. They brought the body of Johnson

Mulkey, the mail, the express treasure box, and the baggage from the stagecoach.

As the wagon neared Dalles City, James addressed his passengers. "I'll be stopping at the Umatilla House to unload the mail, the treasure box, and everyone's baggage. I'm right sorry this all had to happen. You've all been real good companions and I've got to thank you for not complaining or making a fuss."

"Thank you, Mr. James. We need to find out where they took Mr. Riddle and the others," said Glover.

"I hope they are all going to be alright. We'll find them first thing," said Bolton.

"Oh, dear Lord, none of them knows about Mulkey," cried Wilson.

"I'll go with you," said Niles. "We'll break the news together."

Upon reaching Umatilla House James sent a hotel runner to seek Lawrence Coe. Coe would take charge of Johnson Mulkey's remains as he had those of John Jagger. James supposed the matter of Mulkey's Tracy Express receipt would be the responsibility of the Wasco County Sheriff. He sent another hotel runner in search of the Sheriff.

Kaufman thanked James and said brief farewells to Welch and his other companions before hurrying up the street. He had been away for almost six months and was understandably anxious about the state of his shop. He had left a clerk in charge and was hoping the man had been honest.

Welch bid the rest of the men good luck, and shook James' hand. "Thank you for the ride," he said. He went inside the Umatilla House and got himself a room with a view of the Columbia River. He figured he might have to stay in Dalles City for several weeks before the weather would allow him to continue back home.

The hotel clerk registered Niles, Glover, Bolton, and Wilson while telling them their friends had been taken to the Army hospital. The four men decided to hike up the steep rise and visit Jeffries, Wellington, Riddle, and McDonald.

"Let me talk to Riddle first," said Glover. "I been with him and Mulkey since Walla Walla, and walked from Wells Springs to Willow Creek with them. We been through a lot."

Entering the hospital building, the men first met Doctor Hogg. He let them know how the patients were doing. McDonald and Wellington would probably need no surgical treatment. Riddle and Jeffries, however, would each lose a foot to the effects of frostbite. Doctor Hogg permitted Glover to talk to Riddle in private. Riddle had a room to himself, as did Jeffries. McDonald and Wellington shared the large, echoing dormitory.

Glover, hat in hand, stood in the doorway of Riddle's room. At first he wasn't sure Riddle was awake. The man looked strangely smaller than Glover remembered. Glover cleared his throat, and Riddle opened his eyes.

"Remember me?" asked Glover.

"Glover, my boy, of course I do," said Riddle.

Glover came to stand by Riddle's bed. "How are you doing?" asked Glover.

"Not good. I just, oh I just ... The doctor told me I'm going to lose my foot. Not just some toes, but my whole foot. My foot!" Riddle complained. "What am I going to do without my foot?" Tears glistened in his eyes.

Glover reached out to touch the older man's shoulder. "I'm right sorry to hear that, sir." Glover sighed, gathering his courage. "I'm right sorry to have to tell you this, too. We lost Mr. Mulkey. He never rose from his bed there at Graham's hotel."

"Oh no, no, not Mulkey," whispered Riddle, tears streaming down his face.

"I'm sorry. I thought you had a right to know. We been through a lot together," said Glover.

"You were kind to come and tell me. We have been through a lot. Thank you, son. Poor Mulkey. Do you think you could come back later? I just want to be alone to think about this for now," said Riddle, closing his eyes.

Glover quietly left the room. Suddenly, the air seemed thick with all the medical smells. Glover hurried, stumbling out onto the steps of the hospital. He spit repeatedly into the snow-covered flower beds, barely controlling his nausea. He had no idea that visiting Riddle would affect him so badly. He guessed that maybe he was a little worn out and showing the strain himself. He waited outside on the hospital steps for Bolton, Wilson, and Niles. He couldn't bring himself to go back into the building.

Niles, Bolton, and Wilson visited with McDonald and Wellington first, congratulating them on coming through their ordeal almost undamaged. With Jeffries they were more sober, knowing that he was facing surgery, and wishing him a speedy recovery. Their visit was brief. Finding Glover out on the steps, they all headed back downhill to town.

The four companions located Moody and Gay later in the afternoon. They repeated the news about Mulkey and their wishes for a speedy convalescence to the patients.

Moody and Gay expressed their regrets over Mulkey's fate, but tried to make light of their own situations.

"I'm just a little numb around the edges yet, but Doc Hunter says I'll be fine," said Moody.

"I've never known what earthly good little toes are, anyway. I believe I'll do alright without mine," Gay bravely declared.

◆━◆◆◆━◆

Irvin, O'Brien, and Poole spent Monday and Tuesday searching for some sign of Pat Davis and Frank Allphin. They lost the trail repeatedly and had to circle around to find it time and again. They finally came back to the Deschutes River home station cold and exhausted, fearing the task was hopeless.

I had gone out on my own again, searching for Frank ever further to the east and south. I came back to Graham's hotel on Wednesday, January 22th. It was late afternoon. I could think of only one other direction to look.

It may not have been likely, but it was possible that Pat Davis had been able to rouse up Frank and get him walking again. If he had, then the two men could have walked due north to the Columbia River. Perhaps they walked to Celilo, to the steamboat dock, or to the Indian village west of the mouth of the Deschutes River. I knew it wasn't likely. They would have had to pass right by Graham's home station. But maybe someone had found them out in the storm. There was a slim possibility that the two men were at the dock or the Indian village now. I would spend the night at Graham's hotel and take Napoleon to the steamboat dock and the Indian village the next day.

———◦•❖•◦———

On Thursday, January 23th Doctor Andrew Hogg amputated Riddle's left foot above the ankle. Riddle was generally in poor condition, having been frozen all over. His feet had been repeatedly frozen since before reaching the home station at Willow Creek.

Jeffries had also been frozen all over. Doctor Hogg had to amputate part of his right foot.

Wellington and McDonald were lucky. They would recover without surgery.

———◆◆◆◆———

At Graham's hotel, Nichols was recuperating from mild frostbite without the benefit of trained medical attention. He was staying close to the fire, drinking lots of hot coffee and putting away a great deal of Harriet Graham's good cooking. Nichols would take his time and spend another two weeks with the Grahams before borrowing a horse to ride to Dalles City. He found that he no longer was in any hurry to go anywhere.

There was still no word about the fate of Frank or of Pat Davis.

I went to the steamboat dock and to see the Indians on the Columbia River at Celilo. The dock was deserted, but The Colonel Wright was there, secured to the pilings. A watchman was aboard, and he said he hadn't seen anyone or heard anything. He told me Captain White was staying at the Umatilla House eight miles downriver until the weather got better. I went to see the Indians next. I was on good terms with them, and they made me welcome at the village. Unfortunately, they had seen nothing of Frank.

———◆◆◆◆———

Returning to Dalles City, I had a very important chore to complete. First, I went downtown to Kaufman's haberdashery. I selected the best heavy overcoat from Kaufman's stock. I paid the tailor and had him wrap the coat in brown paper. I then walked the four blocks to the residence where Gay and Moody were recuperating. After knocking, I was admitted with my bulky package.

"Mr. Moody, giving your overcoat to my brother could have been the death of you," I said. "Please accept this one to replace it with all my gratitude."

"I wish I could have done more," said Moody with tears in his eyes. "I'd give anything to have done more."

"There's no one on this earth who could have done more than you did," I said. "And there's many a man who would have done a lot less. You're a kind man, sir. You did all you could."

CHAPTER TWENTY

In Portland, Oregon, the temperature did not rise above freezing during the entire month of January 1862.

I carried the sad news of Frank's almost certain demise to Allie Ann on January 28th. I helped her pack up and brought her and the boys back to Dalles City before accompanying them to Tom and Louisa's home in the Willamette Valley.

In the future, someone else would have to take care of Miller's Willow Creek home station.

It would be the last week in February before the first men on snowshoes could get in or out of Florence, Washington Territory.

On March 14th, the Oregonian newspaper in Portland carried the notice of the funeral of Mr. I.E. Jagger, to be held on Sunday, March

16th. Deepest regrets were expressed throughout the entire community regarding his deplorable loss. Sincere sympathy was extended to his family, especially his widow and young child.

Jagger was interred in the Corbett family cemetery, located behind the Henry Corbett residence on the southeast corner of Southwest 5th and Southwest Taylor Streets in Portland.

———◆·◆·◆———

Lacking any instructions regarding Johnson Mulkey, Lawrence Coe had him interred in a cemetery in Dalles City.

———◆·◆·◆———

Doc Gay and W.A. Moody traveled together back to their families in Eugene City in the middle of March. While Gay now only had four toes on each foot, he was a rich man. Moody was wealthy, too. Both were thankful to be alive.

Doctor Hunter had released Moody from his care three weeks before he released Doc Gay. Moody got himself a room at the Umatilla House, but spent every afternoon with Gay, helping him learn to walk again with a stout stick and eight toes. Moody commissioned tailor Kaufman to make them each new suits for traveling.

There was the beginning of a vast wave of men coming through Dalles City. They were all going east, to the gold mines. At the ticket office for the Oregon Steam Navigation Company, Moody found he could have the choicest of accommodations for the trip to Portland. Very few passengers wished to go in that direction.

Moody and Gay traveled in style, wearing fine clothing, eating the best foods, enjoying fine drinks, and sleeping in feather beds. Arriving in Portland, they traveled by coach to Oregon City. Once there, they secured tickets on another river steamer to Eugene City. Arriving in Eugene City, the friends did not say good-bye. They arranged to meet the following Tuesday, and every Tuesday thereafter, at noon, for lunch and drinks downtown.

Frances Gay could hardly believe her eyes when she saw Doc walking down the front path. He looked good, though perhaps a bit thin. He did use an ebony walking stick, but he did not limp or stumble. Doc was soon engulfed in a wave of female relatives. They nearly knocked him off his feet.

"Now girls," said Frances, "Give Daddy room to breathe. Give him some room, let him sit down, and I'll fetch our new addition."

Frances gave Doc a kiss on the cheek as she handed him the new baby. "I know you wanted a boy real bad, but here I've got to introduce you to our very own Florence. You won't have to go away to see Florence, now."

Doc studied the baby who was studying him in return. "A boy might have been nice, but I can see that this here girl is a mighty fine one. A lot like her sisters, and her Ma," Doc said.

———◆•✦•◆———

It was the end of March when the ice finally broke up on the Columbia River. Steamboat service resumed first between Astoria and Portland and then between Portland and Dalles City. On the Dalles City to Wallula run The Colonel Wright was joined by the Tenino and the Okanogan, newly built for the upper river. Business was very good. Okanogan paid for herself on her maiden voyage.

My houseguests, Merrill Short, his wife, and small daughter returned to Columbus Landing. They got home in time to supply The Colonel Wright with firewood when she made her first upriver trip of the season.

———•+•+•———

Riddle and Jeffries had undergone more extensive surgery than Gay. It took longer for them to heal. Doctor Hogg finally permitted them each to travel at the end of April.

Jeffries disembarked from the Willamette River steamboat at Butte Landing. He used a crutch to walk with. He hired a man at the landing to drive him home to the Bethel District in Polk County. The roads were muddy, and the drive took about five hours. Jeffries was exhausted when he climbed down from the wagon and bid the man good-bye.

Teddy heard the wagon out in the dooryard. He came running to wrap his arms around his father, stopping him in his tracks. His cries of "Daddy, Daddy, Daddy" brought Susan running from the kitchen. The little family group stood hugging each other in the dooryard for a long time. "I'm home now," declared Jeffries. "I won't ever leave again."

———•+•+•———

When the snow started to melt, there was more flooding. In Dalles City Front Street, Second Street, and Third Street were all submerged. Eighteen inches of water stood in the dining room of the Umatilla House Hotel. The official high water mark was forty-eight feet, ten inches above the normal water level. I tell you Tommy, if I hadn't a been there I wouldn't have believed it myself.

———•+•+•———

John Irvin and I searched diligently for Frank's body when the snow began to melt in March. For a country known as an open, most-ly treeless waste, the Columbia Plateau was proving surprisingly dif-ficult to locate a man's body in. We had been up and down all the main trails and side trails, riding slowly in both directions. This had yielded nothing. Unfortunately, Frank had not died within sight of any trail, making the search even more difficult.

We expanded our search, carefully quartering the area from the John Day River crossing west almost to the Deschutes River. We ranged north and south of the Oregon Trail, trying to imagine the land under three feet of snow, with more coming down. We tried to guess where men would walk in those conditions. The work was te-dious and unrewarding. We rode and searched all day, then camped out, eating and sleeping under the stars. The days slipped by, each one pretty much like the rest.

Every few days we would ride back to the Deschutes River home station to get supplies and see if there was any news. Supplies were always plentiful, but Graham and Poole, though sympathetic, never had any news. No one else had found any bodies in the melting snow.

On the twenty-fourth day of our search, John and I had covered about twelve miles from the Deschutes River when I thought I saw something in the winter-killed grass. There was a lumpy form part-ly hidden by dead grass and sagebrush. Urging Napoleon closer, I could see that it was part of a body. There were a leg and a foot, also a long soldier's overcoat. My hopes soared, then crashed as I saw the man's head. This man had long, gray hair. It could not be Frank, and it couldn't be red-headed Pat Davis, either.

We carefully searched the entire area. The head, leg, and foot were all that we could find of the body. We found a leather purse with three hundred twelve dollars inside near the overcoat. Scattered pa-pers proved to be payment vouchers from the government, the pay-ees listed as J.W. Knight and Ned Clough.

We wrapped the head, leg, and foot in the coat and buried them. We covered the gravesite with a pile of rocks, hoping this would discourage wild animals from digging up the remains. We would turn the papers and the purse with the money over to the Wasco County Coroner when we next reached Dalles City.

It was the first week in April and the thirty-sixth day of our search before we found Frank's body. He was in Big Grass Valley Canyon, about a mile from the top. The wild animals had left him alone, but his body was badly decomposed. This made identification difficult, but since the body was wrapped in Moody's overcoat, had brown hair, and wore Frank's boots, I was sure it was indeed him.

We decided not to try to move Frank, but to inter him where he was. It took several hours for us to gather enough rocks to form a cairn for him. While John went in search of a few more rocks, I sat with my brother's body for a bit to think about him and say farewell. I assured Frank that his Allie Ann and young William would be alright.

———————•◆•◆•◆•———————

April 5th, 1862 I read an advertisement from the *Oregonian* newspaper, Portland, Oregon. It confirmed for me that life goes on, despite past tragedies.

New Steamer *Tenino,* White Commander, will leave Des Chutes for Wallula Every Tuesday. Returning, leaves Wallula every Thursday at 6AM

Passage from Portland to the Dalles,	$8.00
Portage at Cascades extra.	
Animals from Portland to Dalles	$5.00
Passage from Des Chutes to Wallula	$15.00

No Extra charge for meals.
J.C. Ainsworth, President O.S.N. Co.

———— ❖•❄•❖ ————

Despite a foot of snow still on the ground, the first pack animals of the season arrived in Florence from Slate Creek on May 10th. Three-fingered Smith was there to greet them.

———— ❖•❄•❖ ————

After escorting Allie Ann and the boys back to Tom and Louisa's, I had a serious discussion with your Aunt Mary. We each felt that Dalles City just didn't seem like home anymore. We didn't have the heart to stay.

That's when we went back to the Willamette Valley ourselves, settling in Albany. I bought a saloon and ran it for many years.

———— ❖•❄•❖ ————

On the bright morning of July 3rd, a lone rider came tearing into Florence, shouting his news at the top of his lungs. "Gold! Gold strike in Elk City! Rich beyond your dreams! First men there will get the best pickin's. Gold! Only fifty miles away! Gold!" he shouted. Within forty-eight hours over four thousand men had abandoned Florence, heading for Elk City. Three-fingered Smith was among them.

———— ❖•❄•❖ ————

"Well, Uncle Jack, what happened to everyone else?" asked Tommy curiously.

"Well, Tommy I suppose they all went on livin' their lives just like we all did, but I tell you one thing I know for sure. Ain't none of them ever gonna forget that winter of 1862," I replied.

AFTERWORD

———— ✵ ————

Boone Helm was caught and returned to Florence late in the month of July 1862. The place was virtually deserted. There were no witnesses to any murder to be found. Helm was released due to lack of evidence. However, this did not buy "The Kentucky Cannibal" much time. On January 14th, 1864, over six thousand witnesses watched while the Montana Vigilantes hung Boone Helm and several other men associated with the Plummer gang. Helm was credited with at least eleven killings. He proudly claimed to have eaten part or all of three of his victims.

————•◦•◦•————

The widow Eliza Jagger married Mark A. King in Portland, Oregon in 1865. Eliza may have been widowed again before 1880. Sometime after 1870, Hattie Jagger went to live in Alameda, California with her grandparents Robert R. and Harriet Thompson. She still resided with them in 1880.

Robert R. Thompson died in California on July 22, 1908. His estate was valued at over three million dollars.

Cara E. Corbett, wife of Henry W. Corbett, died July 27, 1865, at the home of her father, Ira Jagger, in Albany, New York. She was survived by her husband and two sons, Henry Jagger Corbett, age eight, and Hamilton Corbett, age six.

The elder Ira Jagger died in April of 1891 in Albany, New York. He was survived by two sons, Franklin H. Jagger of Albany, New York and Henry Corbett Jagger of San Francisco, California.

———————

In 1870 Lewis Day was no longer with Oregon Steam Navigation Company but was still living in Walla Walla with his wife and four children, and working as a carpenter.

John C. Ainsworth was successful in various business ventures in Oregon. He moved to California and died near Oakland in 1893.

Cyrus Jacobs, the owner of the supplies stored in Tom Scott's barn, was born in Pennsylvania in 1830. He moved back to Pennsylvania again before 1870.

———————

By 1870 Doc and Frances Gay were the parents of five daughters and four sons. In 1900 Doc and Frances celebrated their fiftieth wedding anniversary. They still lived in Lane County, Oregon. Doc Gay died in 1903.

In 1870 Charles "Swede" Wilson was living in East Portland, Oregon. He was working as a farmer.

Richard Bolton was still single and living in Portland in 1880. He still listed his profession as miner on the federal census.

Thomas S. Jeffries continued to live in Polk County as a farmer. By 1880 his family included his wife Susan, son Theodore, nephew Harley, niece Julia Jacobs, and his mother-in-law Hannah Nichols.

William H. Riddle returned to the Canyonville area to farm. By

Allie Ann McClain Allphin Farrier in 1873, age 29. *After the death of Frank Allphin, Allie Ann married George W. Farrier. She, her nephew Allen, and her son William survived the 1862 blizzard despite low supplies of food and firewood. At the time, Allie Ann was only 18 years old. (Courtesy of Charlene McLain.)*

Frank Allphin in 1860, age 26. *Frank ran the stagecoach station at Willow Creek, east of Dalles City, Oregon. He perished in the 1862 blizzard while trying to bring food to his family. (Courtesy of Charlene McLain.)*

1870 he was widowed and living with the family of Watson Minot. He still resided with them in 1880.

Nichols continued to mine and was working at Olive Creek in Grant County, Oregon, in 1870.

The body of Pat Davis was never found.

———•◦•◦•———

William Graham and his family were still living at the mouth of the Deschutes River in 1870. Graham listed his profession on the federal census as farmer. In 1885 Georgia Graham, a daughter of William and Harriet Graham, married Logan P. Mulkey, a son of Johnson Mulkey.

Thomas Scott was living alone on Willow Creek in 1870, farming. In 1880 he was living on lower Butter Creek in Umatilla County with his wife, two sons, and a daughter.

John Irvin still lived at West Dalles in 1880, farming for a living. His household consisted of his wife Catherine and five children.

———•◦•◦•———

C.H. Johnson owned land near Umatilla Landing from 1860 until 1918.

Fred Stocking was still living in Wasco County in 1900.

Doctor J.C. Shields moved to Eugene City and was practicing there in 1880.

W. Allen McClain married Mary Griggs on May 16, 1875. In 1880 they were farming land near Syracuse, Oregon and had one daughter. Subsequently, he served as Marshall for Albany, Oregon. In 1900 Allen and Mary still lived in Albany with their two daughters. At that time Allen listed his profession as night watchman. Until at least

William Allphin in about 1864, age about 5. William was the son of Frank and Allie Ann Allphin. (Courtesy of Charlene McLain.)

W. Allen McClain in about 1865, age 14. McClain was Allie Ann's nephew. He later became a lawman in Albany, Oregon. A photograph taken after 1890 shows him wearing a star-shaped badge on his vest. (Courtesy of Charlene McLain.)

1920 they still made their home in Albany. W. Allen McClain died in Bremerton, Washington September 2, 1923.

Frank and Allie Ann Allphin's son William married in 1885. In 1900 he and his wife Nancy were living near the Santiam River in Linn County. They had four children. By 1920 William was widowed and living in the Fairmont District of Benton County with two of his sons. William Allphin died in 1926.

The widow Allie Ann Allphin married George Washington Farrier, farmer and step-brother of Frank Allphin on July 24, 1862. During their twenty years of marriage, they lived in Linn County and had at least seven children. Farrier died in 1883. Allie Ann married Asa Burbank in 1896, and they remained married until Burbank died in 1913. Allie Ann died on January 31, 1941. She was ninety-seven years old.

The town of Champoeg was never rebuilt. The site is now an Oregon State Park.

The site of Graham's Hotel and the Deschutes River stagecoach station is also now an Oregon State Park.

The Umatilla House Hotel burned down twice and was twice rebuilt. The third incarnation of the hotel was torn down in 1930. Lewis and Clark Festival Park now occupies the land where the Umatilla House Hotel once stood.

The cairn of stones marking the gravesite of Francis Marion Allphin was still evident until sometime after 1940. Since that time several major floods, including the Christmas week flood of 1964, have eradicated all trace of his final resting place in Big Grass Valley Canyon.

———•+•+•———

The Miller and Blackmore Stagecoach Company had only just been established in 1861. It did not last long after the blizzard.

In the spring no regular schedule of service was possible. There were places where the snow was slow to melt, causing delays. Also, Emmitt Miller found it almost impossible to find anyone to stay at the Willow Creek home station. No one had any specific complaints about the place, but no one would stay long. There also seemed to be a certain lack of public confidence in the stagecoach company after the tragedy.

By early 1863 other operators were running stagecoach routes both to the east and to the south out of Dalles City.

———•+•+•———

There is no official record of the number of fatalities from the 1862 blizzard.

———•+•+•———

Mary Allphin passed away in 1902.

Jack Allphin was eighty-four years old when he died in 1912.

———•+•+•———

Rafe Garrity, Fred Wilcox, Marv Knowles, Joe the hosteler, and Irish Mike the hosteler are fictional characters. Some real person held their jobs, but their names are unknown.

Surgeon's Quarters, Fort Dalles, The Dalles, Oregon, in about 1919. *Medical facilities at the fort were made ready to treat civilian victims of the 1862 blizzard. (Oregon Historical Society)*

AUTHOR'S NOTE

I've spent over twenty years researching the blizzard of 1862. I visited a dozen county historic societies, the Oregon State Archives and the Oregon State Library. I scrutinized satellite images of the terrain in Big Grass Valley. I traveled the stagecoach route and contacted the present owner of the land west of the John Day River on the Oregon Trail.

I've found a brief, sometimes garbled, mention of the blizzard in about a dozen books. I believe this is the only book that details the tragedy of the blizzard of 1862.

SOURCES

Books

Lost Mines and Treasures of the Pacific Northwest by Ruby El Hult

One Woman's West, Recollections of the Oregon Trail and Settling the Northwest Country by Martha Gay Masterson 1838-1916, Edited by Lois Barton

Northern California, Oregon and the Sandwich Islands by Charles Nordhoff

Knights of the Whip: Stagecoach Days in Oregon by Gary and Gloria Meier

Maps of Historical Oregon by R.N. Preston

Thunder Over The Ochoco by Gale Ontko

The Golden Land: A History of Sherman County, Oregon by Giles L. French

Reminiscences of Eastern Oregon by Elizabeth Lord

History of Washington, The Rise and Progress of an American State by Clinton A. Snowden

History of Oregon, Volume Two by Hubert Howe Bancroft

Oregon's Golden Years: Bonanza of the West by Miles F. Potter

Fifteen Thousand Miles by Stage by Carrie Adell Strahorn

The Story of the Outlaw: The Story of the Western Desperado by Emerson Hough

The Passing of the Frontier, A Chronicle of the Old West by Emerson
   Hough
Lyman's History of Old Walla Walla: Embracing Walla Walla, Columbia,
   Garfield and Asotin Counties, Volume 1 By William Denison Lyman

Newspapers

Oregon Statesman newspaper, Salem, Oregon
Albany Democrat newspaper, Albany, Oregon, Impressions and
   Observations of the Journal Man by Fred Lockley
Idaho Statesman newspaper, Boise, Idaho, Idaho History: Hurdy-
   Gurdy Girls on Frontier Danced With All Comers by Arthur
   Hart
Walla Walla Statesman newspaper, Walla Walla, Washington
Olympia Overland Press newspaper, Olympia, Washington
Oregonian newspaper, Portland, Oregon
The State Republican newspaper, Eugene City, Oregon
Schenectady New York Cabinet newspaper, Schenectady, New York
Albany Evening Journal newspaper, Albany, New York
Oregon Sentinel newspaper, Jacksonville, Oregon
The New Northwest newspaper, Portland, Oregon
Oregon City Enterprise newspaper, Oregon City, Oregon

Other

Florence, Idaho County, Idaho, Miller's Creek Mining Claims,
   Summit Creek Mining Claims
Federal Population Census, 1850, 1860, 1870, 1880, 1900,
   1910, 1920, Territory and State of Oregon, Territory and
   State of Washington, Territory and State of California, State
   of New York
1941 Interview with F.M. Allphin's 97-year-old Widow by Leslie
   M. Haskin for Works Progress Administration

The Quarterly of the Oregon Historical Society, No. 3, Volume VIII,
September 1908 thesis, Oregon's First Monopoly – The Oregon
Steam Navigation Company by Irene Lincoln Poppleton
Linn County, Oregon Marriage Records, Marriage Book "A"

Internet sources
The Oregon Encyclopedia – oregonencyclopedia.org
Find a Grave – findagrave.com
Sweethearts of the West – sweetheartsofthewest.com
Google Maps – google.com/maps

Credits
The stagecoach passenger rules used in this book are based on both
an 1877 *Omaha Herald* article, "Wells Fargo's Rules for Riding
the Stagecoach" and similar rules in the Gale Ontko book
Thunder Over the Ochoco, Volume III, Lightening Strikes!, copyright
2007, Seven Locks Press.

ABOUT THE AUTHOR

Lenora Whiteman is a fourth-generation Oregonian with interests including history, gardening, and geology. She has worked as a hardware store clerk, a surgical dental assistant, and a community college instructor. She has also worked in antique malls and a traditional English tearoom. She is a past vice president of the Allphin-McClain Family Association and a life member of the Sons and Daughters of Oregon Pioneers.

CPSIA information can be obtained
at www.ICGtesting.com
Printed in the USA
LVHW050435020720
659505LV00003B/485